The Underground

Ilana Katz Katz

Merrimack
MEDIA

Published by Merrimack Media
Custom Universal ISBN: 10: 0615640400
ISBN: 0615640400

Merrimack
MEDIA

A Merrimack Media edition.

For Shira
In gratitude for so many things

Chapter One

"What do you think?" Janice said, twirling as if she were a perfectly proportioned Barbie doll.

"You look beautiful," Nathaniel said, forcing a smile. Beautiful was the last word he thought of when looking at Janice. Not just because her doughy body was tightly packed into a sausage skin of a dress. Years of inebriation made her skin sallow. It wasn't surprising since she was drunk most of the time, and Janice was a nasty drunk.

Still, being with Janice beat mandatory castration, his likely fate without her marriage proposal. He was grateful for that, but it didn't quell his resentment.

Her perfume of stale cigarettes mixed with sour breath was constant. She leaned in to kiss him. Luckily, the doorbell interrupted.

"Your party guests are here!" she said, pulling away. A string of Janice clones stumbled in, chattering loudly.

"We need some drinks!" she yelled in Nathaniel's direction, snapping her fingers at him as she greeted her guests.

"No vodka, no happy Janice," he muttered to himself as he slipped back into the kitchen.

"My birthday party has begun," Nathaniel announced sarcastically to Janice's Uncle Chester, once the kitchen door closed behind him.

"You mean Janice's friends are here and they want booze?" Chester joked, while rotating trays of hors d'oeuvres between the counter and the oven. Nathaniel found it hard to believe that this kind man was Janice's blood relative.

"You got that right. The last time we ran out of vodka, it was after 11 p.m. which is not a good time of night for a man to be out. I tried to tell Janice, but she didn't care about my safety, just about getting more booze. I ran to the liquor store and barely outran them," Nathaniel said, letting his words trail. His near miss with the military police, or Tasers as they were commonly called, paled in comparison to what Chester had suffered.

From the outside, Chester seemed to have a decent life. Almost 50, he had a successful bakery with lines snaking out the door each morning. If it wasn't for the dime-sized purple "Spot" tattoo to the left of his Adam's apple, which all men received on their castration day, Nathaniel would never know he had gone through such a horrible ordeal.

"Thanks for all your help. I couldn't have done this without you," Nathaniel said, motioning to the platters peppered with Chester's artful garnishes. There were cut up vegetables with homemade artichoke dip, baked Brie with apricot jam and crackers, and Chester's signature award winning mini muffin tops.

"It's the least I can do for your birthday," Chester said.

"Why don't you take these drinks out to Janice and I'll finish up in here. Just tell me what needs to be done," Nathaniel said.

"You know I'm more comfortable in the kitchen. Help me finish getting the rest of this tray ready and then get out there and mingle. That is most important."

As they wordlessly chopped vegetables, Nathaniel felt thinly insulated from Janice's favorite electronica music. The drums suddenly pulsed louder, triggering his nerves. It sounded like rhythmic bombs, much too close for comfort, right outside the kitchen door. Nathanial put down the knife and met Chester's eyes.

"I'm too nervous to go out there. When she turns the music up like that, it means she's pretty drunk and I just never know what she's going to do. I hate to give her more fuel," Nathaniel said, motioning to the vodka sitting on the counter.

Chester quickly peeked out the kitchen door, before ducking back in and locking it.

"It's alright. She's just dancing and having a good time. You'll be fine. Before you go out there, I have something for you," Chester said. He wiped his hands on the apron bearing his bakery's name, Chester's, before pulling a wrapped package from underneath the table.

"Happy Birthday," he said, holding it out to Nathaniel.

"On top of everything else, you got me a gift? You really shouldn't..."

"Open it," Chester whispered.

Nathaniel took the package and began to tear the brown wrapping.

"Careful!" Chester snapped.

Nathaniel's hands started to tremble as the black leather cover revealed itself. The embossed gold letters were half faded and worn away, but still clear enough to read.

REMINDER OF TRUTH

By Anonymous

"Is this what I think it is? I can't believe this really exists," Nathaniel said, hoping his voice didn't sound as shaky as he felt.

"Thank you," he said trying to look Chester in the eye.

Nathanial tentatively ran his fingers across the cover and started to open it.

"Put it away," Chester said, tersely.

Nathaniel quickly rewrapped the book wondering why the hell Chester had it but was too afraid to ask. Castration would be a picnic compared to what would happen if the Tasers found Nathaniel with this contraband. According to legend, it described a time long ago when there was equality between the sexes. It was impossible to imagine.

Nathaniel quickly stashed the ancient book at the very back of the cabinet under the sink, behind all the cleaning supplies. Janice would never look there since cleaning was men's work. As he closed the cabinet, Janice's familiar cackle bled through the kitchen door, setting him on edge and bringing him back to reality.

"We're in good shape here," Chester said, releasing the lock and stepping aside. Nathaniel was about to leave the kitchen, but stopped. What if she dumped him on his birthday? She had been engaged two other times and had done exactly that. He caught his reflection in the glass cabinet door, and while he didn't love his buzz haircut that Janice had mandated, at least he wasn't going bald like other men turning 25. He looked good. Years of manual labor for the Cambridge Public Works kept his body toned. He was six feet tall. His warm blue eyes contrasted his dark hair. He could see in his reflection his chiseled jaw visibly tense.

"Go on out there," Chester said, as if to break his spell.

"You sure you don't need help?" Nathaniel said. He was nervous about getting through the night, but that wasn't the only problem. There were four months until their wedding, and getting through that time period really weighed on him.

Chester shooed him away.

"Just one more thing…I told Janice that I made the platters. I said you just came to help at the end," Nathaniel said.

"Don't worry, I can keep a secret." Chester winked at him.

LONG LIVE THE QUEEN!
LONG LIVE THE QUEEN!
LONG LIVE THE QUEEN!

Nathaniel first heard that familiar chant as a child. Still, he wasn't desensitized to it. Each round grew louder. As he opened the kitchen door and stepped out, he felt like a caterer at someone else's party.

He couldn't help but think about *Reminder of Truth.* It supposedly chronicled an era when men weren't afraid to walk outside. Nathaniel couldn't imagine that. After all, Nathaniel felt like he was heading into a minefield, and he was only walking from the kitchen into the living room of his apartment.

LONG LIVE THE QUEEN!...

He tried to let the words wash past him, but the women glared at him as they raised their fists in unison, rhythmically punching their words with lacquered fingernails. He was the only man there, besides Chester in the kitchen, so it wasn't surprising that the aggression was entirely aimed at him. Nathaniel fought against the adrenaline urging him to run away. Instead, he pretended he was playing a role in a movie as he made his way toward his fiancée.

No matter how hard he tried to give himself a pep talk, he couldn't deny his fear. What if they attacked him? What if Janice hated her drink?

"HERE COMES THE BIRTHDAY BOY!!" Janice yelled from the chair she stood on, high above all the others as she broke the chorus she had been conducting. The synchronicity deteriorated into comments thrown at him like rocks. *"Tick Tock, one year closer to the C Center..." "...You dodged a bullet. Well not quite yet, but soon, assuming she really does marry you, Nathaniel."*

He couldn't hear them all, but a few rose above the cacophony of taunts riddled with a laughter that didn't stem from anything he thought of as funny. He tried to block them out.

This was not how he envisioned his life. When Janice silenced them with a single wave of her hand, he felt a nanosecond of gratitude to her for making them stop. He shivered inside as the moment stretched. The final few steps toward Janice made his nerves jump as she beckoned him with her finger. It took effort to keep the tray steady as he felt a single bead of sweat slowly fall down his forehead to sting his right eye.

"I brought your favorite," he said, holding the beautifully presented hot dogs in pastry dough as though it were a diamond he hoped was big enough for the Queen, herself. He held it to her with a display of reverence he didn't feel. Whispers abounded as everyone waited. Janice gobbled two at a time and said nothing, holding the moment like a long musical crescendo.

"You're right, pigs in blankets are my favorite, but they do make me thirsty," she finally said, handing him her empty glass and giving him a shove that made him stumble and nearly spill the rest of the food onto the floor.

After regaining his balance, he walked toward the kitchen. With each step, the path seemed to stretch. Along the way, the women pawed his tray as if each hors d'oeuvre was a winning lottery ticket. He focused on the kitchen door ahead, his heavenly gate to a few moments of peace. Just as he made it inside, the electronica abruptly reignited.

"I don't know how I'm going to get through this," Nathaniel said, the moment the kitchen door closed behind him.

"You will because you have to," Chester commanded. Nathaniel had never heard him speak that way. The veins running through the purple tattoo on Chester's neck swelled. It was like a badge that he had earned, but never wanted.

Nathaniel wondered how Chester summoned the energy to lead his life following castration. It wasn't like he just plodded on. He had a successful business. Chester's Bakery won a slew of "best bakery" awards. That would be a noteworthy accomplishment for anyone, but for a Spot it was particularly significant.

"Janice is insisting on another drink," Nathaniel said.

Chester wordlessly pulled a perfect pitcher of Janice's favorite mixed vodka drink from the fridge and handed it over. "Hurry."

Nathaniel did as he was told, even though all he really wanted to do was sit down and ask Chester about *Reminder of Truth*. How did Chester get that book and why? Chester seemed like the kind of person he could open up to, but there never seemed to be the time. Chester was either working at his bakery or else they were with Janice.

Nathaniel realized there would be plenty of time to talk with Chester. After all, for better or worse, Nathaniel DeLuca had a lifetime as Janice's husband ahead.

Chapter Two

It was nearly 11 p.m. when Nathaniel forced his last smile for the evening and closed the door behind the final guest. He turned and surveyed the damage. Spilled drinks patterned the wooden floor, and food littered the apartment like confetti. Women are such pigs, he thought, as he assessed the damage.

Chester offered to stay and help clean up, but Nathaniel insisted he go home. It was a work night for each of them, but Chester's day at the bakery started practically in the middle of the night. Nathaniel felt a little sorry for himself with the job ahead. Luckily, Janice was already passed out on the couch eliminating the possibility of obligatory drunken sex. If she was semi-conscious, she would demand it.

Still, he had to get her to bed. He scooped her up, which was no easy feat. Just as Nathaniel strained to lift her, his cell phone sounded with Brigg's ring tone. "Damn," he muttered, furious at himself for leaving the ringer on. He couldn't risk putting her down, so he quickly carried his snoring bride-to-be over the bedroom threshold. He gently laid her down on the bed and looked at her. There was a momentary peacefulness, but as the phone stopped ringing, Janice started talking like a broken string-pull doll.

"Anna Marie, sing-it-with-me…long-live-the-queen-longlivethe queenlonglivethe…"

Nathaniel held his breath.

If there is a God, I pray that you listen. Please make Janice stay asleep. Please, as a birthday gift for me.

He felt silly begging to an entity he didn't believe in. As abruptly as she began to speak, Janice's talk dissolved to a snore and Nathaniel wondered if there was a God listening. Maybe he should pray more often.

He glanced back at her before quietly closing the bedroom door and checking voicemail: "Good luck, old friend, and happy 25th.

I hope this is a good year for you and I'm sorry I couldn't be there. I'll take you out some night when she's working. My treat. Give me a call if you're still up or else I'll see you at work."

Nathaniel loved celebrating past birthdays with Brigg, but Janice didn't allow Brigg an invitation to this party. She was too jealous, having only known Nathaniel for a year. That timeframe was no match for a lifetime of friendship that Brigg and Nathanial shared.

Nathaniel was usually annoyed at how she tried to keep Brigg away, but on this night it was a gift. He was ashamed that he had turned into the exact kind of pussy-whipped guy that he and Brigg used to make fun of when they were teens. Now, he kissed ass just like all the other men trying to save their balls, and he understood why they did it.

Things could be a helluva lot worse, he repeatedly told himself over the next two hours as he cleaned the dishes, emptied the ashtrays, and mopped the stickiness off the floor. He found food between the seat cushions, and scrubbed the vomit-laced bathroom, as well as any man-servant could.

Nathaniel then tucked his head back into the bedroom to be sure Janice was still asleep before returning to the kitchen. He locked it from the inside, as Chester had done hours earlier, and his heart boomed as he pulled the book from underneath the kitchen cabinet. Nathaniel wanted to know who gave it to Chester and why. This was probably the most dangerous illegal possession in the country.

He looked at the book cover and almost put it back in its hiding place. If there was another kind of life in another time, maybe it was better not to know about it.

If it hadn't been for the flat tire he got precisely one year earlier, he might never have walked into Eva's Diner and met Janice. And he might still have the threat of castration hanging over him.

"Can I help you?" Janice said, cracking her gum, as she flashed a smile. Even then he could tell she thought herself sexy by the way she sashayed in her stained polyester uniform, as though she was walking the red carpet at a Hollywood premiere.

"Flat tire," he said, shaking his head. "My ride meets me here in an hour, so I thought I'd get a cup of coffee while I wait."

"We've got more than coffee!" she said.

"Here you go" she said a short while later as she set a burger with fries in front of him, along with coffee. She also sat herself down, as though invited. She was attentive that night, but never again. Since then, Nathaniel served her. Always.

"Wow, I only ordered coffee," he said, feeling funny about her attentiveness.

"I know, but I thought you might be hungry," she said, flirtatiously, leaning in to him, as though studying every pore of his face.

"Thank you. It's my birthday dinner," he said, feeling a little self-conscious.

"Today's your birthday? How old are you?" she asked.

"Twenty-four," he said. He felt uncomfortable admitting he was getting closer to that life defining birthday.

"Hmmm," she said, thinking for a minute before she asked for his number. It was a good sign, at the time, and when she proposed a few months later, that was even better. Didn't he owe something to Janice? She was kind sometimes, and he couldn't help but remember that she didn't have to propose.

As he looked at the cover of *Reminder of Truth*, he wondered if reading the book would make him feel better or worse. Should he feel guilty for even considering it? He was grateful for Janice's proposal and indebted to her. But, he repaid her every day in too many ways to count.

This lure of reading the truth that the Queen tried to hide was too much to ignore and he opened the book.

REMINDER OF TRUTH

By Anonymous

A yellowed corner of the first page flaked off, falling to the ground like a snowflake. He didn't stop to pick it up as he was transfixed on the text:

There was a time long ago when men and women were equal. There was no monarchy or Tasers, nor were there castration centers. Yes, dear reader, there was such a time and I lived in it! I have nearly nine decades behind me. Until my death, I will pray for the balance in our country to be restored. Dear reader, I am writing to offer you a "Reminder of Truth."

"Can I please pay you?" Nathaniel asked Chester the next morning, as Chester handed him a bag containing his favorite: a large coffee and an oversized blueberry muffin.

"Not a chance. Family doesn't pay," Chester said, sitting across the tiny café table nestled into a corner of the crowded bakery. He always sat with Nathaniel for a few minutes each morning. "Thankfully, I'm blessed with plenty of customers who do pay." He whispered this, so the throngs of people patiently waiting in line wouldn't hear.

"Thank you," Nathaniel said.

"Everything go alright last night? You okay?" Chester asked, raising his eyebrows in question. Nathaniel wondered if he was referring to *Reminder of Truth,* but knew it wasn't safe to mention specifically.

"I'm tired. It took a while to clean up. I also stayed up late to do a little reading, thank you, which raised a lot of questions for me," he said, knowing full well they wouldn't be answered today.

Chester said nothing, but gave Nathaniel a dark look that he had seen the night before. It felt like a signal of something new and secretive between them. Did Chester know the author? By now, "Anonymous" was surely deceased, judging from the aged book. Nathaniel wanted to find out more. The very idea that an American society existed without mandatory castration was mind-boggling. As a Spot, Nathaniel wondered how Chester felt about the book. Did it make him hopeful or resentful?

"Can I ask you a question?" Nathaniel said, leaning in toward Chester.

"You can ask me anything."

"It's personal," Nathaniel said, wanting to make sure that Chester wouldn't mind or be surprised.

Chester nodded.

"How were you able to start the bakery after…?"

Chester's jaw visibly tightened.

Nathaniel immediately regretted his intrusion. "Sorry, I shouldn't have asked. It's none of my business."

"No, it's okay, really," Chester paused for a moment. The way Chester touched the dime sized purple tattoo on his neck belied his words. "It happened so long ago, and I try not to think about it, but the C Center changed my life's path. You've seen the statistics of homeless Spots who just plain give up. As horrible and as wrong as I believe our system is, I vowed not to become another unproductive Spot who goes through life feeling sorry for himself."

"I'm sorry," Nathaniel said.

"For what?"

"For what you went through, for asking you…"

Chester shrugged. "You didn't make the laws. Keep reading your book. Maybe your generation still stands a chance." Abruptly, Chester stood up.

Nathaniel walked toward the bakery door, wanting to ask more, but knew this wasn't the time or the place. He was about to step out the bakery door when a strong hand gripped his arm.

"Tasers!" a stranger said, discreetly, staring outside.

Nathaniel was sure they were coming for him! They found out about the book!

The Good Samaritan was gone before Nathaniel had a chance to thank him for the warning. Peering out the storefront window, he saw a man being dragged away by the Tasers with his mouth duct-taped. It was a common sight, but Nathaniel never grew accustomed to it.

Nathaniel wondered how many Parties of Availability that guy attended. He looked decent enough – not overweight, but still he clearly didn't get picked for marriage.

That could be me, Nathaniel realized before gingerly stepping outside and heading to work. A few minutes later, he walked in the door of the Cambridge Public Works and breathed a sigh of relief, though he was still rattled. He couldn't wipe away the look on that guy's face as he was being dragged away.

Nathaniel tried to force that image from his head, but realized how goddamn lucky he was to have Janice.

Nathaniel's thoughts consumed him as he walked down the corridor, and the more he tried to suppress his true feelings, the more he could not. His blood boiled at the thought of that man going through a horror. Still, abuse of men was considered the norm.

On top of everything, Nathaniel now worked for the Queen's daughter, Shayla Smith, at the Cambridge Public Works. People claimed she wasn't as extreme as her mother, but Nathaniel didn't trust workplace gossip.

After the chaos he witnessed on the way to work, he relished the silence of walking alone through the hallway. He needed it. The only sound was the echo of his shoes on the cement floor, with each step. The hallway walls were off-white, lined with photos of woman supervisors in action. There was a consistent theme to the pictures: Supervisors yelling through a megaphone, giving orders to the staff of nervous men. He knew that feeling and hated it. He stopped looking at the photos and moved a little more quickly, but then paused as he approached Shayla Smith's office. She had hardly been there a few weeks, and her freshly engraved nameplate shined and greatly contrasted the oversized steel office door to which it was affixed.

SHAYLA SMITH, CHIEF OFFICER,
CAMBRIDGE PUBLIC WORKS

Maybe it should say: "The Queen's Daughter – Better Kiss her Ass"

He pulled out a coffee from his brown paper bag as he stared at her nameplate but realized his bag was still heavy. He discovered a second coffee and muffin. Nathaniel supposed it was Chester's way of offering comfort.

Nathaniel looked down the hall, both ways, and impulsively set down the extra cup of coffee and muffin in front of her door before hurrying along to meet Brigg.

He didn't know what made him do it, but less than thirty seconds later he thought it was a mistake. They'd probably fingerprint the cup and come arrest him, somehow manipulating a simple gesture of kindness into Nathaniel stalking her. He turned back and thought of retrieving it, but it looked tiny from a distance. He took two steps toward it but stopped.

Nathaniel decided he couldn't live in fear of everything. Besides, how much trouble could giving a coffee and muffin possibly cause?

Chapter Four

"Couldn't you at least have warned me?" the Queen said stiffly to her daughter. "Hiding my surprise from reporters wasn't easy."

"Take me off speakerphone, mother?" Shayla said, before hearing the click of the handset.

"I just want to understand *why* you didn't tell me. I've got enough on my plate without being blindsided by something my daughter should have told me."

"Must we rehash this every time we talk?" Shayla said. She couldn't believe that her mother was still harping on the fact that a few weeks earlier Shayla had taken a job as head of the Cambridge Public Works.

"I promise not to bring it up again if you answer my question. Why didn't you tell me that you were taking that job?" the Queen asked.

"Because I thought you'd try to talk me out of it," Shayla said.

"You're damn right I would have!" Queen Amanda said, escalating her voice with each syllable.

"I want to help the men there. They need someone to stick up for them. Their working conditions are awful," Shayla said, knowing she was undoubtedly fueling her mother's fire. She didn't care anymore. She was finally doing what she believed in.

Cambridge, Massachusetts was known to be liberal, and seemed like a good testing ground for her goal of helping restore men's rights. Ultimately, Shayla had bigger changes in mind. Much bigger.

"You just don't get it, do you? You have it so goddamn good, you forgot how your great grandmother saved our country. Maybe I should force you to sit down and watch the historical footage to remind you," the Queen said.

"I know, mother. The President was assassinated and great grandmother was the Vice President and took over. I don't need to hear about it again," Shayla said.

"Clearly you do. She inherited a government that was defined by corruption. Our country had no credibility around the world. Our economy collapsed. Looting was common, and sex crimes were rampant and she restored this entire nation in all ways. Don't take that for granted."

"I don't." Shayla said, feeling indignant.

"Then why are you sticking up for men like this. They're the ones who made the mess. The country trusted her for a reason. She knew what she was doing. Let things be. I'll get you another job," the Queen said.

"I *like* what I do and where I work. I believe in it!" Shayla yelled back.

"Alright. If I can't stop you, at least let me get you a security detail, please," the Queen said, sighing.

"I'm fine." Shayla knew that her mother would probably put a detail out on her anyway, but they'd be discreet. At least she wouldn't have a mess of bodyguards surrounding her every trip to the bathroom.

"If your father were alive…"

"I've got to go. I have a meeting in a little while. Goodbye," Shayla said.

She hated when her mother started down that path: *If your father were alive.* Shayla tried not to think about how the world would be and the type of leader her mother could have been if her father hadn't died. Even as a young girl, Shayla remembered how her father tried to convince the Queen to banish mandatory castration for any man unmarried by age 26.

"Bring back equality. You have an opportunity to make history, Amanda," he used to say, with young Shayla sitting with them at the dinner table.

The day her father died, so did his dream. Shayla started thinking that if he lived, maybe the Queen would have changed, but Shayla stopped herself. Allowing her mind to enter "what if" land was pointless. History and the laws were cemented, along with the Queen's bitterness.

Shayla walked toward her office checking email on her phone, nearly causing her to trip over the bag outside her door. She thought about calling security, but when does a bomb smell that delicious? She carefully picked it up and looked inside. Coffee and a muffin?

She placed her hand up to her office door sensor, and it quickly unlocked. Shayla stepped inside, closed the door and could practically hear her mother scolding her for even considering eating what was there. "You have to be careful! Someone might want to poison you!"

Perhaps to spite her mother, or because she was hungry and tired, she took a sip of the coffee. It was still hot. It was probably the best coffee she had ever had, prepared just the way she liked it with just a little milk. She took a bite of the muffin and decided it was even better than the coffee. She justified eating it since she needed her strength for the morning meeting. If it poisoned her, it was worth it. The muffin was *that* good.

Until now, she had only observed the worksites and studied the existing processes at the Cambridge Public Works. Today, she would begin to unveil her agenda. Treading carefully was vital.

She read the logo on the side of the cup. She had heard of Chester's Bakery. The fact that the bakery came to her, so to speak, suited her fine. Maybe it was one of her 50 subordinates trying to suck up. It wouldn't work, but that didn't mean she was going to let it go to waste.

No man in his right mind would think it was okay to leave something for the head of the Cambridge Public Works. Yes, it had to be from one of her subordinates. She decided to bring the coffee to her morning meeting to see if someone confessed.

"Good morning," she said, trying to mask her uneasiness as she entered the meeting. It was the first step to improve working conditions for the men. At least that's what she hoped.

"I'll get right to the point, unless anyone has a pressing issue." Shayla paused to take a sip of her coffee as she surveyed the crowd.

"Effective immediately, field workers will have breaks every two-and-a-half-hours," Shayla declared. "Let them smoke or sit or get a drink or whatever, but make sure they get a ten-minute break. Not six minutes, not eight. Ten full minutes, and they can talk amongst themselves. Any questions?" she said, feeling happy. She waited for expository reactions, but all she saw and heard were gasps as the women shifted in their chairs.

"Are you lowering our quota requirements?" one brave soul asked.

"The quota requirements remain. Anyone else?" Shayla said, tersely.

"It's going to impact productivity. The men don't need so many breaks," said the same spark-plug of a woman.

"I agree," said another.

"Ten full minutes, every two and a half hours," Shayla repeated. Her voice grew louder as she leaned into the microphone for emphasis. While Shayla's message was opposite anything the Queen ever declared, Shayla copied her mother's communication tactics. She spoke forcefully, with confidence.

"A little more rest for the men will do the opposite and improve productivity and morale. Respect begets respect," she said, waiting for some kind of reaction, but the room was silent.

"Questions? Good." She left the meeting with her mother's quick gait and heard the room begin to buzz with discussion. Most likely they were bashing her behind her back. She couldn't blame them. They were used to getting their way and having full power over men who worked for them.

Nobody else could get away with the kind of change Shayla made. As the Queen's daughter, they wouldn't dare speak against her, at least not right away. Shayla knew that even with her status, her stance was risky, perhaps even treasonous.

Eventually, her mother would find out, but hopefully not too soon. She hoped her mother wouldn't publicly denounce her, as that wouldn't be publicly pretty either. That was just about the only thing she had in her favor.

As she neared her office, her father's voice rang in her head.

"The balance of equality in the country needs to be restored. Never forget. Promise me that." He told her this over and over when she visited him at his sick bed. Even as a young girl, she knew the day to turn around the tradition of female intimidation and live out her father's dream would come.

Pleased with herself, she took the last sip of her coffee. She was certain that after the meeting, whichever woman had left it would not do so again.

Chapter Five

"Can you believe she's giving us those ten minute breaks?" Nathaniel said to Brigg, before holding up his empty glass and nodding to the bartender. "Another Maker's, neat and straight up, please."

Nathaniel knew not to drink too much as he still had to get home to take care of Janice, but one more wouldn't hurt. In fact, it might actually help.

"Let's drink to new policies and Miss Shayla herself," Brigg said.

"Here, here," Nathaniel said. As he clinked his refreshed glass with Brigg's, he thought of Shayla and smiled.

"You look like the Cheshire cat with that smile," Brigg said, laughing.

Nathaniel's smile vanished. Despite Nathaniel's discretion as he left breakfast over the last few weeks, it occurred to Nathanial that Brigg might have seen him, or was he being paranoid?

"What's up with you and Janice, anyway. Things getting better?"

"No," Nathaniel said. Just hearing Janice's name wiped the smile off his face.

"Things weren't always so great with Grace when we first got together," Brigg said casually.

Nathaniel grew irritated when Brigg brought up Grace, as though she and Janice were interchangeable. Grace wasn't an alcoholic. She treated Brigg like a decent person and had forward-thinking views on men. On top of that, she was attractive.

"You've got a great wife. You can't possibly understand," Nathaniel said.

"Look, I'm just trying to help," Brigg said, with compassion.

"Well, you can't. Okay. Just accept that my life with Janice can't be better," Nathaniel said, bitterly, before draining his glass.

"Maybe there are ways to make life with her more palatable that you haven't thought of," Brigg suggested.

"She's a raging alcoholic. I clean up her vomit, and the thought of fathering her children, which she talks about all the time, makes me sick. You keep telling me it'll get better, but it's not going to change. Ever," Nathaniel said, pulling money out of his pocket and slapping it on the bar. He headed straight for the stairs and took them two at a time, exiting the Black Hole quickly.

"Wait!"

Early dusk met Nathaniel as he stepped outside. Brigg caught up and grabbed his arm.

"What do you want?" Nathaniel asked Brigg, not giving him room to answer. "… You wanna give me yet another lecture about how I should have gone to the Parties of Availability with you when I was 18? Let's just get this out of the way… Yes, you were right, okay… I should have gone. I should have pandered at those stupid fucking parties, so that maybe just *maybe* I'd get chosen for marriage by someone I could get along with before I turned 26. But I didn't go because I didn't want to be humiliated. That's all those women do at those parties from the moment they see a fresh 18-year-old walk in until the day he turns 26 and gets dragged off to the C Center. Do I regret not going to those parties now? Yes. You happy? Maybe I would've found someone a little better, or at least a woman who isn't a drunk. Still, I'm lucky. Janice is my savior. Hallelujah!" he said sarcastically. "She is my lifeline and life sentence at the same time."

"Keep your voice down!" Brigg said. "And watch what you're saying." Brigg dragged Nathaniel down an alley so they would be less vulnerable to Tasers who might walk by. "You seemed like you were doing okay for a while, and clearly you are not. I was just asking. I thought I could help," Brigg said.

"Nobody can help me," Nathaniel said, with a smile that felt scary, not happy. "I'm a man with my biological clock attached to a bomb on my balls. And it's just about gone off. I can't move, man. Can't you see that?" he whispered to Brigg.

"Do you trust me?" Brigg whispered back, close to his friend's face.

"Of course I trust you," Nathaniel said, annoyed, and shaking his arm free from Brigg.

"There is a way for you to be happy," Brigg said. He was absolutely resolute.

"Not with Janice."

"I'm certainly not going to argue about that."

"What are you talking about?"

"Look, I know some people who can help you."

"How?" Nathaniel said, holding onto his frustration.

"I can't say," Brigg said, pleading. "But you have got to trust me."

"Who could possibly help me?" Nathaniel asked, hoping to wear Brigg down.

"Call this number, and tell them I said you should call," Brigg said jotting down a phone number on a cocktail napkin that he had had in his hand from the bar.

"I can't tell you the details. I can only say that this is a chance for you without Janice."

"What is it... some sort of murdering service?!" Nathaniel whispered.

"Of course not!" Brigg said.

"What then?"

"Look at yourself. You're miserable. I'm giving you a chance for something more," Brigg said firmly pressing the number into Nathaniel's hand.

Nathaniel clutched the napkin tightly in his pocket as he walked home. It had been a long time since he felt any hope. Forget about love, all he could think of was his future with a woman he despised. He tried, unsuccessfully, to quell his yearning for fulfillment. Just as Nathaniel started to feel sorry for himself, he passed a group of Spots and reminded himself to be grateful. He threw the napkin in the next trashcan he saw on the corner, knowing he shouldn't screw up what he had.

He had only walked a few steps when he saw a woman walk by him.

"Hello," she said to Nathanial, without a threat. Her tone seemed almost...pleasant.

"Hi" he said nervously back, trying to keep his eyes on the

ground as she passed by. Was this a trick? Women weren't generally friendly like that, but what if some women could be like that? What if there was something better? He turned around and went back to the trash can. He fished out the rumpled napkin and smoothed it out so he could read the number.

Chapter Six

As soon as he got home, he saw Janice's note.

Nathaniel, I got out of work early and came home, but you weren't here. WTF? I called your cell. No answer. Thought we were having a late dinner, but I couldn't wait, so went down to Zelda's for a drink and a bite with Janey.

Did you find out about the wedding photographer? You were also supposed to get information about liposuction. You know I'm still hoping to get this done before the wedding. In any case, even if there isn't enough time for my procedure, you need to get Botox in that wrinkle between your brows and those crows' feet you have. There is no way our wedding photos are going to have your face all wrinkled.

Call when you get this.

Love,

Janice

There had to be a better life. Nathaniel looked at his phone and she had, in fact, called four times. He really should have been more mindful as he knew there wasn't cell service in the Black Hole, since it was a basement bar fully underground. Cursing, he dialed her cell nervously.

"Hi love!" he said, hoping his upbeat tone might gloss over the fact that he didn't tell her he might not be home on time.

"Where..ya..been?" she said, slurry.

"I was making calls about liposuction and missed your calls."

"Oh, well what'd you find out?" she said.

He suppressed a sigh of relief. She bought it.

"There's not enough time for the surgery and recovery before the wedding."

"Yeah, but what about the Botox? That's done in a doctor's office. Hmmm, maybe I could get some on the Internet and do it at home even," she said, making him shudder at the thought of a drunken Janice jabbing his face with poison after watching some how-to-inject-Botox YouTube video.

"The Botox is possible. I'll certainly make an appointment for that, but I'm talking about the surgery you wanted. I still don't understand why you would want to do that silly surgery anyway," he said. "You are gorgeous exactly the way you are."

"Nathaniel DeLuca, you are just the sweetest man who ever walked the earth," she said, laughing. "I'll be home in an hour. Janey and I are finishing up. Can't wait!" she said.

"Me too!" he said, forcing himself, but feeling relieved her mood sounded upbeat.

He immediately went into the kitchen and turned on the timer for forty minutes, in case she came home early. He opened the lower cabinet and reached all the way to the back. He touched the worn cover respectfully, thinking of the many times it had been read. Perhaps fifty. No, maybe twice that, he thought. He flipped through it slowly, caressing the washed out text.

...The world changed before my eyes when I was young. Our country had a male President who was assassinated. The Vice President, a woman named Madeleine Smith took over. While there was chaos in our country that she restored, she took things too far. She demanded to be addressed as "The Queen." Everyone feared her and obliged her wishes, and this was the first mistake. Her new policies began to infiltrate the country:

- *She released full reports with fabricated or exaggerated statistics about the prevalence of sexual assaults by unmarried men aged 26 to 35.*
- *She went on the Webavision to tell her story. She had been gang raped as a teenager and her mission as Queen would be to abolish sexual assaults.*
- *She chipped away at male rights while she encouraged women to take leadership roles. She also passed outrageously tough laws ensuring that women stayed in power.*

Little by little, the Queen stripped men of basic human rights. It is up to you to turn back time. I am old, or depending on when you read this, already dead. I can do nothing more than remind you of how it used to be.

We must all work to stop the injustices and barbaric treatment of men! Look around you. There, but for the grace of God, go I. If it happens to others, it can happen to you. Dignity is the path to happiness. Without it, life is worthless.

You must hold onto these thoughts. Work with other men to make changes, big or small, to restore our country's balance between genders.

Nathaniel carefully returned the book to its hiding place a few minutes before Janice was due home. He placed a bottle of Windex innocently in front as the words he read echoed in his mind. He had to do something. He could no longer look the other way. He nervously pulled the crumpled napkin out of his pocket.

He took a deep breath, and hesitated before finally calling the mystery number. Was he crazy for making this call? What if the phone was bugged and he got arrested for talking to the wrong people who were somehow affiliated with *Reminder of Truth?* After all, it was illegal to possess it.

He knew he should hang up. Just as he was going to disconnect, he heard a voice on the other end.

"So it's you," Shayla said, eyeing him suspiciously as she snuck up behind Nathaniel as he set down the bag in front of her office.

Nathaniel turned around, afraid for his job, his testicles, and even his life. Surely, the Queen's daughter could call in her pick of punishments with ease, if she deemed him a stalker. He tried to think of what to say if she became angry. She could send someone to search Janice's apartment and they'd find the book and then… he couldn't let his mind go there. Be polite. Be respectful and it will be okay, he told himself, hoping this was true.

"Who are you?" she asked, but Nathaniel was frozen, his mind swirling with possibilities.

"I asked your name." She folded her arms across her chest.

Her look was entirely feminine, but her energy was tough.

Nathaniel tried to say something. He had never been so close to her, and she was far more beautiful than the Webavision photos revealed. Her shiny dark hair framed her face, falling perfectly to the middle of her back. Her deep cinnamon eyes drew him in. He couldn't look away.

"I'm Nathaniel DeLuca," he said nervously, once he was able.

"Mr. DeLuca," she said before pausing for some passersby. "Why don't you come into my office?"

To Nathaniel, her words sounded more like a command than an invitation. He panicked before following her inside the office he had passed by a thousand times before. He imagined the inside to be as majestic as the Queen's daughter, but it was a dump.

The scuffed ancient desk was from the same era as the squeaky vinyl chair that she sat in. It was a great contrast to Shayla's polished look. Nathaniel was immediately mesmerized by Shayla's honey vanilla scent that contrasted the cigarettes and alcohol breath to which he was, unfortunately, accustomed. She was like the colorized part of a black and white photo with her rose chiffon blouse beneath the blue wool suit that hugged her like a second skin.

"You can sit," Shayla said matter-of-factly, as she motioned to the chair next to her desk.

Nathaniel tentatively lowered himself to the chair, but remained mute as his eyes darted around the office. The room wasn't large, but every item had its place: piles of labeled backup drives neatly stacked, and three large computer screens that spanned the desk, probably allowing her to check data and watch workers via remote cameras. He'd never seen such an elaborate setup. Everything was orderly, with one exception.

The books that sat prominently on the corner of her desk had nothing to do with construction or utilities or Cambridge Public Works policies. These were novels, the most recent bestselling authors. Pristine hardcover books. Few people read real, physical books anymore, as 90 percent of stories were accessed via electronic tablets.

Nathaniel was very curious about why she had novels on her desk. Reading was his mental escape and her desk boasted many of his favorite authors. There were classics like *Oliver Twist* by Charles Dickens, *Wuthering Heights* by Emily Bronte, and *Sacred Turns* by classic modern authors like Pedro Antflick and Aarin McCormick – Nathaniel's favorite.

Why did she have them at work?

"I was just wondering why you did it?" she asked, looking at Nathaniel with concentration as her question sounded very much like he had committed a crime. This was it. Everything was over. He was going to get castrated. Today.

"I asked you a question," she said, her voice getting louder.

He wasn't sure what to say, wasn't even sure he knew the answer, but somehow the words floated out. "I wanted to do something nice for you."

"Thank you. I appreciate that," she offered with a puzzled look. "I still don't understand why, though," she said, with a wrinkle in her brow. "Look at me," she commanded.

The real reason that he put it there on the first day was because he wanted to be defiant, but there was no way he could say that. Beside, his reason had changed since that time. His motivation came from a place of appreciation now.

"You're a good boss. A nice boss. You gave us breaks. Nobody has ever done anything like that. I guess I wanted to thank you," he said, before allowing his eyes to meet hers. He tried not to second-guess himself, but there was something about her that made him feel comfortable being himself. Considering she was the Queen's daughter, his boss, and she had ammunition to ruin his life, it surprised him. The longer they sat there silently looking at one another, the more certain he was of this feeling.

"I'm just doing my job," she said dryly. "I must admit, these are the best damn muffins I think I've ever had," she said. She broke into a grin that accentuated her perfectly supple lips and Nathaniel felt his fears ease.

"They're from Chester's Bakery down the street," he said, suddenly feeling great pride for Chester as the ice in the room thawed. He wondered whether the simple mixtures of sugar, flour, and butter just might, ironically, save his balls.

"Would you mind continuing to bring them? It helps when I don't have to stop and grab breakfast in the morning."

"No, ma'am. Not at all," he said enthusiastically.

"I like the banana ones best, and the blueberry are a close second. How much is it?" she asked, reaching for her purse.

"Actually, there's no need for that. You see, Chester, the owner, is my Uncle-in-law to be," he said, almost smiling. "He won't let me pay for anything."

"I insist," she said, handing him a large bill. "And, by the way… you don't need to call me ma'am."

"Okay," he said, not sure what to say.

"When you are in my office, call me Shayla," she said as she handed him a large bill. "When this runs out, I'll give you more. I pay for my own breakfast, understood?"

Nathaniel hesitantly took the money from her, feeling a zing of pleasure from just brushing his hand against hers, however briefly. There was no way that Chester was going to take money from him, and there was no way in hell that he was going to tell Chester who the extra muffin went to.

"Thank you, Nathaniel." He loved the way she said his name and that she might say it again sometime.

"You're very welcome," he said.

She got up and opened the door. She peered out, making sure nobody was there, and gestured for his exit. He closed the door, his heart beating wildly at the thought of what went on, the absence of punishment, and Shayla's personal request for a daily muffin and coffee. Should he just leave them outside her door as he had been? Or, now that she knew who it was, should he wait until she was there and bring it to her door? She hadn't asked for anything different, so he decided to just keep leaving them outside her door.

Continuing to his morning post, he knew better than to

tell anyone. As much as his coworkers appreciated Shayla's policies, she was still a woman, and not just any woman. She was the daughter of man's biggest enemy. Even Brigg would see it as buttering up the other side.

"Heard you made the call," Brigg said quietly, the moment Nathaniel sat down next to him.

"Yeah," he said with his mind adrift to the cryptic conversation the previous evening that ended with a scolding…

"Yes, there is something better for you. We were told you might call. You did the right thing, now you need to be ready to go."

"Go where? I don't understand," Nathaniel said, his heart beating wildly as he wondered what he was doing.

"To a better place."

"That's what people say about dying," Nathaniel said.

"Do not call this number again under any circumstances. You'll be given further instructions soon. Do you understand?"

"What is this? How will I know…"

"We will contact you."

"For what?" Nathaniel tried to ask again, but was cut off with a firm click that scared and angered him.

Nathaniel unpacked his coffee and muffin, preferring to think about Shayla and how she was enjoying the same simple pleasure.

"The voice was so familiar…just tell me who it was. I won't say anything," Nathaniel whispered, hoping Brigg would trust him.

"I can't."

"Can't or won't," Nathaniel said, slightly annoyed. That phone call unnerved him.

"Please," Brigg pleaded, his jaw tightening visibly.

Nathaniel was too tired to argue with Brigg. After all, Nathaniel had a secret, too.

Chapter Seven

After dropping off breakfast for Shayla each day, Nathanial looked forward to seeing her tour the worksites most mornings, coffee cup in hand, with Chester's Bakery logo side out. He kept hoping for her eyes to rest on him, but she was all business. He felt an undeniable desire as he watched her beautiful lips take a sip from that cup. She even looked sexy when drinking coffee.

While Janice might own him and his actions, she didn't own his thoughts. Nathaniel unapologetically enjoyed the fantasy visions of himself in Shayla's embrace.

One morning, he was about to make his coffee and muffin drop off when he noticed the light from underneath her office door. After making sure nobody was looking, with his heart pounding, he offered a wistful knock. He knew he probably shouldn't do it, but he wanted to see her again, even just for a minute.

"Would you like to come in, Nathaniel?" she said after opening the door and smiling once she saw who was there.

Nathaniel glanced up and down the hallway, and stepped inside thinking about how he liked the sound of his name from her mouth. She closed the door behind him and he felt like they were in an alternate universe.

"You can sit down," she said, motioning to the chair. She eyed the bag that he nervously clutched.

"Thanks," he said, staring at a faced-down novel on her desk.

"Yes, I sometimes read before work, before things get crazy around here," she said, as if reading his mind's question.

"Are you a big fan of Deahn's?" he asked.

"You like Deahn?" she asked, noticing his eyes stuck on the cover.

"I just finished that one," he said carefully not offering his opinion of the work he thought masterful. Berrini Deahn was one of his favorites, with suspenseful stories that swooped Nathaniel neatly outside of his world, which was exactly what he needed.

"Really?" she said with great surprise. "What did you think?"

He noticed she was in the middle, and felt the test of her question.

"I don't want to ruin it for you," he said noncommittally.

"Did you like it? That doesn't give anything away," she said, sitting back in her chair, observing him in a way that made him feel like he was in an interview.

"I thought it was pretty good, and I've read them all," he said, wondering if he should say more.

"All of them, huh," she said, biting the end of her pencil as she pensively surveyed her own private Secret Santa Claus of muffins and coffee.

"Yes, ma'am," he said, feeling her survey him.

"Ahh, ahh… call me Shalya. Now, which one is your favorite?" she asked, smirking at him in a way that made him blush.

"*The Torrent*," he said.

"Oh, come on! With all those goofy space ships?" she said, laughing. He loved her animated smile and the lightness it brought to her eyes. He felt happy around her, such a rarity as he faced his coming-of-age dilemma. Either marry Janice and face a lifetime of unhappiness or be castrated.

"I like fantasy. It's better than my real life," he said, with more bite than he had intended. He was momentarily embarrassed. Shayla seemed unfazed, but tilted her head as if studying him.

"You are entirely entitled to your opinion," she said in a way that felt so respectful. It was refreshing to hear that from a woman, but it was especially unexpected from the Queen's daughter.

"Thank you for saying that," he said. A moment of quietness followed and felt nice. "What about you?" he finally said, starting to feel at ease.

"My favorite is *The Revengers*. I love the way the protagonist got back at all the people who had wronged her and her family," Shayla said with a seriousness that changed the air.

"Different kind of book really, but I like that idea. Righting injustices is something we don't see enough of…," he said trailing his thought, realizing he was about to say too much.

"In Deahn's stories?" she asked, clearly intrigued.

Nathaniel was quiet for a moment, weighing the consequences of the truth, but he had spent the previous evening reading more of *Reminder of Truth*. Clearly, the messages were getting under his skin and coming out of his mouth.

"In this country," he clarified, as he looked her directly in the eye, laying the thoughts between them that no man dared to bring up in front of her.

"Go on," she said, putting her pencil down and looking Nathanial square in the eyes, but Nathaniel was hesitant to say anything. A flood of words was barely being levied at the back of his throat.

"What I really think is…"

Her phone rang, and Nathaniel's heart leapt at the sound. She answered, listening intently, and Nathaniel was glad for the interruption.

"I've gotta get out of here," he whispered. She held up her finger and mouthed he should wait just a minute, but he stood up to leave.

Shayla covered the mouthpiece of her phone. "I'll be off in just a minute," she said.

"I have to be at my post in 3 minutes," he whispered.

"I'll call you right back," Shayla said, before immediately closing her phone.

"Just finish what you were saying," she said. He felt her focus nearly force him to sit back down.

"Nothing important," he said, shaking his head feeling incredibly nervous. As he picked up his coffee and muffin bag, she lightly put her hand on his arm, startling him. He jumped back, nearly knocking over the chair.

"I'm sorry," he said, setting the chair back in its spot as he couldn't bear to meet her eyes as the awkwardness returned. Once again, she was in charge. Without another word, he hurried out of her office door hoping he would make it in time. After all, there was no way anyone would believe he was late because he was sitting having coffee with the Queen's daughter.

"Nathaniel!"

He sprinted into the kitchen, the moment he heard Janice's familiar shriek.

"You said you cleaned up after dinner, but the kitchen just seems kind of…"

"What else would you like me to do?" he asked, his adrenaline making him cut her off mid-sentence. He could see that she was drunk.

She turned her head and looked out the window, leaving him hanging for a moment before she turned back. "Clean the kitchen. Thoroughly. Top to bottom," she said, clutching her glass like a security blanket. She took a sip, but ice was all that remained.

"Right now?" he asked, having a really hard time masking his disappointment. The day started early with work, and then he bought groceries, and cooked dinner. He just finished doing the dinner dishes. He wanted to sit down and read for a while before going to sleep. He had purchased one of the books he had seen on Shayla's shelf, and he had been trying to sneak in time here and there to read, but Janice kept finding tasks that "needed" doing, immediately.

"You have something else more important to do?" she asked, staring at the electronic tablet in his hand, which she seemed to hate as much as anything that diverted his attention from her. He had given up so much. He didn't want to give up reading, too. He hoped to get a chance to discuss the book with Shayla, but there had been no light on under her door the past few mornings, and he figured that might be for the best. He wasn't sure how long he could keep quiet about what was really on his mind.

"No, certainly not," he said to Janice, reassuringly, nodding, fearful of speaking further.

She shook her glass gently in his direction. The ice cubes tinkled together like a bell summoning him. He wordlessly went to her, intent on refilling the glass, but she tightened her grip just for a moment when he tried to take it. Why did she have to do this? He knew better than to try and figure it out. He had learned it was better, and easier, to simply try and do what she wanted. Obey, rather than understand her moods.

"With a little more lemon this time," she said, hovering closely as he poured the chilled vodka into her glass, adding a little ice, and a splash of cranberry juice. He took a fresh lemon and sliced it clean in half before squeezing it with all his might into the glass. Janice's eyes penetrated him, as he scurried around the kitchen.

He handed her the drink and waited. His insides churned as he tried to prepare for the next criticism. She'll probably say there is too much lemon.

"Good job," she said to him finally, as though he was a dog, surprising him with a smile as she walked out of the kitchen.

"If you need another drink, or anything else, just let me know," he said as she wobbled away.

When he heard the Webavision turn on in the other room, he breathed a momentary sigh of relief. He picked up his electronic tablet and turned it off before bringing it into the bedroom and setting it on his nightstand, so it wouldn't even tease him while he cleaned.

"Don't forget to clean out the refrigerator, too!" Janice yelled from the other room.

"Of course!" he replied, and decided to begin there. He set the entire contents of the fridge on the counter before going underneath the sink to retrieve the Windex. He peered behind the Windex. lured him like a beacon. He wanted to know about the real history that he had never known, and he wanted to talk with Shayla about it. He knew that speaking his mind to her, of all people, was insane.

But he had to admit that the last time he was in her office, she seemed almost disappointed when he had to rush out of her office. Was that his imagination?

He reminded himself that she was his boss. He was her employee and nothing more. Sure, he brought her breakfast, but he made breakfast for Janice, too. Once a servant, always a servant.

Nathaniel picked up the Windex and began to clean the refrigerator, refocusing on the only true reality.

"Looks good," Janice slurred, checking in a while later. He didn't hear her enter the kitchen.

"Thanks," he said, feeling worn down. Sometimes he wished Chester had never given him that book. When he didn't know about men living free lives, his mind didn't think about such possibilities. What if he had been born in another time?

"What's the matter?"

"Nothing," he said, trying to pull himself together.

"Are you sure?" she said, approaching him, touching his face in a way that made him cringe. She smiled as she guided his face toward hers. "You wanna go in the bedroom?" she whispered, her forehead touching his.

"Don't you want me to finish cleaning here?"

"Finish it later," she said, running her fingers through his hair as she leaned her cigarette flavored mouth onto his lips.

She pulled him into the bedroom, and he didn't think he could perform, but knew he had to.

"Leave the lights on," she said.

"It's sexier with them off," he told her, as he took her to the bed in the dark, for once going against her wishes. Closing his eyes, he thought of Shayla, allowing the fantasy of her beckoning him to her bed until he could feel himself erect. He held onto those visions of Shayla so he could comply with Janice's requests.

He bore himself into her as she cried out with pleasure. Even in that moment, he longed to feel something for Janice other than hatred, but knew he never would. He could only imagine Shayla opening herself up to him, responding to his fingers exploring her body. He wanted to give her the kind of irresistible pleasure that she had never experienced.

When he felt the pulsation of his climax, he saw Shayla in his mind, but reality quickly set in. A few minutes later Janice's snoring reminded Nathaniel who was by his side and who would be there forevermore.

Chapter Eight

"What the hell happened to you? You look terrible!" Chester said, as they sat at the corner table in his bakery.

"I haven't been sleeping well," Nathaniel said, wanting badly to confide. He knew that Chester would listen, but complaining to a Spot, about anything, seemed wrong to Nathaniel. Plus, this was Janice's uncle. He may have given Nathaniel *Reminder of Truth,* but that didn't mean it was open season to bash her. Maybe he would talk to Brigg later, maybe not. Discussing his frustrations seemed futile.

Chester took a sip of coffee and eyed him. "You gotta take care of yourself," he said, shaking his head.

"I'll be fine. I just need a good night's sleep, that's all," he said as he got up, wishing that was true. "Thanks for the coffee," he said.

"My pleasure, as always. You're gonna be alright," Chester said, giving Nathaniel a hearty pat on the back before Nathaniel left.

As he walked to work, he fantasized that Shayla showed up early and was waiting for him, but he doubted this would happen. Still, he turned the corner toward her office with nervous anticipation.

As he moved down the corridor, his eyes shot to the bottom of her door. No light. He bent down to pretend he was tying his shoe as he looked at the shy crack at the bottom of the door, to be sure. Maybe if he stayed there long enough, he could will the light on, the door would spring open and Shayla would welcome him.

He knew this was ridiculous. He was just about to set the bag down when he heard someone coming. He pretended to be tying his shoe again.

"Hey," she said, nearly out of breath as she approached her office.

"Hi," Nathaniel said, feeling his face heat up.

"Want to come in?" she asked.

"Sure," he said, feeling his heartbeat boom in his chest.

She's your boss. You're her employee. She's just being polite because you serve her breakfast each day. Don't forget that!

As she placed her hand on the sensor that unlocked her door, she was quiet and kept her eyes on the door. As soon as they crossed the threshold into her office and the door closed, all formality vanished. The outside world fell away, as if they were tucked away in a cabin in the woods. He loved this comfortable feeling, just as it pained him to know it would never amount to anything.

Nathaniel sat down without waiting for an invitation. He watched as she quietly set her briefcase down and removed her coat that she carefully hung up. It offered him a moment of looking at her from behind. She caught the focus of his eyes when she turned around and gave him a slow, but knowing smile, clearly entertained. The smile alone made him stiffen, and he shifted the Chester's Bakery bag to his lap as he crossed his legs.

"So, how long have you been working here?" she asked, once she sat down.

"I've been here forever, since right after high school. Never worked anywhere else, really," he said. "This," he said, gesturing around "is my life and probably will be forever."

"Do you like working here?" she asked. Nathaniel kept his eyes focused on the floor, as an uncomfortable feeling began to settle in. How could he answer that?

"What you tell me is between us," she told him, as if she could read his quandary about whether to please her or be honest.

"I like working hard and earning a living and am grateful to have a job," he said.

"Oh, c'mon, Nathaniel. You sound like a goddamn commercial for bipartisanship!" she said, laughing. "Tell me the truth. I don't have anybody here to tell me how things really are," she said, her voice softening. "I'm just the new girl here, you know," she said, laughing.

"I think I'd better go," he said. He had been wishing to have the opportunity to sit exactly where he was, and now realized it was probably better kept as a daydream. He had to get out of there and motioned to stand.

"Sit," she said, looking at her watch. "You've got plenty of time."

"It's not that," he said. She smiled at him with a relaxed, pleasant smile that he wasn't sure how to interpret. He had seen a zillion photos of her over the years, but they didn't come anywhere close to capturing her true beauty.

"I don't know how I'm supposed to answer you," he said, simply.

"We're just having a conversation over coffee," she said shrugging. She pulled the other cup of coffee from the bag in between them and offered it to him. He couldn't help but think about how Janice held her glass out to him the previous evening, tricking him by gripping it tight when he went to take it. Shayla's fingers momentarily touched his as he took the coffee. How he wished they could linger there, but knew that he needed to banish those thoughts. *You are her employee and she is your boss*, he reminded himself yet again. That didn't help him manage the allure of her.

He took a sip of coffee, hoping this conversation would go somewhere else.

"Now tell me, how do you like working here?"

"I like working here as much as any man probably likes working anywhere," he said, "which is to say, not very much."

She tilted her head and looked at him with a curiosity that didn't make him feel threatened.

"It's challenging…," he continued, feeling like he still wanted to tread lightly.

"I'm listening."

"I can't say anymore."

"Nathaniel," she said, leaning toward him. "I'm asking you because I want to know. I really do. I want to know why you don't like it and I want to make it better. Nothing bad is going to happen to you for speaking the truth."

He laughed out loud at the irony of where he sat, who was talking to him, and what she said.

"Why are you laughing?"

"The tension in this room is so big that I'm surprised either of us can breathe," he said, looking straight at her. "I don't want to get myself fired," he said. "Or worse."

"I give you my word. Just tell me."

He took another sip of his coffee and pondered, wondering if this was a trick, but he trusted her. Maybe he shouldn't, but he did.

"Last time I was here, you told me about your favorite book," he said.

"The Deahn book?"

"Yes, the one with the revenge theme," he said with emphasis. "Let me ask you a question. How do you think all the men feel working here or anywhere for that matter? Don't get me wrong," he added quickly. "I think you have made things better for men in the short time you've been here. Still, the changes you made are small, compared to what we need."

"And that is?" she asked.

"I truly believe that inside every man in this country is a desire for equality," he said, feeling liberated and afraid all at once. He had never said any of this aloud and certainly not to a woman. He hadn't talked about this with anyone but Brigg.

Shayla looked at him with compassionate eyes, the kind that he had never ever seen from a woman.

"This is hush, hush," the Queen said over the phone, excitement filling her voice. "Male infants will have micro chips injected under their skin while still in the hospital. It'll track them as they grow up. Women can point smart phones at men to read all about them at the Parties of Availability. The Tasers also benefit from this technology for immediate access to a man's age, medical records, but also the database of prior arrests, employment history etc...."

"I think you're making a huge mistake," Shayla said. She was haunted by Nathaniel DeLuca's honesty. He had finally opened up and his words echoed the sentiment of her father's: men feel the burden of injustices that start with the Parties of Availability, and segue into total servitude, especially once married. It wasn't a surprise, but it was difficult to hear because she knew her mother, and previous grandmothers before her, were responsible for the way men were treated. She knew it wasn't going to do any good to stand up to her mother, but she had to at least try.

"Some day, my dear Shayla, you will understand. I hope," the Queen said, quietly.

"Aren't you going a little overboard? I mean, what if men treated women this way?" Shayla asked in a purposely moderate voice. She knew it would enflame her mother, but she had to speak her mind. She thought of Nathaniel. She had already been on the path to pick up her father's legacy, but hearing Nathaniel's opinions made all her plans seem urgent.

She had even gone home the previous evening after hearing Nathaniel's candidness and pulled out her copy of *Reminder of Truth*, the gift from her father on his death bed. She hadn't read it in quite a while. If her mother ever found out she had it or where it came from … Shayla couldn't imagine what she would do.

"Look at the rate of sexual assaults in America compared with other countries? We are LEADERS because we are forward thinking! Can't you see that?" The Queen asked with rhetorical venom.

"Okay, mother. You are right. You are always right." Shayla should have known better than to speak her mind to her mother. She almost reminded her mother of all the homeless Spots but knew it would fall on deaf ears as she would undoubtedly talk about how they were "comfortably sheltered." Yes, that's true, as long as one considered "comfort" personal space the size of a refrigerator box with food that was akin to gruel from a Dickens novel.

"Do I have to remind you that your great grandmother was raped at age 14?"

"I know, and that was terrible, but not all men are rapists and evil the way you make them out to be," Shayla said.

"Sexual assaults and violence have been eradicated from our

society. The only reason you can walk through a city park after dark with ease and freedom is because our first Queen passed mandatory castration laws. I'm proud of her and what she stood for."

"Are you proud of the fact that we're the oppressors? Just today I walked by a Taser who had a man strapped to a chair, in the middle of the park, with duct tape on his mouth…Isn't that assault?"

"We do that to keep the men safe. They crave that discipline, deep down," the Queen said, not letting Shayla finish. "At the core, men are uncontrollable animals. It's not their fault, you understand. We must help them, and that's what we have done. It's for their own good. It's for everyone's own good."

"That was a long time ago, mother. Things have changed," Shayla said, growing weary of this argument.

"They are dangerous. Studies and history have shown…"

"What about Daddy? Was he a monster, too? After all, he was a man!" Shayla yelled. This time it was her turn to bring her father up. She hated doing it, but had to prove her point. Shayla closed her eyes, feeling bad for using his memory this way, but she knew he would have understood.

"You sure you want to defy me, Shayla?" the Queen said, with a cunning stronghold in her voice. "I don't care how old you are. If you were here, I'd wash your mouth out with soap," her mother said before hanging up on her. Shayla was shaken more than she cared to admit, but her thoughts were interrupted with a knock on her office door.

Chapter Nine

Again, Nathaniel saw light underneath her office door and knocked. As she opened the door, he was, once again, lost in her aura.

"Come in," she said, smiling, but her voice was flat. Maybe he was wrong and his thought of her enjoying his company was purely in his head.

"You sure? I could just leave this if you're busy."

"Please," she said, stepping away from the door and sitting at her desk. He sat down and took the coffee from the bag and held it out to her. She gently took the cup, her quiet gaze resting on his. Usually, she asked how he was right off the bat, but she said nothing.

"Is something wrong?" he asked carefully.

"I can't really talk about it," she said.

"I didn't mean to pry…" he said.

"You're sweet," she said, her smile returning, along with a glimpse of the woman with whom he had become acquainted. Her warmth melted his heart.

"Well, if there is anything I can do…"

"You have already done something, Nathaniel DeLuca, and you don't even know it," she said with a lightness that made him feel something deep inside.

"I hope it's something good," he said, smiling back.

"For one thing, you bring me breakfast each morning, and well… I've been thinking about what we talked about the last time you were here."

"I was afraid I said too much," Nathaniel said.

"I'm glad you said what you did. You spoke the truth, and I know that was difficult, not because you're dishonest, but…" she said, her voice growing quiet. Nathaniel looked at her and the silence between them thickened.

"I'm afraid," he said. "All men are afraid."

"You don't have to be afraid of me…"

Shayla was silent and took the muffin from the bag, setting it on her desk. She observed it, as though strategizing about how to approach it. Finally, she pulled a small piece from the edge, and popped it in her mouth.

"I believe you. I trust you," he said. "But I still wonder. What am I doing here?" he said.

"Do you know how things used to be? You probably don't even know about my great grandmother, the first Queen," Shayla said.

"I know of another era," he said, cautiously.

"Have you read about it?" she asked.

He felt like she was talking in code and it made him uncomfortable because he wasn't entirely sure.

"Maybe I should go," he said, blushing.

"No," she said with the authoritative command he was accustomed to hearing when she spoke to supervisors on worksites.

Shayla rose from her seat and locked the door. She pulled a dark velvet bag from deep inside her purse and held it out to him. Nathaniel looked at her and she nodded.

He opened the bag and pulled out a book that he never thought he would see one time, let alone twice. *Reminder of Truth.*

"I've read it," he said quietly, his hands shaking as Shayla stood over him. She took the book and set it gently on the desk and engaged his eyes before silently leaning over and kissing him softly on the lips. Nathaniel couldn't hold back. The kiss was slow and gentle, and as she took his hands and guided them, he inhaled her sweet smell that he had been starving for since the moment the scent first tickled his nose. Each kiss made the flutter in his stomach reach down immediately making him hard. He walked down her neck with his lips and she let out a soft purr of pleasure that let him know each kiss was just right.

Shayla's hands touched the thick calluses on Nathaniel's hands, as if they were Braille and she was memorizing them. She looked into his eyes before feeling his biceps and instinctively straddled him unabashedly, feeling the tenseness of his muscles, making her unable to ignore the excitement between her legs. They both thought only with their bodies as they explored one another, gently but firmly. It was a curiosity that needed satisfying.

When there seemed to be no other place to go beyond the boundaries of their clothing, Nathaniel stopped. While his hardness wanted nothing more than to feel his skin against hers, he knew better than to assume. She touched his stiffness and smiled at him.

"What now?" he asked softly, hoping for an answer that would fulfill his sexual excitement.

She silenced him with a kiss and began to take off her clothes.

He thought of himself as a gentleman caller who was courting his ladylove with muffins and coffee, instead of flowers.

"I'm sorry, but I've got an early meeting," Shayla said with sadness as soon as he came in, squashing the moment that had become the jewel of his routine over the last month.

Nathaniel's face showed obvious disappointment. Shayla grabbed him and gave a passionate kiss, showing her preference for their morning's usual routine.

"I have to go, but I wish I could stay here," she whispered flirtatiously, as she fondled him.

"Don't get me all excited, then!" he joked, as he couldn't help but grow hard with her hand wrapped around him.

"You gotta go now," she said, "but give me my coffee and muffin," she said, playfully grabbing the bag from him.

Nathaniel walked toward his post, waiting for his hard-on to soften. He resorted to the only sure way to get it to crawl back inside. He imagined Janice in one of her 'sexy' outfits. It was always a full-proof way to squelch his sexual desire. He hated to do it but learned this trick in high school when his hormones controlled him completely -- Think of something disgusting and your hard-on instantly disappears. Otherwise, there was no break from the sexual tension.

As the morning dragged, Nathaniel focused on work, alongside Brigg, until their first break of the day.

Brigg took a long drink from his water bottle as they sat on the curb. "It's gotta be a hundred degrees. Thank God for this break."

"Don't you think we should thank Miss Shayla?" Nathaniel said.

Brigg nodded. "Thank you, Miss Shayla," he said, sounding a little sarcastic to Nathaniel.

"It could be worse," Nathaniel said, using a towel to wipe his forehead. He felt like he had been rolled in charcoal, and the dust was baking into his skin. Still, he wasn't as irritated by the heat as he used to be. His mornings with Shayla took the edge off of the heat, the supervisors, and even Janice.

"Am I sitting next to the same guy who used to whine constantly? Why are you so fucking happy lately?" Brigg said.

Nathaniel shrugged, grinning.

Brigg eyed him closely.

"Break is over!" their supervisor yelled.

"It wasn't really a full 10 minutes," Brigg whispered to Nathaniel, but apparently, he hadn't done so quietly enough as their supervisor turned and glared at them, before walking over.

"What'd you say?" she asked.

"Ready to get back to work," Brigg said, his voice barely masking a quiver. She was known to be harsh. Rumor had it that she had sent two men to the C Center before they were 26, deeming their behaviors "dangerous and erratic" and therefore causing a threat to women's safety.

"Good. You two are back on jackhammer duty for the rest of the week."

Jack hammering was known to be the toughest assignment, and they were done with it for the week. They each knew better than to speak up and remind her about Shayla's new policy that only allowed fifteen hours per week of jackhammer duty, which they had just completed.

Nathaniel and Brigg silently walked over to the jackhammers that were used to break up the top layer of the street for repaving.

Without emotion, they put on their goggles and protective ear gear and began the work that vibrated their bodies and souls.

"DeLUCA!"

"Yes," he said, turning off his jack hammer not an hour later. The same supervisor yelled his name again. Brigg caught his eyes for a moment, and Nathaniel saw his own worry reflected back.

"This is for you and apparently it's an emergency so I am instructed to let you go," she said, eyeing the well-sealed envelope that she reluctantly handed him.

Chapter Ten

Nathaniel quickly showered at work and put on another set of Cambridge Public Works clothes, as that was all he had. He then hurried through the streets until he got to the hotel. Walking through the lobby, he felt self-conscious in his work uniform.

He glanced at the note one more time, in his lover's unmistakable handwriting as he waited for the elevator.

Room 314. Cambridge Marriott. Now!

The lipstick kiss at the bottom made him want to smile when he first got the note, but his supervisor was standing close by. It took effort to maintain his composure.

"What is it?" his supervisor had asked suspiciously.

"I've got to go," he had simply said, and shoved it into his pocket. He couldn't wait to get out of there. Obviously, Shayla couldn't wait either, he thought, grinning. It was highly unusual to be called away from a job site in this way. Even for the Queen's daughter, sending such a note felt too risky.

As soon as he was out of there, he relaxed a little, and now he was nervous again. Nathaniel tried to appear nonchalant when boarding the elevator, but was unaccustomed to being inside such an elegant building. Even the elevators were stunning with green marble walls and hand-carved wood trim.

He made his way to the room. As soon as Shayla let him in and closed the door, she opened the hotel's insignia bathrobe to reveal her sheer black negligee. The matching black garters perfectly complemented her sexy body.

"I've waited a long time to share a bed with you," she said.

With an unhindered smile, she led him to the bed before she began to peel away her lingerie. She stood still for a moment, teasing him toward her as he admired every inch of her body as she touched her own breasts invitingly. They were perfect, ample, and accentuated her petite waist. The dip of her flat belly invited him to what was below. As she began to tug at his buttons, he put his hands on hers to help her slowly undo the fly and then he removed his standard issue Public Works uniform of a blue polyester button-down shirt. All the while, his eyes stayed on hers as she began to touch the muscles that defined the lines of his taut body.

He kissed her long and hard until she pushed him away to quickly pull her negligee over her head. He pulled her close again, cupped her breasts and leaned down to softly suck on her nipples until they tightened with pleasure.

She backed away after a moment and sat on the bed. Clad only in a g-string, she spread her legs to reach in the panties where she touched herself, watching for his reaction. He wanted her so badly. Nothing would keep him from her as he went to her.

Her eyes met Nathaniel's for a moment before she began to kiss her way down his body, teasing him slowly until she reached his granite hard-on. She put her hands around him, before taunting him further, pretending she was going to take him in. Finally, she began with the tip in her mouth, tasting the pearl of saltiness on the end. He had to concentrate to control himself once her lips enveloped him completely. The smoothness of her mouth rapidly on him was too much and he felt his release too soon.

When she was done, she brought her face to his. "This is so perfect in a place like this." he said. He looked into her eyes deeply for all the nights they'd been apart, for the dinners they hadn't shared, and the public strolls around town that would never be. "Thank you," he added, holding her, caressing her soft skin with a relaxed pleasure that was unlike anything he'd ever experienced.

His hardness soon returned and he mounted her with unrestrained passion. They rocked together in perfect rhythm. She moaned with bliss as he wrapped her legs around him. She shuddered as Nathaniel felt his orgasm blast through her.

He said, "I wish…"

"Shhh…" she said, stopping him with her finger on his mouth. He felt relaxed as never before, but he wanted to say so many things as he gazed into her welcome eyes. Instead, he held her tightly, sadly wondering if he would ever have this opportunity again.

✣✣✣✣✣✣✣✣✣✣

As Nathaniel stepped outside, he was greeted with the rush of people heading home for the evening. A surge of guilt and fear rose up in him and he decided to go by Eva's Diner, since it was on the way, and surprise Janice. The wedding was still a month away and he needed to keep her happy. He hadn't planned on cheating when he agreed to be her husband. He knew it wasn't okay and he also felt bad about harboring this secret from Brigg, too. Since they were kids, they'd always trusted one another. But this was different. He had to keep it to himself, for everyone's safety.

As soon as he stepped inside Eva's Diner, he saw the unbridled excitement on Janice's face. She ran to the door and gave him a big kiss and hug.

"What a great surprise!" she asked happily. "Oh, you smell so clean! Is that a new soap? I like!" she said, leaning close. He was very glad to have taken an extra shower after sex with Shayla. Better to smell of soap than anything else.

"I showered at work," he said, offering only a piece of the truth. While he didn't love Janice, she didn't deserve to be cheated on.

"What brings you here?"

"I was going home from work and thought I'd come visit my love," he said. He had to lay it on thick as much to assuage his guilt as he did to try to undercut his growing mountain of feelings for Shayla.

Janice lunged at her boss. "Eva, can I take my break now?"

"You lovebirds take your time," Eva said.

"Let's go outside so I can have a smoke," Janice said, grabbing Nathaniel's hand, as she stepped out the door and led him to a bench out front. The fresh air felt good, until she lit her menthol cigarette that traveled in slow waves toward him. Although she made no effort to shield the smoke, he didn't complain.

"Does my special man want me to take him out to dinner tonight?" she asked as she ran her index finger lightly over his hand in small spirals.

"I don't mind cooking, but I'm happy to go out too," he said lightly, not responding to her touch. He knew he should, but his mind ran elsewhere the moment she lit that cigarette.

"Great. Let's go to Antonio's and have a real nice meal. Can you wait for a late dinner?"

"Perfect," he said, trying to sound upbeat before leaning into give her a quick kiss on the lips.

"Great. I'll pick you up at 9:30 and we'll go straight from there. I gotta get back to work, even though I'd love to knock off right now," she said softly before giving him one more nicotine kiss, this one longer. He resisted his urge to pull away and grab a mint.

Antonio's was crowded, but Janice had been going there forever, and they were seated quickly.

"I had a fitting today for my dress," she said with excitement when they sat down. "It's so beautiful. I can't wait! Did you get your botox appointment?"

"Not yet, but soon," he said.

"Nathaniel, you must do that! It's 29 days until the wedding! You need to get that done so there will be time for it to settle down a little!" she said. He placed his hand on hers, and she visibly softened. His stomach knotted as he realized they were each counting the days for entirely different reasons.

"I'll make the appointment tomorrow," he said. "I promise."

As they walked home, she carried on about wedding details, making his stomach tighter and tighter, as he could only think of Shayla.

Soon after they got home, Nathaniel settled onto the couch in the living room, hoping to read. Janice soon joined him, clad only in a red see-through negligee that had accompanying crotch-less panties. She softly said his name as she showed him the intentional hole in her outfit, which repulsed him. He looked where she pointed, but the ripples of cellulite that surrounded her belly button turned him off completely as he couldn't help but compare it to the negligee and beautifully smooth body of his true love, from earlier in the day.

"I'm a little tired, love," he said. He didn't know if he could manage another erection, especially if it wasn't for Shayla.

"I need you," she said. "It's been a while…"

"You know I love you. It's just that I've been working with the jackhammers in 100 degree weather. It's so exhausting," he said, pulling her close, the sour alcohol smell infusing his space.

"Are you sure that's all?" she said, and he felt a new twinge of guilt for Janice. He had never heard her insecurity so blatantly. Of course he should have forced himself to have sex with her on a regular basis. Even though it would be a challenge, he made a mental note to do so moving forward – at least twice a week.

"Of course that's all," he said, trying to be reassuring as he held her close. He let the hug linger, and lovingly stroked her head, as if she were Shayla. He realized that he couldn't put it off forever. "We'll make some special time this weekend to be together," he said.

"Okay," she said, pulling back and looking into his eyes with a tentative smile. He held her gaze, but his heart quickened, as he worried that she would see into his mind. He had to be careful or she might dump him. He had no backup plan. It wasn't as if the Queen's daughter was going to drop everything, give up her place in the Palace lineage and propose to a laborer like Nathaniel DeLuca.

She pulled out a bottle of vodka from the cabinet and retreated to the bedroom. It was uncharacteristic of her not to have him fix her drinks. He was happy to be left alone. Shayla had given him a hardcover book as a gift and he pulled it out and opened to the page he had last read. As much as he tried, he couldn't concentrate. He closed the book and set it on the coffee table in front of him, wondering whether he preferred to have Janice bossy or insecure. Bossy Janice, at least, helped him justify the love he had found elsewhere.

He checked in on her a little later and saw she was asleep

next to a half-empty bottle of vodka. He put the lid on it before turning off the light and closing the bedroom door. He retrieved *Reminder of Truth*, which he had read with a new fervor since he had seen Shayla's copy. They had discussed their favorite passages, and he turned to one of those that fueled him when he felt unsure of how he was going to make it through another day, with all that he juggled.

...You must foster the change, dear reader! Give love and make love, and show the women our compassion. We must show women and the world that not all men are violent, rapists, or cruel. This is the truth and it must be revealed.

He reread it and absorbed the meaning before closing the book. He carefully replaced it under the sink, hidden away. It was late, and he was headed to bed when the nighttime silence was subtly interrupted with a tapping sound that caught him off guard. At first, he thought the noise came from their grumpy refrigerator, but he realized this stray sound wasn't coming from the kitchen.

He stood in the center of the living room, listening. Adrenaline surged from within him, moving toward his fingertips. He couldn't pinpoint its origin until it changed to a quiet knock on the door and he moved toward it.

It was nearly midnight. Who could be at the door? It could only be a neighbor from inside the building since anyone else would have to ring the buzzer to get past the initial set of doors. The knocking sound started again. He hesitated.

"Who's there?"

"It's Brigg. I know it's late, but can I come in for a minute?"

Nathaniel felt his muscles relax as the familiar voice calmed him. He was confused as to why Brigg didn't use the cell to at least text him and let him know he was coming. As he unlocked the door, he again wondered how Brigg got into the building without a key.

As soon as the door opened, Brigg came in.

"What's up?"

"I have some people I want you to meet," Brigg whispered, pulling him into the hall.

"Now?"

"Yes," Brigg said, and out of nowhere four men clad in black quietly overtook Nathaniel. One covered his mouth with a gag, two others helped hold him down while the fourth prepared a syringe.

"Hold still and it'll hurt less," Brigg said, but Nathaniel squirmed. What the hell was going on? Why was Brigg doing this?

"This is for the best, my friend," Nathaniel heard Brigg say from the distance as he felt a shocking pierce to his arm, and after that everything went black.

Chapter Eleven

"Brigg!" he managed to croak through his cottony-dry mouth. If his friend was in the front of the van, surely he would help. Nathaniel's head boomed in sync with the highway's jostling ride. With effort, he roused his body to a sitting position, feeling a plethora of aches – presumably from being bumped around in the van for God knows how long.

"Brigg, come on, man!"

"One more yell out of you and I'll pull over and put that gag back on," he finally heard in an unfamiliar bark.

Nathaniel looked around the back of the van, shades drawn on the windows so the only light came from the edges. Everything he looked at had a haze. He felt thirsty, like a dehydrated plant. What the hell did they inject him with?

Most important, he felt no pain in his groin. There had been rumors about people randomly being captured and taken directly to the C Centers before their time. The government propaganda swore it wasn't cruel since full anesthesia made it so that there was no discomfort. Nathaniel lacked any faith in the government, let alone the C Center literature. To wake up as a Spot would be a permanent hell. Then again, maybe that's where they were headed.

Nathaniel silently cursed himself. It must have to do with Shayla. How foolish he was to think that he and Shayla could get away with spending an entire afternoon in a hotel. It was a blur of tangled lovemaking and room service. Someone had seen them.

He guessed that they weren't on the highway anymore as the road suddenly grew bumpy. His nerves rattled with each turn. The motor finally ceased and the driver door squeaked open and closed with a slam. Adrenalin and fear tore through Nathaniel. The back door of the van flew open and the shock of daylight blinded him.

"I'll do anything you want. Please, just don't castrate me! PLEASE!" he said as a primal desire for the survival of his manhood made him plead. Two masked people subdued him once again.

Shayla tried to stay focused, but the thought of Nathaniel being castrated made her ill. She hadn't heard from him in more than a week and shuddered to think that he had been picked up by the Tasers, 26 years old or not.

She knew something was terribly wrong. His work record was impeccable. He hadn't missed a single day of coming to her office door since they'd become lovers. He would never just vanish. Above all, he would never abandon her.

Shayla had lived her first 28 years without this man, but she was suddenly desperate for him. She hated that, but there was no turning away from her feelings. Her worry, anxiety, and sheer longing permeated every thought and at the end of another long day, she found herself exhausted but unable to sleep.

She reluctantly took a sleeping pill.

"*Help! Shayla! help!*"

Shayla woke up suddenly, her heart racing as she regained her bearings. She was home in her own bed. It was only a dream. But the comfort was short-lived. What if it was a premonition, or worse, what if this already happened? She had seen the C Center logo in the dream as he was being dragged into the building. Her fingers nervously trembled as she picked up the phone, and made the call, against her better judgment.

"Good morning, Shayla," she heard. It was Gerald, her mother's right-hand man. What was he doing answering her mother's direct line? Shit. Shayla looked at the clock and realized it was morning-briefing time.

"I didn't realize the time. I'll call back later," she said, hoping Gerald didn't hear the worry in her tone. He knew her well. Technically he was a servant, but he had been like a father to Shayla, certainly a more hands-on parent than her mother ever had been.

"Not a problem. I will get your mother. Just a second," he said, before she had a chance to back pedal. Shayla's rapid heartbeat contrasted the relaxed music that whispered from the speaker into her ear while she waited for her mother's unmistakable voice, the very voice that frightened her as a child. Even now as she waited, she feared the sound.

"Is everything alright?" her mother asked as soon as she was on the line, concern penetrating her voice.

"Oh, I'm fine, mother. Just calling to say hello," Shayla said. She tried to sound casual, but knew it was useless. Shayla rarely called to say hello, and certainly not at 6:10 a.m. As she woke up, a thought came to her. Maybe her mother was behind Nathaniel's disappearance. It was certainly possible! Why didn't she think of this before? Her mother had wanted to have a security detail follow her. While Shayla forbade it, that didn't mean that her mother listened. One thing was for certain, if her mother did have her followed and found out she was dating a manual laborer, it was entirely possible that she had Nathaniel kidnapped.

"That's good to hear!" her mother said with the jovial attitude that defined her public persona. "What can I do for you then, dear?"

"Anything new?" Shayla managed to say, realizing again what a mistake it was to call.

"Well, my dear, I'm trying to figure that out as I am in the middle of my morning meeting. You sure you're okay?" the Queen asked.

Shayla knew her mother's keen intuition had already detected something was amiss.

"Fine, I got up early and didn't realize what time it was. I'll let you get back to your…"

"Just a second," her mother said, interrupting. She heard her mother's muffled voice in the background. Shayla twirled the end of her long dark hair, a nervous habit from childhood that hadn't surfaced in years.

"I'm all yours," her mother said.

"You didn't have to cancel your meeting! I'm really fine. Besides, I've got to get ready for work myself," Shayla said. She winced at the nervous sound of her own voice.

"How is that new job of yours, anyway? You getting that out of your system?" her mother asked with the judgmental zing that Shayla knew well.

"I love the Cambridge Public Works and the people. I'm learning a lot," Shayla said, with emphasis.

"You'd learn more elsewhere, but I'm glad you're happy," her mother said with audible reluctance.

"There is, ah, actually something you can help me with, come to think of it," Shayla said, trying to sound casual as she furiously twirled that lock into a Shirley Temple curl. There was nobody else to turn to with the means to locate him. Wherever Nathaniel was, and whatever happened to him, Shayla had to know the truth.

"Of course. What is it?" she asked.

"Do you think you could find someone who is missing?" Shayla asked, trying to edit the fear out of her voice.

A moment of dead air quickly cooled their warm connection.

"What do you mean someone's missing?" the Queen asked with concern. "Who are we talking about?"

"A friend of mine just disappeared a little over a week ago. He hasn't shown up to work and nobody he knows has heard from him. I just didn't know if you might…"

"Of course, I'll help if I can. It sounds rather strange. Are you sure this person didn't run away?"

"Yes, mother. I'm sure," Shayla said impatiently.

"Okay, okay. I'm just asking. Who is it?"

"A friend."

"I can't help if you won't give me the name, now can I?"

"It's a friend from Cambridge. His name is Nathaniel DeLuca."

"Is he just a friend?" the Queen asked coyly. Shayla could hear the smile in her voice.

"Mother. This is serious. My friend has vanished," she said choking back tears, once again considering the possibilities.

"Okay, okay…what's his name again?"

"Nathaniel DeLuca."

"I'll put some people on it immediately. I promise. In the meantime, why don't you come home for a few days and relax?" she said.

"I need to be here now," Shayla said softly.

"Nonsense, you need to be with your mother. I'm sending a plane. A few days off will do you some good."

In one sense, her mother was the last person on earth she wanted to see, but there was something appealing about going home to the Palace's insulation. Her mom wasn't always easy to be around, but Gerald always offered comfort.

"Let me think about it."

"I've gotta go. Someone needs to speak with me. I'll call you later, but thank you for looking," Shayla said, not looking to see who was calling in as she clicked over.

"Is this Shayla Smith?" the voice asked in a slur. Shayla's heart beat fluttered with fear.

"Yes. May I ask who is calling?"

"My name is Janice. I think you know who I am."

Chapter Twelve

The musty basement smell woke him. On top of that, he was shivering. He flipped on the lamp beside him on the floor. The raw brightness from the naked bulb stung his eyes as he surveyed the chilly environment. The room had two doors. One looked like a fortress exit with multiple locks, and the other was open, with a toilet in view. He searched unsuccessfully for a clock before glancing at his chafed wrists, where his watch - an engagement gift from Janice - used to be.

After going to the bathroom, he returned to the makeshift bed; an old mattress on the floor with a few dirty blankets. His head boomed with each step. It felt like a hangover, but it definitely wasn't from enjoying too much Maker's Mark. They had injected him with something. That much he remembered.

A clicking sound startled Nathanial. One by one, he saw the door locks unlatch, making his fears intensify about the uncertainty of what lay ahead.

A towering man entered, turned and carefully turned all the locks back before facing Nathaniel. A long, deep scar hovered above his left eyebrow. He had no laugh lines, but rather vertical lines deeply set between his brows. His stance was like a military guard, his eyes had the intensity of a jaguar.

"I'm Simon. In case your little brain hasn't figured it out, you're in the Underground now," he said, folding his thick arms across his chest, each one a braid of muscles. "And in case you haven't already become familiar with us, our mission is to help rescue young men, like you, who are nearing the age of castration and have not yet found a mate. It is our understanding that you have a mate, and normally we wouldn't take such a case. But, there were circumstances in your favor that allowed us to rescue you. Namely, your connections," he said with an obvious emphasis to signal that he disagreed with this intervention.

"Why the hell did you need to bang my head and drug me with whatever the fuck that was?"

"We can't take chances of getting any form of resistance from those we rescue, until we are sure they – or you – understand that we are here for your benefit."

"Where's Brigg?" Nathaniel asked hoarsely, feeling the soreness of his throat, ignoring the bullshit that this guy was giving him. Nathaniel didn't trust him.

"Did you look under the bed?" Simon asked sarcastically, not missing a beat before scratching his crew cut. "In case you hadn't noticed, he's not here. Just me and you," Simon said with no further explanation.

"Where are we?"

"I already told you. You're with the Underground, and that's all you need to know," he said loudly, almost yelling. "We've got to get going," he said staring hard at Nathaniel with the look of a bull about to charge. "Now, don't try anything funny. We're on your side, pal, and we'd like to keep it that way. Understand?" he asked.

Nathaniel slowly nodded, even though he was more confused than ever. The Underground?

A knock at the door broke the tension, and Nathaniel was grateful. Simon answered the door, and took a cafeteria-style tray from mysterious arms that Nathaniel was barely able to see.

"We're leaving in 20 minutes," he said as he placed the tray on the mattress next to Nathaniel. After he left, Nathaniel heard and watched each lock click into place, reinforcing his imprisonment. Nathaniel inhaled the food, very soggy cereal with raisins in milk, and cold, dry toast. What he really craved was a cup of coffee, even if it wasn't from Chester's Bakery. But this certainly wasn't like the hotel he had just shared with Shayla where room service was delivered in style. This wasn't the kind of place where you could order anything.

After eating, he splashed freezing water on his face. No soap, but it was better than nothing. He still felt ripe with sweat from the journey. With nothing else to do, he sat on the mattress, the old blanket wrapped around him as he tried to keep warm and wondered what might be next.

"Time to go," Simon said when he returned.

"You're not going to lasso me again, are you?" Nathaniel asked.

"As long as you won't give me a hard time. One wrong move, though, and I'll have to tie you down. Deal?"

"Deal."

Being on Simon's good side seemed imperative. Nathaniel walked through the building sandwiched between a masked guard in front of him and Simon behind. The corridors were lined with closed doors, and while he could hear movement and voices behind them, there was nothing distinctive to hold onto as they quickly walked.

"Is there any chance of seeing Brigg today?" Nathaniel asked Simon.

"No. There is no Brigg, so don't ask about him," Simon snapped as they led him to the back row of a humongous garage. There had to be a hundred black vans in it.

"Get in," Simon said.

Nathaniel climbed into the van. One of the masked men secured him into a rear-facing vinyl seat with yellow foam popping out where the old seat cushion stitching had given way. Nathaniel was grateful to be in a seat. He was neither hog-tied nor drugged. This was a limousine ride in comparison to the last one. Wherever he was going, it had to be better than the C Center. For just a moment he felt relieved, but then the motor started.

Simon was glad there was just one more stop with this Grounder. The new ones were always full of questions, but answering them was not part of his job.

Better to leave the Underground's orientation to the instructors who were more patient. He knew his limitations. Plus, that gave each new Grounder a uniform experience with clear, consistent rules, regulations, and training.

Simon preferred to stick to his job's strict delivery parameters: Pick them up at point A, and drop them off at point B. No small-talk, no bullshit, no glamour, but very necessary to the organization's success.

And Simon wanted the Underground to succeed. Badly. Actually, he wanted them to exceed their mission. He wanted more than just equality for all men as the Underground's mission officially proclaimed. He wanted that evil bitch that America called the Queen to be filleted, but he knew it wasn't prudent to broadcast that. Technically speaking, it was outside of the Underground's official agenda. Still, if he ever got the chance, he would do it. She deserved it as punishment for all the men castrated under her rule. Yes, she inherited the laws as they were, but there's no question she could change the laws. That's the kind of power, unfortunately, the Queen held.

"Simon here," he said, answering his cell phone as he drove along the highway, dusk turning quickly to darkness along the country's plains.

"You close?"

"Be there in a few hours, why?"

"Got another assignment for you. Not close to home, but important. Drop him off and then you'll be off again."

"Got it. I'll be ready," Simon said, hanging up and knowing this meant a short overnight at the Underground headquarters.

"I've gotta take a crap, are we almost there?" he heard Nathaniel yell. Simon didn't answer. Some new Grounders grated on his nerves more than others. This guy was a needy pain in the ass. Where's Brigg? Where's Brigg? Are we almost there? Simon wanted to smack him. Nathaniel didn't need help, as far as he was concerned. Simon couldn't understand why he, and countless others, had to risk their lives for a guy who already had a fiancée. If Simon's brother had had a fiancée, he surely wouldn't have been castrated and then committed suicide from his depression.

Nathaniel must be pretty connected because they didn't rescue people who were engaged. Simon tried to dig up the dirt on Nathaniel, but all he learned was that the guy's fiancée was difficult. Poor boy. Maybe he didn't love her. After all Simon had seen, he didn't believe in love. Lust? That was another story. He still enjoyed occasional trysts with Eudora, the head Underground Sexpert instructor. The thought of that made him smile. He hoped she was free tonight. He could use a good fuck after all this driving. She was, technically speaking, his wife, which she had done to keep him out of the C Centers.

"How much longer?" Simon heard from a hoarse sounding Nathaniel.

Simon turned the on stereo, selected his favorite CD and cranked the volume, not giving a shit if Nathaniel was an AC/DC fan or not.

Nathaniel knew Janice was either worried sick or sick from drinking. Either way, she would surely blame Nathaniel for his disappearance even if she found out at some point that it was against his will. She was probably drinking vodka by the bottle to "calm her nerves," as she used to say.

He couldn't worry about Janice right now. He had his own shit to deal with, like figuring out who the hell he was traveling with. He tried to think of any unusual past disappearances. He didn't know anyone who had gone AWOL. Maybe some people who went on the record as murder victims were really members of this Underground? Would they declare him dead after he was gone for a certain amount of time?

Still, he felt a little bad for Janice, but not as bad as he did for Shayla. She would expect a phone call if he wasn't coming to work, and Nathaniel never missed work.

"*I don't want you to go*," she playfully said as she grabbed him one last time before he got dressed when they were in the hotel. "*I wish you could stay the night*," she pleaded.

"I do too, but I will see you in the morning with a blueberry muffin and coffee," he had whispered in her ear the day before he was kidnapped.

"Come early."

"I promise," he had said before a lingering kiss.

Just the thought of it made him grow hard. He didn't think he could last without her. He had to contact her somehow, and soon.

When the engine finally turned off, Nathaniel was escorted from the van into an elevator that went down for so long he felt the pressure in his ears. This was not an elevator with an inspection sticker signed by the state. It was not that kind of place.

The elevator doors opened to a dark hallway, illuminated only by humming fluorescents. Nathaniel noticed the words painted on the wall behind the guard's desk: *Keep your Laws off my Body. Equal Rights and Justice for all Men.* He knew these words well. *Reminder of Truth* had them at the end of each chapter, and he would soon see these words everywhere. The Underground's mantra was painted on the shower stalls, cafeteria, lining the warren of hallways that were his new home and in every cell men slept in.

"Welcome back, Simon," the guard said without fanfare.

"Barely here for a rest, but here is my delivery," he said, as though Nathaniel was a box of office supplies. Nathaniel nodded quietly, which seemed safest.

"Good luck, son. You'll need it," Simon said before heading down a corridor.

"Thank you," Nathaniel managed, but Simon didn't turn back. Nathaniel hoped that appearing polite and appreciative might help him get off on the right foot as the next set of chaperones watched closely. While his expectations were low, he hoped they were friendlier than Simon. They simply had to be.

He was led down a long corridor lined with metal doors, each having a keypad on the wall to the left. His escort stopped in front of one, punched in a code and the door unlocked.

"Wait here," he was told, and knew better than to question authority.

As the door locked behind him, Nathaniel was relieved to be alone, but his nerves were frazzled. There were two chairs around a small table. A single bulb dangled from above. The light rattled on and off, threatening complete darkness at any moment. There was a stainless steel prison-issue toilet in the corner, and nothing else inside the grey cinder-block room. Not a picture on the wall to focus his thoughts or a pad of paper, pencil, book, pamphlet or magazine. He sat on one of the two folding chairs and put his head down on the small cold metal table for what seemed like forever.

When the door finally opened, Nathaniel sat up quickly and a small man with closely cropped black hair and a well-sculpted goatee walked in. A black uniform, that everyone seemed to wear, covered his petite 5-foot frame. A tiny pink triangle dangled from his left ear lobe, a distinctive decoration compared to the others.

"Sorry to keep you waiting. I'm Crosby. Welcome to the Underground," he said followed by a sparkly smile as he held his hand out. Crosby's gesture was one of a friendly salesman, greatly contrasting Simon's curtness.

Crosby spoke quickly, not allowing Nathaniel a word. "Now, I know you probably have a lot of questions, and I'll try to answer as many of them as I can. First things first. Look over this family history to make sure it's one hundred percent accurate. Then, we'll move on," he said smiling as he handed Nathaniel a thick printout, clipped to a board with a dangling pen attached. "Oh, and I'm guessing you're a little hungry, so here's something to tide you over," Crosby said. He put a tightly saran wrapped submarine sandwich and a big bottle of water on the table.

Nathaniel warily took the sandwich, ripping it open and greedily took a bite. Would they poison him if they didn't like how he'd behaved so far? He hoped not, but was too hungry to let that stop him.

"I'll be back soon," Crosby said as he closed the door behind him.

"Thanks!" Nathaniel said, before devouring the large sandwich. He had hoped for meat, but there was only tofu and vegetables inside. Still, food was food and he was starving and thirsty.

He picked up the booklet Crosby left. It was filled with such precise information about Nathaniel's life that it was downright creepy. Not only did it list his birthplace and family tree, but there were also details about his childhood that weren't so easy to dig up. They mentioned that he had a scar on his left ankle and noted it happened after he fell off his bike at age ten. How did they know? They had a copy of his first place certificate for an engineering contest, from high school, where he had to fix a broken engine in a fixed time period. Winning that opened the door to his job at the Cambridge Public Works.

There were addresses, health records, and work records. It also had a chronology of the few women he dated, including an in-depth description of his unpleasant relationship with Janice. It was as though someone had gathered Nathaniel up and summarized him in 40 sterile pages. Now he was supposed to sign off on the accuracy. It felt strange to read. Someone had done his homework, presumably with a lot of help from Brigg. Not a word about Shayla was mentioned, and he felt keenly satisfied keeping this secret. He feared for her safety. While she was the Queen's daughter, she had taken pride doing without a full-time security detail, and these guys didn't appear to be the law-abiding types. If they knew about the two of them… he didn't want to think about what could happen.

He read the full summary a second time, since there was nothing else to do. Occasionally, he heard steps echo quietly on the concrete corridor outside his door. He hoped to hear them halt and enter, but it was quite sometime before that happened.

"Was all the info okay?" Crosby asked as soon as he walked in, flashing a quick smile.

Nathaniel nodded.

"Can I ask some questions?" Nathaniel asked, hopefully.

"Not yet, but soon. I promise. I'll be back. Sit tight," he said with a sing song excitement before disappearing as quickly as he had entered.

Nathaniel's patience waned, but he knew that lashing out was useless. He was far outside his own territory, and alienating anyone was unwise. Besides, Crosby seemed nice.

True to his promise, Crosby reappeared a few minutes later. After locking the door, he sat down, crossing his legs in an exaggerated effeminate way.

"I'm here to orient you to the Underground. After I'm done, I'll do my best to answer any questions you have," he said in a friendly tone. "The Underground was started 25 years ago by a great man who decided it was time for men to regain equality. He believed mandatory castration must stop and he provided the seed money for The Underground. If you are wondering how this all works, we induct men into our system and retrain them to be very attractive to women in all ways. We then strategically place men, called Grounders, around the country. As the powerful women in our nation select Grounders for marriage, we infiltrate the country's power-system to meet our goal. We are already making headway with our network of Grounders married to high-powered women."

"So how do you know I'll be snapped up so quickly?" Nathaniel asked, his mind flooded with questions. From where he sat, no man had gained anything. Castration was as rampant as ever.

"As I said, you will be trained. You will, in fact, remain here until you have all the qualities that our Master Instructors believe are necessary. Believe me, they know what they're doing. There is a lot of market research behind what we do. Lucky for you, your sole purpose during your stay is to improve yourself, and to learn about women. It's a marvelous, educational experience," Crosby said enthusiastically, as though Nathaniel was going on an all expense paid trip to Paris.

"How long will this take?" Nathaniel asked, already dying to get out of there.

"It may not take that long for you because most likely you won't need plastic surgery, since you're so good looking," he casually said, squinting his eyes as though sizing him up.

"Plastic surgery? I should hope not!" Nathaniel balked, feeling sick at the way Crosby glibly spoke about this. Heck, he didn't even like the idea of the stupid Botox that Janice was going to make him get before they got married.

"It's not a huge deal. It's done all the time," Crosby said, gesturing as though it was nothing.

"It would be a big deal to me."

"It's not for you to decide, or me for that matter. All I can do is tell you I wouldn't worry. If the powers that be think you can look better at the hands of our surgeons, then you shall have surgery. That's just the way it is, but think about it. It's certainly better than the other kind of surgery, don't you think?" Crosby said.

"Well…"

"Well, what?" Crosby asked, with an innocence that seemed genuine. "Look on the bright side. You have a lot going for you. Your history says you're a quick study. Your records are impeccable and after dealing so well with that Janice woman, I think you'll take very well to what we have to offer. It's a spectacular opportunity!" Crosby said with an excitement that Nathaniel thought quite odd, considering he felt imprisoned.

Crosby quickly flipped through some pages of a document that he held close, as he put on a pair of wire-framed reading glasses. "Ah yes. You are in here, essentially, for some advanced training and a roll-back," he said turning his attention back to Nathaniel. Nathaniel wondered what else was in Crosby's private notepad.

"What the hell's a 'roll-back' and what kind of training?"

"A roll-back is when we transplant someone back into society with a new birth date that makes him younger to allow a little bit more time to find a woman after the training. We also, of course, give him a new identity and release him into a different part of the country. It's actually quite exciting," Crosby said, his grey eyes growing bright. "We've seen great success. You're 25, so we'll probably release you as 21. You won't have a problem drawing in the women. No siree," he said raising his eyebrows to show Nathaniel what he thought. "You'll be a fine catch for some lucky lady. I'd like to catch you myself, but I'm not your cup of tea, am I?" he said with a laugh, not waiting for an answer.

"For now, you are in training. Our day begins at 6 a.m. with group lectures and group classes. There is also one-on-one instruction. Afternoons are for physical exercises, which most people find refreshing after being sedentary so much of the day. Although," he said pausing for a moment, "come to think about it, not all our classes are sedentary," he said laughing to himself.

"Also, quite obviously, we don't get government subsidies, so everyone needs to help maintain our facility. Evenings are reserved for homework. After that, you'll be tuckered out. Mark my words."

"What kind of classes?"

"From our profile, you need help in Social Confidence and Manners, Basic Romance, Work Enhancement, and Sex-Skills. Okey dokey? All set then," Crosby said, standing up to leave.

"Are you kidding me? I have a thousand questions! First of all, what the hell am I doing here?"

"You have a friend or two who thought this was better for you, as far as where your life was headed," Crosby said. Nathaniel knew that Brigg was part of this, but who else could there be?

"How long will I be here, and for God's sake who decided I need to take sex classes? And where the hell are we? I mean, am I in Nevada? It just all feels so weird," Nathaniel said before Crosby waved his hands in an attempt to silence him.

"Nathaniel, my good man! Don't worry so much. I can't tell you, technically, our location, but you are Underground. You seem like a bright, energetic young man. If I had to guess, you will be here six months or so. But don't hold me to that. You won't leave until you are ready and I don't know where you'll go, but it won't be back to Cambridge, Massachusetts. That's for sure, but you'll be happier elsewhere. Take advantage of our classes. We teach you to think like a woman. It's a truly enlightening program! And, the sex classes?" he said with a laugh. "Don't worry. Everyone takes at least one sex class. That won't start tomorrow, so don't be nervous. It's extremely educational and the lab for that class is a one-on-one with one of our beautiful Sexperts. I'm sure you'll love it. Anything else?"

Nathaniel sat in silence, not knowing what to say. Crosby seemed so happy and worry-free, quite the opposite of how Nathaniel felt. Thoughts of Shayla bled into every moment and he wondered if she would look for him.

"Come, I'll show you around," Crosby said, leading Nathaniel. "This used to be an old military facility a long time ago. We purchased it through one of our dummy corporations. It's not fancy, but it fulfills our needs.

Crosby whisked him into the locked room that would be Nathaniel's private home during his stay. It was tiny, with a single bed. A freestanding chrome sink stood behind a curtain, next to a puny toilet. "Showers are near the Gym, so you can shower after your workouts."

"Can I ask why the doors are locked all the time?" Nathaniel asked with as much care as possible. He certainly felt safer questioning Crosby, compared with Simon.

"We keep things locked for everyone's safety. If you need something, press the little red button here and someone will come to you in a jiffy. So, it's really not that bad," Crosby said, like a real estate agent showing the finer points of a property.

"Now, let's move along," he said. Nathaniel's cell was located near a small library. Books to read! Maybe it wouldn't be so bad here after all. It was like a dream to Nathaniel to have the time and peace to browse through stacks of books and read. He hoped to capitalize on it as long as he would be here. This was the first place where Nathaniel saw people other than the black-clad Underground staff. A handful of men sat at long tables, studying intently. He longed to ask them about their journeys, see how they liked it in here. While people looked up to see him, nobody made eye contact, and that made Nathaniel apprehensive. There was a seriousness in the air. Nathaniel felt the burning eyes of the silent guard who stood at the library's entrance.

"May I take a look around?" Nathaniel cautiously whispered to Crosby.

"Sure, for a moment or two. We've got to get on soon. A splendid lunch awaits us, and I'm famished."

Nathaniel walked through the aisles checking titles waiting for one to grab him. There were books on romance, women's sexuality, women's psychology, women's anatomy, and it seemed to go on in that vein.

"Any good novels in this place?" Nathaniel asked hopefully.

"Well, there is a small section of novels, in line with our purpose, but I'm afraid there aren't too many. You see, this library isn't to entertain. The books in this library focus on helping you understand women. "It's also a lovely place to study, as you can see," he whispered. "Come on, let's go eat!" he said, flashing his quick smile.

As they approached the dining line, it made Nathaniel think of his junior high school cafeteria. They each picked up a tray. Nathaniel followed Crosby. As Crosby went through the line, everyone gave him a big hello. They asked how much he wanted. When Nathaniel walked through, he just got the stock amount of whatever they served. A plop of the glop, like an assembly line plant.

"What are we eating?" Nathaniel asked when they sat down. Some of the foods were unfamiliar. He was still gobbling everything with hungry abandon.

"We have a vegetarian, low-fat, low-sodium diet. All the meals are balanced. Desserts are a no-no. Well, that's not entirely true. Sometimes there is a fruit sorbet. Let's see, today we have a miso soup, which is an option almost every meal. Very healthy. Then, there's a low-fat tofu stir-fry, with veggies. We usually have spelt rolls with soy butter," he said pointing to a whitish watery looking spread that somewhat resembled mayonnaise. "The cooks here are really quite talented, indeed!" Crosby said taking a bite of tofu. "Mmm, mmm good!"

Nathaniel laughed. It was the first smile he felt since he arrived. He couldn't help but like Crosby who seemed to appreciate the bright side of every cranny in this dark hole.

"May I ask who is in charge of the Underground?"

"A very wise man," he said not missing a beat as he chomped on some ground tofu and vegetables. "This is really delicious," Crosby said, pointing to a beige mountain of food that Nathaniel couldn't identify. He had the passion of a restaurant critic eating at a five-star Michelin restaurant.

Nathaniel knew that the explanations were over. He finished his meal and followed Crosby back to his quarters. He was too tired to ask anything else.

"Home sweet home!" Crosby said when he got into Nathaniel's room. Some night-time reading and a good night's sleep await you," he said, motioning to the bed that had a neat stack of linens, sitting alongside an electronic tablet.

"Turn on the electronic tablet and read the document that comes up. After that, get some rest. Tomorrow is a big day for you! Now I've got to go and tend to some other things."

"What am I doing tomorrow?"

"It's your first day of school. You'll need all your energy. Our classes are fast-paced," Crosby said, snapping his fingers like firecrackers.

"What am I studying first?"

"All good stuff. In the meantime, if you need something, just click the red button. Ta ta!" The cheeriness left the room with Crosby, and Nathaniel was uncomfortably lonely. He glanced at the single clock that hung high on the wall. It was 5:30 in the afternoon, just about the time Shayla was beginning to wind down her day.

Chapter Thirteen

"Ready to reconvene the meeting?" Gerald asked the Queen as soon as she got off the phone.

"Give me five minutes," the Queen answered.

"Is something the matter, your majesty?" Gerald asked, and the Queen knew her voice gave her away, at least to Gerald. After a quarter century of service, he knew her better than anyone else.

"Anything I can do?" Gerald asked, raising his eyebrows in concern.

"Actually, there is," she said.

He walked inside her office and closed the door.

"It's Shayla. It seems she is a bit down about a *man* who she says is a *friend*. He is missing. I told her I'd try to find him. Would you make sure that the head of security gets right on this? No one is to know of this, understood?"

"Perfectly."

"I want her to work on it directly, the Queen said as she copied the name Nathaniel DeLuca and handed it to Gerald. He raised an eyebrow as he saw the name, and the Queen figured Gerald had some thought, but was glad he kept it to himself. The Queen had bit her own tongue when wanting to lecture Shayla about how it was utterly impossible to truly be "friends" with a man – unless the man was a Spot. Otherwise, they really couldn't be trusted, but the Queen knew that saying this, or anything close to it, would earn a tongue lashing from Shayla.

"Do you think he was picked up by the Tasers for some reason and sent to the C Center…?" Gerald started to ask.

"I'm not sure…" she said, glancing away from Gerald's warm hazel eyes down to a piece of paper. She found it hard to look Gerald in the eye when talking about castration. She knew the castration system was important for the country's well-being, but wondered why he, in particular, never drew in a mate. It was something they never discussed. She reminded herself that he had a wonderful job, career and life since coming out of the C Center, straight into the Palace where he worked his way up and now lived a rather privileged life in the grandeur that most people only dreamed about.

"Well, I'll get right on it and get back to you just the moment that I hear anything," he said matter-of-factly. A trademark nod of his head and he left her office, quietly closing the door behind him.

The Queen looked out the window into the Square. The Tasers were beating a man. She sighed, feeling sorry for the man, but it was proven that this was the only way they learned. He had certainly, unfortunately, done something to deserve it. Still, it was a shame. She turned away and returned to reading her briefing since the meeting would resume shortly. The man's faint cries seeped up the twenty stories and through the screened window, accompanied by a light breeze that felt refreshing. She turned on her favorite Vivaldi concerto, The Four Seasons, loud enough to drown out that distracting annoyance.

Even so, she couldn't focus on the briefing. There was something about her conversation with Shayla that disturbed her.

"*He's very dear to me. Please, can you help?*"

Those words echoed in her head, and she vowed to find out about this man who had softened her daughter's heart.

✣✣✣✣✣✣✣✣✣✣

As Shayla hung up the phone, she cried harder, knowing that Nathaniel really was missing.

She looked at her heart-broken eyes in the mirror. Her mother considered crying weak. "Big girls do not cry." That's what her mother said when Shayla was little, no matter the reason.

Her father would hug Shayla. "It's okay, let it all out," he would whisper, as long as the Queen wasn't around.

Shayla regained her composure and called the office.

"I'm going to Washington for business," she said to the Cambridge Public Works facilities coordinator, with the authoritative voice she inherited from her mother. As much as Shayla hated being on the receiving end of this tone, she was grateful to have that voice in her toolkit to mask any lack of confidence.

"Did I miss a meeting on the schedule?" the office manager nervously asked.

"It just came up. I'll let you know as soon as I have my return date. Damn, just a second, somebody is calling in. Actually, I'm going to take it," she said, grateful for the interrupting call so she could avoid further questions. Maybe it was Nathaniel. She hoped for this with each phone call.

She clicked the phone and looked at the number. A rumble of anger and nervousness went through her body. Janice sure was a piece of work. The first drunken rambling phone call had been pretty nervy. "I know you have him. Where is he?" she had slurred.

That's what I'd like to know myself, Shayla thought, as she hurriedly got off the phone last time.

Shayla pressed the Ignore button on her phone, knowing that she needed to take care of that. It might be time to enlist the help of her mother's head of security since Janice was becoming a nuisance. But the thought of bringing her mother into this would open up a rat's nest. Shayla didn't feel like explaining her circumstances to her mother, not yet anyway.

"I have strict orders to bring you to your mother as soon as you arrive," Gerald said as he greeted Shayla, giving her a fatherly hug, just as his cell phone rang.

"Your majesty?" Gerald said, but Shayla mouthed "no" to him as she moved her head back and forth.

"Yes, she has arrived, but isn't available in the moment," he said like the perfect butler. He had always been a liaison between Shayla and the Queen and Shayla couldn't imagine what she would do without him.

"Yes, your majesty," he said several times before wrapping up the call.

"Whew!" Shayla said. Gerald nodded and she knew he understood that she wasn't quite ready to see her, "But it will be nice to be home for a few days."

"A few days? The Queen inferred you'd be coming to stay," he said, surprised, his eyebrows pressing together.

"Well, you know my mother. She thinks all words from her mouth are the law. It may be true in most ways, but not in terms of controlling my whereabouts," Shayla said feeling angry at her mother's continued attempts at manipulating her. "I really am here for just a few days," Shayla said.

"You're not leaving your job?" he asked with surprise.

"No, did she say that? Never mind, I don't want to hear it," Shayla said, rolling her eyes.

"Well, whenever you are here, short or long, it's a treat," he said, smiling. He was her family and she loved being around him.

As he escorted her down the grandiose corridors that Shayla still found breathtaking, various staff members greeted Shayla looking pleased and surprised. As Shayla looked up at the twelve-foot tall ceilings with the Victorian-era moldings that were pristinely maintained, she couldn't help but think about all the men who worked at the Cambridge Public Works and would never even see such beauty as their view of the world mostly consisted of the rat-infested underground world below the city streets.

"How is my mother doing anyway?"

"Oh, she's fine, perhaps a little more stressed than usual. She is always trying to keep a lid on her policies, but lately she seems a little more unnerved by the situation than usual."

"What situation?"

"I'm not certain, exactly, but there is always a small vocal group protesting, but she seems more worried lately. She has been putting together a state of the nation speech that she will deliver live on the Webavision."

"Do you think she should be worried?" Shayla said, stopping in her tracks and turning to face him. He wasn't an easy read, but he had always been honest and level-headed, which marveled Shayla, especially considering he was a Spot.

"There is always talk, Shayla. I don't want you to worry and am sure the Queen wouldn't want that. I shouldn't have said anything. You know I only hear dribs and drabs so please don't take my word as anything more than secondhand news."

"Have you heard anything about…oh, forget it," Shayla said.

"What is it?"

"It can wait," she said. Shayla didn't have the energy to bring up Nathaniel. She could barely keep her tears at bay. It's not that Gerald hadn't seen her cry a million times. He had brushed off all the childhood bumps and bruises that her mother scoffed at, particularly once her father died and her mother's involvement in child rearing fell entirely off a cliff. Since Gerald couldn't become a father in the usual way and she lost her father at a tender age, it worked out well.

"I'm going to do a little work from my suite," she said as she walked toward her room.

"Let me know if you need anything."

"Just one more hug," she said, smiling.

"Gladly," he said, leaning into her. "It's great to have you home," he said.

She couldn't agree more, but didn't say so as she knew the words would have crumbled to tears and she didn't feel like bawling in the hallway with elephant-eared servants swishing by.

Later, there would be another opportunity to get this secret off her chest to him.

Shayla punched the code to her suite and slipped inside. The room had been preserved in the palatial childhood pink décor she had insisted on as a child.

The servants had drawn the curtains open so the afternoon sunlight illuminated the frilly but faded pink canopy bed. She plopped down on the mattress and looked out over the capital city, which made her smile, but her mind kept circling back to Nathaniel.

She almost called her mother to ask about him, but stopped herself. Her mother detested weakness and desperation.

Somehow, she would wait the four plus hours until dinnertime to find out.

Chapter Fourteen

"*Keep your Laws off my Body Equal Rights and Justice for all Men. Keep your Laws off my Body Equal Rights and Justice for all Men.* ...."

Saying it ten times in a row each morning in unison with an auditorium of Grounders gave Nathaniel a sense of camaraderie, despite the fact that they were all forbidden from befriending one another.

"Amen."

Just as their voices spoke together, they ceased with crisp precision and each man immediately downloaded his daily schedule to his electronic tablet. Nathaniel pressed the button and nervously waited, as he did each morning.

Nathaniel's Daily Schedule

7:30 a.m. to 9 a.m. Chores – Bathroom Cleaning

He had already taken – and mastered - "Bathroom Cleaning, From Toilet Base to Countertop," so he was confident he could do an excellent job of using the right cleaner and tools for the job. If he didn't meet the Underground's high standards, the inspector would make him do it over.

9:15 a.m.

The Reality of Women –Part 2: Decoding a Woman's Mood

This pragmatic seminar offers tools to manage her moods. Learn how to temper her after she has had a long day at the office. What if she has bad PMS?

What if she is irrational at some other time of the month? This course teaches what to do and what not to do.

Nathaniel thought of living with Janice as the ultimate primer for this course. Surely he would pass quickly. Still, there was always more to learn, especially when it came to the subject of women and moods.

11:30 a.m. Intermediate Romance
You've passed 'Beginning Romance' so you already know the basics: How to make a woman feel special and interesting whether she talks about hair styles, politics, fashion or advances in medicine. This course takes it up a notch: Know when to draw her a bubble bath vs. when to have a cocktail prepared. Learn the subtleties of asking her for something – from money to a night out with your male friends. These skills are key to the Underground's mission of luring and keeping a woman.

Nathaniel was concerned about mastering the nuances of understanding a woman's mood. Still, he had already mastered a lot of other foreign subjects: …"Vegan cooking," "How to Dress – All Occasions," "Gift Buying and Wrapping." He breezed through "Quickie Meals and Gourmet extravaganzas: How to Pull Together a Party in 20 minutes or Less." After living with Janice, Nathaniel considered himself an expert in this area and could probably teach something to the Underground's Master Instructor.

He was most proud of graduating from the seminar about "Understanding Women's Emotions." That was a killer. He didn't feel he understood women, but learned the appropriate behavior modification techniques. "It doesn't matter if you ever understand why, but knowing what you must do is what's important," his Master Instructor said. That made so much sense and freed his mind.

Somehow, he would muddle through these latest classes, he thought, as he continued to read the schedule.

1:15 p.m. Lunch
2:00 p.m. Study
3:15 p.m. Gym and Shower
5:30 p.m. "Into the bedroom…Sex to Please Women
– Learn the Ins and Outs of Satisfying Every Woman's Desires

His palms were sweaty at the thought of actually being observed and graded for his sexual efforts. He knew this day was coming, but still…He had the whole day, until late afternoon, to fret about it. What would they grade on? What if he couldn't perform? Did they expect men to perform oral sex?

"Did you take…" he started to instinctively ask the guy next to him, but stopped himself mid-sentence. He kept forgetting the Underground's rule of no communication with Grounders except in a classroom environment.

Nathaniel quickly swallowed his words and turned away from the guy, but not before noticing that he was clearly recovering from some kind of surgery. The purple/yellowish swelling below the man's eyes, coupled with a white bandaging and stitches at the base of his nose told him that, at the very least, this man had a nose job. It looked painful.

"Line up," one of the guards said in the trademark drill-sergeant voice they all had, regardless of what they looked like.

Nathaniel, along with the other Grounders, were silently escorted through the Underground corridors and dropped at their respective assignments, one by one as usual.

"Do I have to clean this whole thing myself?" Nathaniel asked the instructor who motioned for Nathaniel to go in the bathroom. There were 25 stalls and an equal bank of sinks.

The instructor did not acknowledge Nathaniel's question. He turned on his heels and left. That's your answer, Nathaniel, he thought.

As Nathaniel picked up the buckets of cleaning supplies, he focused on mixing the floor cleaning solution, precisely as he was taught in class. He examined the tiny floor tiles and assessed the best mop for the job. Much like in the class he had graduated from, the cleaning supply closet held many choices.

As he began to move the mop across the endless floor, thoughts of Shayla welled up. How he missed her raw honesty, her compassion for men, and feeling her silky body moving beneath his in rhythmic sync. His stomach knotted as he wondered if he would ever see her again.

He'd been gone nearly three months and he wouldn't be surprised if she was dating someone else by now. The thought of her kissing another man sickened him and he suddenly realized he had stopped cleaning and was sitting on the floor. He got back on his feet quickly and looked at the job in front of him – the floor, the sinks, and all those toilets.

He vigorously began to clean the floor, needing to banish Shayla from his mind. He knew he had no right to her, but couldn't help how he felt.

"*Keep your Laws off my Body. Equal Rights and Justice for all Men. Keep your Laws off my Body. Equal Rights and Justice for all Men....*"

He said it aloud over and over, and it soothed him like a drug.

✣✣✣✣✣✣✣✣✣✣

"Darling!" the Queen said, offering a statesman kiss to Shayla.

"You're all dressed up," Shayla said to her mother who was sporting her trademark silk sari.

"I had meetings all day and haven't had a chance to change, but let me look at you!" the Queen said giving her daughter a once-over. The Queen thought Shayla looked fine, but her manner of dress was boring business suits. How she wished her daughter would take a little fashion advice from her, but she knew that wasn't going to happen. Of course what she really wanted was to formally groom her daughter to not only dress a little more like the Queen, but to see her duty and embrace her future role as the Queen. It was inevitable, so why fight it?

Shayla's plastic smile didn't fool the Queen. She knew her daughter too well. She recognized that look. If not for that, Shayla looked like her carbon copy from thirty years earlier, except for the soft heart that was shining through.

"So? How are you?" the Queen asked, raising her eyebrows as she poured each of them a glass of white wine.

"Not too bad," Shayla said before taking a sip of her wine, and barely pausing before drawing in a little more. The Queen could see the nervousness Shayla was failing to mask. "Any luck finding

Nathaniel DeLuca yet?" Shayla asked.

"Your *friend*?" The Queen said, pausing. "People are working on it. If he can be found, we'll find him," the Queen said matter-of-factly. Okay, it wasn't entirely true. She hadn't found him, but she had found out enough to know that he didn't have anything close to the kind of pedigree that was worthy of Shayla. She had found enough to know that she didn't really *want to find him*. "Who is he again?" the Queen casually asked, sipping her wine.

"He was.... I mean he is one of my workers," Shayla said, taking her eyes away from her mother's and pasting them on the glass of wine that she sipped. "I need you to find him, mother."

"I'm doing my best, dear!" the Queen said, putting on her best insulted tone until her daughter began to tear up.

"You're my only hope."

"What the hell is going on here? Hope for what?"

"I was going to propose to him, or anyway... well, I'd like to, but it's a little complicated."

"What kind of work does he do?" the Queen asked, trying to hide her shock at her daughter considering marriage to a man the Queen had never heard of, let alone met.

"He's a laborer," she said, finally looking her mother directly in the eye.

"You can't be serious, Shayla! You mean a manual laborer as your husband?" she said, shaking her head back and forth. "I think not!"

"He's not just a laborer, he's a person!" Shayla said.

"He's a man, Shayla," the Queen screamed, unable to keep her emotions bottled. She stopped herself from saying what she really wanted to say, as that would only cause Shayla to erupt. Her daughter was too easily seduced by those piranhas. This must be some suave guy. No education to speak of, working in the damn sewers and Shayla wanted to marry him? "I've heard nothing about this man before a few days ago. Now you tell me you want to propose to him? Oh, and he's missing. I'll say that's complicated!"

"Well, even if he were here," Shayla said, lowering her voice, "it's a little more complicated than that."

"I'm listening," the Queen said, refilling Shayla's glass, in addition to her own. She couldn't imagine what else there was.

"He's engaged already, a marriage to save himself. He doesn't love her. He's 25," Shayla said, again knowing her mother would understand the rest fully. "His fiancée is a wretched drunk. I've spoken with her. Maybe he left because he just couldn't face marrying her. I don't really care why he ran off. I'm sure he had a good reason," she said. "I just want him back."

"Shayla, this is sounding more and more like a car chase than a love relationship. You say he just 'up and left?' No note? No nothing?"

"He was just gone, and I know he wouldn't just do that. His fiancée hasn't seen him and neither has anyone else," she said. "What is it? You know something, don't you!"

"No, dear. I'm afraid I don't. I'm completely in shock."

But the Queen did know something. She didn't know Nathaniel DeLuca's precise whereabouts, but she had her suspicions about where he might be.

Chapter Fifteen

Nathaniel, along with thirty other men, sat wide-eyed and silent in the classroom where they'd been deposited. Was everyone as nervous as Nathanial?

"I'm Eudora. Welcome to Underground Sex. Let's be clear that this class is not focused on you getting your rocks off. Alright? It you do get your rocks off, that is a mere byproduct of what happens, but remember you're trying to please her and that is your mission," she said, holding the chalk in one hand and tapping it on her other palm. That same gesture – by anyone else – would evoke nothing, but every micro movement Eudora made was sexual.

"Any questions before I continue? Good," she said before turning around and writing on the chalkboard. A well-cut hole in her outfit on her left buttock revealed a perfect yin-yang tattoo that gave Nathaniel, and probably every other guy in the room, a solid hard-on. When she turned around, she caught him, and probably all of the others, staring, but didn't seem the least bit surprised.

"This list is the general overview of different sex categories. We'll cover all of them, but more importantly, we'll talk about how you assess women's preferences. Got it?"

Gentle Sex
Role Playing and Fantasies
Getting Kinky
Fetishes, S&M and Beyond
Oral Sex
Tantric Sex
Maximizing the G-spot
Sex Props

They all nodded. Nathaniel didn't dare speak, and it seemed that he wasn't the only one under Eudora's domineering spell.

"Good," she said standing silently and looking out at the men for a moment. Nathaniel had seen this woman in the hallways.

Her hard-edged beauty was unquestionable. Eudora wore a black vinyl suit that hugged every curve of her voluptuous body. Her white-blond hair and the angular cut flattered her high cheekbones, accentuated by a tiny diamond stud that sparkled on the side of her nose.

When Nathaniel saw her crystal blue eyes, he felt like she had a laser vision. How did she get involved in the Underground? How did any woman get involved in it?

“Let’s start with the basics. You, as a man, have a big job. First of all, you must work to quickly identify her daily desires and needs. Women get bitchy when they don’t have a sexual release,” Eudora said quite matter of factly. “It’s your job to make sure she’s getting it the way she wants it. Believe me, your life will be better for it. Does she like it soft and romantic? Look for the clues. Does she talk about making love or fucking?” Eudora paused for emphasis, walking back and forth across the wood floor in her boots that echoed with each step. “If it is the former, you put rose-petals on the bed or draw a bubble bath for her. You’re all taking aromatherapy so you’ll know how to determine the perfect scent for her, right?” she asked, rhetorically, but their heads obediently nodded.

“Good. You know you need to master that to get out of here. Above all, always be thinking about her and her needs. Be resourceful,” she said, pausing again.

“Moving along, when you do finally get your cock into her, does she grab and pull you harder? If so, she is telling you she likes it hard and fast. Clues are everywhere. You need to be ready for anything. You need to be in shape because you must be able to deliver. Does she like to receive oral sex? Well, you better know how to do it right. Not some sloppy version of sticking your tongue out for three licks. And for God’s sake, shave! Does she like a lot of different positions? You should be knowledgeable about all of them. Which ones will give her the maximum amount of pleasure? Pay attention all the time and you’ll get the answers from her.”

“Let’s talk about sexual positions. In your reading materials, turn to the first page of The Positions Chapter. We’re going to go through each of these positions fully clothed, gentlemen, to figure out exactly how these work. If you think you can learn them from looking at a piece of paper, you are wrong. There are nuances that you can only know from getting down and dirty. Pick a partner. The last lucky bloke will get to have me," she said without smiling.

"Partners?" said the timid guy sitting next to Nathaniel.

"Sure," Nathaniel said. Nathaniel had seen this guy around. He was slightly heavyset, although he had definitely lost weight since Nathaniel first saw him.

"You play the woman," Eudora said, tapping one person from each partnership on the shoulder. "Don't worry, men, you'll each be playing man and woman several times before this class ends."

Nathaniel felt like an absolute fool as Eudora instructed him, as the "woman," to lie on his back on the floor, with this other man holding his ankles up in the air, spreading them wide.

"Look your partner in the eyes. If you're supposed to be the man, pretend you are looking at a woman. If you're supposed to be the woman… well, you get the idea."

Nathaniel could barely bring himself to look this man in the eye, but when Eudora came around to inspect, he did as he was told. Everyone did.

"Tell her you love her, each morning. Tell her how beautiful she is. If she wants to see a movie, or see an art show, you must enthusiastically agree. Whatever she wants to do, act interested. *This* type of behavior will please her and put her in the mood. Soon, you will get a chance to test this out, so you better fucking get it right," Eudora said.

Nathaniel got a chill as her eyes bore right through him.

"I don't think she should have made that speech," Shayla said to Gerald the morning after the Webavision broadcast. They sat having morning coffee in her pink suite, just as they always did when Shayla was home.

"Remember that she has run this country, quite successfully, for decades. She knows what she's doing," Gerald said, before taking a sip of coffee from the cup that displayed the royal pattern of the Queen's crest.

"But the chip isn't even ready."

"People will find out, and it's better if that information is released in a controlled fashion," he said.

"What do you think of the chip being inserted in baby boys, anyway?"

"My opinion doesn't matter. I work for her and take my duties seriously," Gerald said. As usual, Shayla found his façade unreadable.

"What do you really think, though. Between you and me?" she asked, taking a bite of a blueberry muffin that made her think of Nathaniel and the ones he used to bring from Chester's Bakery. Even the Palace's baker version was sub-par compared to Chester's.

"I think that I should get to work, that's what I think," he said, rising from the couch.

"How can you be so even-keeled?" She said, softly. "C'mon Gerald. You and I both love my mom, but why do you protect her? I think it's time for a change in this country – and not the kind of change that she is proposing. Look me in the eye and tell me you don't agree."

"You had best keep that to yourself," he said curtly.

"If I don't speak up, who will? In a certain way, I am the only one who can really speak up," Shayla said.

"Be careful."

Shayla didn't want to dig further. Would her mother actually go against her?

"Sorry, I didn't meant to dump on you," Shayla said.

"You can always talk to me," Gerald said, a peek of emotion surfacing, like a warm blanket to Shayla.

"There is something I wanted to ask you about," Shayla said. She felt certain that he would always be truthful to her, but still, his loyalties spanned to both her and her mother.

"Anything," he said.

"I have asked my mother to help me find someone who went missing, someone dear to me. Do you know if she's found anything?"

"I'm sorry I can't help you with that," he said, noncommittal, keeping his eyes on hers, entirely unphased. Did he know something? Shayla looked at him and wondered.

Chapter Sixteen

From the outside, the sex chamber had a door like all the others at the Underground. The inside, however, was unlike anything he had seen there. It looked like a real bedroom, not a bunker.

As the guard opened the door for Nathaniel and then locked the door from outside, Nathaniel's pulse elevated. He surveyed the room. There was a lamp in the corner next to an elegant love seat. On the other side of the room was a full-sized bed, the first double-sized mattress he had seen in quite a while. There was even a carpet. The sight of it made him want to remove his shoes and curl his toes into it, but he refrained, remembering Eudora's first lesson. "It's not about your pleasure."

Surely the hidden cameras were rolling. He looked for them in the corners, but they were probably miniscule and could be anywhere.

He was alone, but knew he wouldn't be for long. Should he already have his clothing off and be under the covers when Eudora entered the room? Should he stand in the corner? God, he was nervous. Finally, he settled on the love seat. He tried to wipe the nervous sweat from his palms, but was unable to gain full composure. He had never been put on the spot quite this way. He was very worried that he wouldn't be able to perform.

He quickly realized that if he was able to get hard for Janice, Eudora would be easy to get excited for. She was extremely hot. Besides, he hadn't had sex in months and he could sure use that release. In any case, he *had* to do this.

He considered this a personal challenge, on top of what the Underground declared. Maybe he could get Eudora to smile or at least emit a sound of true pleasure. That would be a feat. As he thought about this, the door opened. Any crumb of confidence dissolved. Of all the zillions of scenarios he pondered, practiced and studied, the vision before him was not one he anticipated. He tried not to show the surprise on his face as this unexpected stranger stepped silently into the room. Where was Eudora?

The woman stood quietly, clearly waiting. His heart pounded as he tried to assess her needs. She was from a different generation, and he knew to take that into account. The lines and wrinkles of age accentuated her frown. Her hair was long and untamed, but not in a beautiful way. She had tried to tuck the wiry gray bundle of hair back into a sensible barrette. She wore a plain dark skirt that flowed past her knees, and a practical long sleeved blouse that did it's best to hide her ample middle.

"I'm Trisha," she finally said with unmistakable shyness.

"I'm Nathaniel," he said, trying to figure out what to do next. She didn't move.

"Would you like to come and sit down here?" he asked, motioning to the seat beside him. She barely nodded as she walked over. He hoped she would say something, but all she did was look at her shoes, which reminded him of his grandmother. It was a thought he tried hard to shoo from his mind. After all, he was trying to prepare himself to perform a sexual act with this woman.

"What do you do?" he asked, trying to sound interested. No reply. "Tell me about yourself, Trisha," he said. Still, no reply. He was growing more nervous, conscious of the cameras. There would be a review and critique after class, frame by frame, like the football analysts did on the Webavision after each play.

It was imperative to connect with her, and quickly. In order to ever leave the Underground, he had to pass this test. He needed to understand how to cater to any woman. But, how?

"You look like you have a lot on your mind." As though unlocking a door, Trish began to speak, quietly and slowly. She spoke about how her brother died, how close they were… how sad she was. She looked down at her hands as she spoke, and Nathaniel noticed her fingernails had been bitten all the way down. He listened closely to her story, trying to appear concerned, as though she was the only woman on earth. While listening, he tried to think of what to do next. That was his goal.

He gently took her hand, and she allowed it. She looked up at him, and revealed more of herself, about her childhood, about what she was feeling. He knew he had broken the spell and as he leaned in to hold her body, he felt her soft flesh snuggle into him. He pulled her closer and realized this was, perhaps, all she wanted.

He needed to pass the test in front of him and hoped he was right. Admittedly, he was more than a little relieved not to have to have sex with this woman who held no spark for him. Some time passed with the two of them cuddling, and he figured things would end soon. He didn't know how he would know it was over, but presumably she would tell him. He had been a perfect gentleman. He smiled to himself, knowing he had done well.

"Would you kiss me, Nathaniel?" she asked, and suddenly he realized he knew nothing at all. He was back at square one. What did this woman want and need? He must always think this way. There was no rest for a man trying to understand a woman.

Without a word, he caressed her ruddy face, and smoothed the wild, course hair that was straying from the barrette that had slumped to one side. He looked into her cloudy brown eyes and gently kissed her. As much as he didn't want to, he knew that it had to be genuine. She kissed him back, and pulled him close before lightly placing his hand on her breast, first it was outside of her blouse, and then she gently guided his hand beneath her blouse, and finally she revealed her big white brassiere that looked about as sexy as a pair of baggy sweat pants. He reached behind her and unfastened the six sturdy hooks that held it closed. Her large breasts spilled immediately downward past her waist. He reached to touch them, consciously forcing himself not to flinch at the softness of her flesh. She was clearly enjoying his touching. He was glad, as he knew it was important to pass the test. He thought back to how he used to please Janice by pretending. Trisha was much nicer than Janice, but she was older, and saggier.

They slowly undressed until they were both completely naked. She wordlessly rolled onto her back and spread her legs, revealing herself to him with a starkness that he did not savor. He wished she would ask to turn out the lights, but she clearly wanted him to meet her eyes with his. As he entered Trisha, he did his best to give her all the pleasure he would need to give to any woman, even though he nearly recoiled at the task. The bed squeaked to the slow rhythm of their movements.

"Keep going. I'm coming. I'm coming, but not yet," she whispered to him. It took an effort to maintain his hard-on, but he managed by thinking about Shayla.

Her climax was obvious with a soft yelp of pleasure that was a signal. It took effort for Nathaniel to come, which he could only do with his eyes closed, picturing Shayla straddling him in her office, which he had taken pleasure in so many times. It had been more than four months since that time.

"You were a little slow picking up on what I wanted," she said, breaking character as soon as she caught her breath, not a minute after he was done. He realized she was a great actress. This woman wasn't shy at all. "First time, so that's okay, but you need to really pay attention to the woman's cues," she said. With that, she got dressed and left.

The next day, he was just as nervous. He hadn't scored that high with Trisha, but now knew to expect the unexpected. It was a different sex chamber, decorated like an elegant hotel room. There was a canopy bed covered in a sheer purple net highlighted with golden sparkles. The bedspread was plush red velvet with a golden cord around the trim, and the embroidered pillows were plentiful. It was very inviting, with the peaceful music piped in to match the relaxing scent of flowing incense.

This time, Eudora entered the room. Although he knew she was a tough judge, he felt a little relieved since maintaining an erection would be relatively easy. He looked for clues in everything she did. She wore a nearly sheer black shirt, and matching pants. It was clear that she had no undergarments on top or bottom, which Nathaniel found both titillating and startling, especially as his eyes made a natural b-line for the inviting perfectly trimmed triangle that sat between her legs.

She smiled at him slyly. Was this the same Eudora who never showed even a remote sign of happiness?

"Show me what you've got," she said. Despite everything, her boldness shocked him. That's all she said as she folded her arms and undressed him with her eyes. Nathaniel noted that she didn't even introduce herself. Was she Eudora or playing some character? He wondered for a moment, but quickly let those thoughts slip away, and followed her lead.

This was a woman who wanted to get right down to it. Forwardness was easier to read. He deduced that Eudora liked it raw and mighty with all the force he could give her every which way.

He kept his eyes on hers, before walking to her. He kissed her passionately, grabbing the back of her head and pulling it toward his own. She kissed him back with a confidence and strength that told him he was on the right track. His hardness was immediate, and he stopped thinking and let his instincts take command.

He quickly pulled her shirt up, exposing her breasts, which she seemed to enjoy as she leaned them toward him. He licked her nipples before biting them, lightly at first and then his teeth closed in a little bit harder, causing her to let out a whimper that he recognized as pleasure.

The next few moments were so fast, with clothes flying everywhere, like fur flying in a cat fight. He picked her up and threw her down onto the bed, before sinking himself into her with a single motion. As Eudora put her hands on his ass pulling him deeper and deeper, he knew that this was no act. He was riding her with a wildness that he was afraid would make him come, and suddenly stopped.

Eudora's eyes grew wide with surprise, and Nathaniel smiled deviously.

"Get on your hands and knees," he said with a commanding voice that he nearly didn't recognize as his own. She scurried into position and he pulled her hips toward him, entering her from behind with a zealous satisfaction. Nathaniel felt like an unleashed animal. He didn't worry whether her quick guttural sounds were of true pleasure or some fake teacher act. He needed this, more than he imagined. His release came more quickly than he would have liked, but he felt satisfaction as he buried himself deep, finally slowing each thrust. His breaths were short, and when he pulled out, he fell back onto the mattress, pleased with himself. He certainly felt darn good. He couldn't be sure, but it sure seemed that Eudora enjoyed her work as the Master Instructor Sexpert. Even Eudora took a few moments to compose herself and get her breathing to a normal pace where she could talk.

"Did it even occur to you to try and talk dirty to me? Ask me if I'd like that?" she said. "You should've seen that I'd be receptive to that kind of behavior or maybe even a little spanking."

"I'm sorry," Nathaniel said, sheepishly, but didn't feel that sorry. He knew she had enjoyed the sex.

"Don't take it personally, Nathaniel. We have a job to do. You're good. You are. I can see you work hard to pick up the nuances of behavior. I saw it in yesterday's tapes and I saw it today. You just need to try a little harder. I know you can do this," she said, pausing. "The Underground needs you, Nathaniel." He appreciated her encouragement. He was amazed how easily she drifted in and out of character.

As soon as she left, his body relaxed. He thought about what she said as he dressed, and vowed to do exactly what she said: Try harder.

Over the next few days, he dealt with women of all body types and moods. He felt like he was getting better, but the sexual acts were still challenging. At the moment of each orgasm, thoughts of Shayla commanded his mind. He knew that his body was Underground, but his heart and soul belonged many miles away.

Chapter Seventeen

"Calling to check in," Gerald said from the cell-phone he kept solely for Underground communication. "It wasn't easy, but I snowed her regarding Nathaniel's whereabouts and deadened that trail."

"How did you do that?" Simon's unfriendly voice spat back.

"I made things up. The Queen would never question information I offered to her. Right now she's preoccupied with her daughter's focus on a lower class man. Truthfully, the Queen doesn't want him to be found. I think she was relieved with my explanation."

"Good work," Simon said, and Gerald couldn't help but think how rare it was to get any kind of complement out of Simon, not that he cared that much.

"How is this Mr. DeLuca doing anyway?" Gerald asked.

"Perfectly well, moving right along," Simon said, non-committal.

"Why don't you let me take care of the Queen. I can do this," Gerald said.

"Don't even think about it. We need you to stay there for the new government. You have Shayla's confidence and we're especially going to need that after the changeover."

"I've been waiting a long time and I know I could handle things…"

"We've all been waiting a long time. You, me and every other Spot wants to be the one to bring her down. You've done a phenomenal job, but you'll get your day. We all will, and soon, so hold onto that. This is about all men."

"I can't forget," Gerald said, rubbing the mandatory tattoo on his neck. "It's not easy to resist the temptation."

"It's not easy for any of us. She is the reason castration is still the law. We're so close."

"You're right. I know. I apologize for even questioning…"

"Don't apologize. Just do your job."

Chapter Eighteen

After seven days of the sex lab, it suddenly disappeared from Nathaniel's schedule. He was relieved that the constant challenges of those encounters were behind him, and yet also somewhat disappointed. He had to admit that the sex labs left him with a kind of sexual confidence he had never experienced. In fact, he was starting to feel surer of himself in many ways.

"Put on your shoes, Nathaniel, there's someone you should meet," Crosby said to Nathaniel that evening, when making evening rounds. In all of Nathaniel's time in the Underground, he had never been allowed out of his room at night. Perhaps he was going to see Brigg! To see his friend's face would be like magic. Nathaniel quickly put on his shoes and followed Crosby.

They walked through the labyrinth of hallways as Crosby hummed, repeatedly using his access codes to unlock deeper corridors of the Underground that Nathaniel didn't even know existed. Finally, they stopped in front of a door, and Crosby paused before finally punching in the access code. When the door finally opened, Nathaniel felt like he was looking inside a fantasyland. After spending months Underground, his eyes were nearly unaccustomed to the rainbow of silken colors that greeted him. The tapestry-covered couches and the sweet incense infused his senses. The carpets were plush, and the paintings on the walls boasted scenes of men giving speeches – seemingly from yester years. The bookshelves took up an entire wall, filled with leather-bound books. He longed to touch everything. This was, by far, the most beautiful room he had seen since arrival. It was so much to take in, but when he turned to the left he saw a sight he could not believe. There, on a yellow embroidered chaise lounge chair was a man in a jasmine colored robe. But this was not just any man. It was Chester, smiling broadly at the dumbfounded Nathaniel.

Chester finally began to laugh, and his purple tattoo appeared to be laughing too. When Chester saw that Nathaniel wasn't moving, he stood up and moved toward Nathaniel, opening his arms. They hugged for a long moment, and when Nathaniel backed away he still couldn't believe it. He tried to speak, but was unable. Chester motioned for Nathaniel to sit across from him on a softly pillowed couch. They sat in silence, as Chester allowed Nathaniel to acclimate to his surroundings.

"Why?" Nathaniel finally was able to ask.

"I wanted to help you," Chester said, pausing momentarily. "While I have no doubt that you would have honored your commitment to Janice, I also saw that she made you miserable, quite understandably. And so I brought you here. I hope you are not unhappy that I did. I saw something in you that I wanted to save."

"I'm stunned," Nathaniel managed.

Chester studied Nathaniel for a moment before walking across the room. When he returned, he handed Nathaniel a bag that made Nathaniel's smile even bigger. It was a bag from Chester's Bakery.

"Open it," he said.

Nathaniel slowly opened the bag and took out two muffins. This time it was Nathaniel who laughed as he playfully pulled a big hunk of blueberry muffin and put it in his mouth.

"Mmm. I can't tell you how much I missed this!"

"There's a banana one too. I would've brought you a coffee too, but didn't think it'd stay hot for the journey," Chester said.

"I'm just...." Nathaniel began, but he couldn't finish. Chester let the silence between them sit while Nathaniel savored the muffin that he thought he would never again taste.

"I joined this group fresh out of the C Center and ended up the leader. A long while ago you asked me how I was able to find a peaceful life. Do you remember?"

"Absolutely," Nathaniel said.

"When you asked me that, it showed me the kind of man that you were, and I knew it was the kind of man we needed here in the Underground. Now you have your answer. I am content because I do work that brings me peace," Chester finally said, looking away, as though he saw himself all those years ago in a twist of physical and mental pain and suffering.

He returned his eyes to Nathaniel's. "I took a personal oath to heal my spirit and continue the work of the founder," he said continuing. "I wanted to help men who felt the same pain I did. I wanted to help men who, if given a second chance, would use it wisely…the ones who had hope and desire for happiness and who could help us gain back what we've lost as men, what we deserved and still do," he said smiling.

"Have you been here all this time?"

"I'm almost never here. We are far from Cambridge, and I've got the bakery to run. I've got to make money, too," he joked, shaking his head back and forth.

"What about Brigg?"

"Brigg has been working with us on the outside for a number of years now, but he is seldom able to get away. I saw him this morning and he made me promise to send you a big hello. He misses you a lot."

"Please tell him I miss him, too," Nathaniel said, grinning. The years of friendship flashed through his mind.

Nathaniel hesitated before asking about Janice.

"Janice is Janice. She looks for wisdom in the bottom of a bottle," Chester said with a distant look in his eye.

"Chester, I don't know what to say."

"There is nothing you need to say. You are dear to me, and I trust you. That's why I sent for you. To the other Grounders, I will remain unknown. I hope you understand this."

"Your secret is safe with me."

"Good. Your days as a manual laborer are behind you now. I have spoken with the Master Instructors and they agree that you have been a top student in all manners. We will be releasing you to the Kansas City area, very soon, into the corporate arena. I wanted to wish you luck. I am certain your life will be better now. The job we get you will give you the opportunity to meet a different caliber of women. You will have a new name, identification number, and address. Your training will provide you with all you need to be successful in your new life. I am positive you will thrive in this new environment. When you go back into the world, we trust that you will hold the oath you take when you leave. You can't contact your old friends, family or anyone at all that you have had contact with," Chester said, pausing. "Ever," he said for emphasis, clearly waiting for Nathaniel to respond.

"I understand," Nathaniel said, thinking about his past and his future.

"I may not see you again, but remember that the Underground always tracks your whereabouts. We will always be in touch with you. I have great faith that you will help our cause, as we win back our rights that we all deserve. I know you will help your brothers all around you, even if they don't know it," he said before rising to show Nathaniel it was time to leave.

Chester gave him another hug, and when they let go of their embrace, Nathaniel saw a tear at the edge of his eye.

"Thank you," Nathaniel said before leaving the room, back into the hands of Crosby who waited patiently in the hallway.

Chapter Nineteen

"I'm sorry I don't have any more information for you," the Queen said to Shayla over dinner. It wasn't exactly true. The Queen wasn't sorry at all. On top of that, while she didn't have an incredibly detailed report on this guy, she didn't need a security report to know this guy wasn't good enough for Shayla.

"Thanks for trying, mother," Shayla said, before turning to look out the Palace window.

"What are you thinking?" the Queen asked, observing her daughter's faraway gaze.

"I was just wondering about Nathaniel, what he's doing, where he is," she said.

"Dear, you're going to have to get over him. He's gone," she said, coldly. Shayla bristled. Quickly realizing her mistake, the Queen purposely softened her tone and said, "It also took me a while to adjust after your father died. We had a nice life together."

"Well, I was trying to have a life with Nathaniel," she said, looking suspiciously at her mother.

"I understand that," she said, rubbing Shayla's shoulder for a moment. It wasn't her natural way, but she knew that Shayla would respond and she was right. Her daughter's face relaxed.

"Thanks, mom," she said, smiling with sadness along with resignation that the Queen took as the green light to further pursue her agenda.

"I have an idea I wanted to run by you," the Queen said, cutting a piece of filet mignon and taking a delicate bite. "Oh, this is delicious, by the way. Have some," the Queen said, lightening the conversation further.

"I'm not hungry," Shayla said, "What's your idea?"

"I got a call from Lorraine, you know, who runs Steelco? She needs a new CEO here in the Washington, D.C. headquarters and asked if I knew of anyone, and I thought of you," she said, taking another bite, observing Shayla.

"I've got a job," Shayla said, but the usual fire in her voice was gone.

"Yes, my dear. I know you do and I don't want you to leave if you don't want to, but just consider talking to her. What do you have to lose, since you're here for a few days anyway? You're so unhappy in Cambridge. Why go back if you don't have to?"

"Maybe you're right," Shayla said. "I don't know."

This definitely wasn't a shoo-in, but waffling was a start, an absolute possibility that wasn't there a month prior. This was good, a crack in the veneer.

"Tell you what, let me just set up a meeting with you and Lorraine. Private, casual, here in the Palace, no commitments, just a conversation. If the position is interesting, you could take this new job and stay on as some sort of advisor to the Cambridge Public Works."

"Maybe," Shayla said, pausing. "But does Lorraine know that my leadership style isn't exactly traditional?" Shayla said, looking dead into her mother's eyes. The strength on her daughter's face was like looking into a mirror.

"Let's not get the cart before the horse," the Queen said, taking a sip of wine avoiding any confrontation that would sideline the headway she was making. Lorraine owed her a few favors and it was high time to collect.

"Your Majesty, they are carrying big posters that read: *Keep your Laws off my Body. Equal Rights and Justice for all Men*."

"How many?" the Queen asked, doing her best to squelch the frantic quality in her own voice.

"Around a hundred, but they are very vocal," the Taser in charge told the Queen. The Queen could hear them chanting, and it made her nervous. She wasn't used to that.

"Round them up."

"And then what?"

"Take them to the prisons and hold them there. Confiscate any phones or cameras of anyone close by, understand?" the Queen said. If this got onto the Webavision, it could start a domino effect.

"We'll do our best," the head of the Taser Force in Washington D.C. said. The Queen could hear the chanting grow louder.

"As long as your best means you get every single cell phone that might have captured any video footage, that's fine," she said, with fervor.

"Yes, your Majesty."

"Make sure I am notified when it is done," she said before hanging up.

Her security detail had been telling her, for the past year, that the equality movement was gaining steam. This was the first real evidence and now she had to obliterate it, no matter the means to that end.

"Come in," she said, to the knock on her door. It was probably the staff to take the dinner dishes away. She had ended her dinner with Shalya shortly after Shayla's agreement to meet with Lorraine. The Queen couldn't be more pleased.

"Gerald? I thought you'd be off by now. It's late," she said, as he peeked in the door.

"I heard from the head of security that there were protests. I wanted to know if you needed anything from me," he said.

"You are so wonderful, always. Thank you, but not right now. I'll keep you posted if need be," she said, feeling blessed with Gerald and his loyalty. That certainly couldn't be bought, or even bred.

"On a completely different note, there is some good news," she said. "Shayla has agreed to an interview with Steelco. I need to get her back D.C., so this is a start. We can cross our fingers about that," she said, although her mind was on the uprising. The head Taser said it was only about "100 people," but that was 100 people too many for her taste.

Chapter Twenty

"How did this happen?" Gerald said thinking about the decades of work and tremendous money spent to keep the Underground's secret and mission intact.

"A few renegade Grounders rallied a group from one of the Parties of Availability. We can't control everything," Simon said.

Gerald couldn't believe he was so glib.

"Do we know who is behind this?" Gerald asked, agitated, sitting in his car in the Palace's garage. Normally, Gerald would never leave the Palace while on duty, especially to call or meet with a fellow Grounder, but the text message used the emergency code.

"I was hoping you could tell me that," Simon said.

"I keep a tight rein on what happens in the Palace. Your job is to do the same outside. The Queen alluded to a protest, but she didn't talk much about it. If she does have those Grounders in custody, they could be interrogated. If they talk, it could literally kill our movement," Gerald said.

"They won't. They're trained."

"Yeah, well, they're not trained very well. They're trained to follow orders not to start a public protest! I should just take her out now before it gets too dangerous and we lose our chance."

"No!" said Simon.

"Why not?" Gerald said, growing more frustrated.

"There's been no breach," Simon said.

"You don't know that. You don't even know who did this."

"And we need you where you are. You are the only one who can convince Shayla to take over before anything happens to the Queen. Once Shayla is in charge, she will need your help. We're getting close. We must have everything in place before we act. I agree the protest wasn't the best timing, but it's not as bad as you think."

"In the memory of our founder, I cannot and will not let his vision be derailed. He is the reason we have come this far. Don't forget that," Gerald said.

"Calm down, we're all on the same page as you and the old man," Simon said, with a condescending air.

"He wasn't just an old man. You never met him. He was a visionary who lived by the principles he believed in and took risks no matter the consequences. I gave him my word… as he lay on his deathbed."

"Regardless, we are in this situation now, and I am the one you report to. You will take my orders, understand?" Simon said.

"Perfectly," Gerald said. He felt angry, but controlled himself.

"Call when you know more," Simon said.

"Yes, sir," Gerald said before hanging up and wondering, for the first time, if he should defy orders because he knew, in his heart of hearts, that nobody truly understood what was best for the country better than he. Not even Chester and certainly not Simon.

He pulled the faded black and white photo from his wallet. To anyone else, it just looked like an elderly gentleman, but he was Gerald's savior. He was Edward Smith, the first, Shayla's grandfather and the author of *Reminder of Truth*.

Dear Mayor Kennedy,

It is with great sadness and regret that I resign my post as head of the Cambridge Public Works. I am sorry I stayed only a short time. I wish you well as you secure a new person to run this wonderful organization that I greatly respect.

If I can be of help during this transition, please let me know.

Sincerely,

Shayla Smith

"What do you think?" Shayla said to her mother, after showing her mother the letter.

"Excellent. It's a fine message," the Queen said.

Working at the Cambridge Public Works had become a constantly painful reminder of Nathaniel's absence, and Shayla had decided it was time to go.

"To celebrate your move back here, I think we should redecorate your suite here. It's high time we did that, long past due really."

"What are you talking about?" Shayla asked, confused.

"Hot pink walls and frilly canopy beds aren't exactly appropriate for a grown woman's living quarters," the Queen said before Shayla interrupted her.

"I am not coming to live at the Palace."

"But..."

"I'll get my own apartment. Besides, I like my suite the way it is," Shayla said, annoyed with her mother's assumptions. She was always so pushy. Shayla hated that.

"If you insist, but if you ever change your mind."

"I appreciate it, Mother, really I do, but..."

"Okay, I hear you," she said, but Shayla could see her mother was holding her tongue. Shayla knew her mother was pleased to have her moving back to town, especially given the stress of the last few weeks. Rumors of a renegade political group were dying down, but there were still murmurs on the Webavision.

She could tell her mother didn't want to talk about it, but Shayla saw the hints of stress in the deepening creases on her mother's face.

"It'll take me a few days to pack up my place in Cambridge, and then I'll be back."

"Back where you belong," the Queen said.

Shayla bristled. She said nothing as she left, but her emotions caught up with her on the flight back to Cambridge. It was good to be at the Palace, but it was good to leave, too. Then again, she didn't really want to go back to Cambridge either. No place felt quite right.

When she walked into her apartment, she didn't want to pack. Didn't she just move in? She sat on her couch and dug out the velvet bag that held *Reminder of Truth*. Reading it was her bridge to the two men she loved. Her father who gave her this book was gone forever, and now Nathaniel might be too. It was difficult to accept.

"Where are you, Nathaniel?" she cried as she held the book and remembered the time they had read it together. She wished he would reappear as quickly as he vanished.

The next morning, Shayla reluctantly went back to the Cambridge Public Works to clean out her desk. As she walked toward her office, she couldn't help but look where Nathaniel used to leave the bag each morning.

"Hey there, good luck in your new position, wherever it is you're going," she heard.

She turned and felt stunned as Nathaniel's best friend Brigg stood before her, piercing her with a look of disrespect she was not accustomed to.

"I'm going back to Washington," she said, uncomfortably. She knew this was Nathaniel's best friend, but she had no idea whether Nathaniel had told Brigg about her.

Maybe Brigg knew where Nathaniel was or at least had heard from him. She was desperate to know anything at all. She tried to gather the courage to ask.

"I'm sure you'll will do well. Unfortunately, we'll still be here, at the mercy of someone new," he said and then turned and walked away without looking back.

Chapter Twenty-One

"Your name is Joe Merino, and you just turned 21. Read your new file. We sent it to your electronic tablet. It has your birthday, your family situation and everything else you need to know. Memorize every detail."

Nathaniel grabbed his electronic tablet and found the recently downloaded file. He thought of the last eight months of his life. It seemed so unreal.

"I'm really leaving?" he asked, thinking of Shayla. How he wanted to see her, even though he knew it was forbidden.

"First, you must become your new identity and then we'll quiz you until you answer each question correctly. When you pass, you may leave. Go study, young man!" Crosby said with joy. "Oh, and one more thing. The Boston accent must go," Crosby said.

"What accent?"

"Trust me," Crosby said, rolling his eyes. "You'll be meeting with our linguistics coach. We didn't know where you'd be going or we would have worked on it earlier. The Master Instructors hope it won't take long, but as with everything, you will be kept here until it is perfect. It is vital that you fit in," Crosby said, with as serious a look as Nathaniel had ever seen from him.

"Joe Merino, huh?" he said to himself as much as to Crosby, while he looked over the opening page of his file.

"That's who you are now," Crosby said, and left the room.

"Nationality?"

"Irish and Italian. Catholic, but not religious."

"Family?"

"Only child, parents – Delores and Anthony – died when I was 18 in a car crash." Nathaniel couldn't help but think of his own parents. He'd never been close with them, left their house when he was 17 to live on his own, but he missed them now. He hoped they were still alive, but he had no idea.

"General background?"

"Grew up in Kansas City and have a strong secretarial background. You've been going at this for two hours and I have not answered a single thing wrong," Nathaniel said, feeling antsy.

"I guess you are ready," Crosby said teasingly.

"When can I leave?" Nathaniel asked.

"Soon."

"You always say that." Nathaniel looked skeptically at Crosby.

"Really. This time I mean it," Crosby said, laughing before he left for the evening.

Nathaniel tried to go to sleep, but thoughts of his friendship with Brigg flooded his mind, along with memories of intimate encounters he shared with Shayla. The physical barrier of the Underground and all its' forced controls made contacting them impossible, but Nathaniel wasn't sure he had the willpower necessary to maintain distance on his own in the outside world.

"Ready?" Simon asked when he entered Nathaniel's room with Crosby the next morning.

"Yes, sir!" Nathaniel declared with vast enthusiasm. Simon's demeanor was entirely different than their last encounter. He no longer looked at Nathaniel with disdain.

"Follow me." With that, Nathaniel took one last look at his cell and walked behind Simon through the maze of hallways that were silent except for the echo of their footsteps and the buzzing of fluorescent lights above their heads. It seemed like they were walking in circles as the hallways had so many twists and turns, but finally they reached the entrance that he hadn't seen since the day he arrived, eight months earlier.

Keep Your Laws Off my Body. Equal Rights and Justice for all Men. Nathaniel looked at the same words that greeted him when he entered the Underground. They were tattooed in his memory, as he had said them aloud each morning along with the other Grounders.

He remembered first reading them in *Reminder of Truth.* That seemed like a lifetime ago. He wanted to remember this mantra as it appeared, painted boldly behind the guard's desk at the Underground's entrance. He stared at it, thinking about what it meant, and how it represented the cause that he believed in, now more than ever.

Crosby said, "Oh Nathaniel. I'm gonna miss you! You go out there and show those women you can take care of them and make them happy. Make us proud! We'll be thinking of you," Crosby said before he threw his arms tightly around Nathaniel.

Nathaniel hugged back, truly sad to be parting ways with Crosby. "Thanks for everything," Nathaniel said.

"Time to get a move on. We have a schedule to meet," Simon said abruptly.

"Cheerio, good man!" Crosby said, choking back tears. Nathaniel waved, and they walked down the corridor. Nathaniel could tell there would be no chains and no rough talk this time. He was leaving in style, and he felt the world was waiting for Joe Merino. And yet he also thought of how his real name, as Crosby just uttered it, might never be spoken again.

As Nathaniel strapped himself into the back of the van, he was grateful there were no guards to subdue him.

"Can we pull up the shades for the drive?" Nathaniel asked, more comfortable talking to Simon than before. He couldn't wait to be out of this dungeon-like garage to see the sky.

"Gotta keep 'em down for at least a few hours. Security reasons," Simon said. His tone was cordial, like speaking to a comrade who well understood what his passenger went through to earn a ticket out.

"Hello, Joe," said a man who hopped in the back of the van next to him, just before they left. Nathaniel was trying to get used to his new name, but it still felt like he was wearing someone else's snug clothing.

"I'm Drew," said the man with the smoothly sheared head that contrasted thick dark eyebrows. His eyes were dark, but friendly, and his voice was too, unlike many of the Underground staff Nathaniel encountered. "I've heard a lot about you. In fact I know more about you, right now, than you do." Drew smiled and strapped himself into the seat alongside Nathaniel. "Don't worry. I'll fill you in on more of the details," he said.

As the van hummed down the street, nervous excitement pulsed through Nathaniel's body. Not a day went by when he didn't envision leaving the Underground. Now that day had come and it felt strange, along with everything else.

"I know you've got the basics down, but there's still a lot we need to go over," Drew said, glancing at his electronic tablet. "Now, let's see… you're going to be living in Kansas City, and you'll be working at a placed called Kelly Boys Temporary Placement Agency."

"I know the name from reading my new identity file, but not much else."

"They place people for temporary office work. You could be working in all kinds of companies around the country. They're based in KC, but travel is likely. You'll be working with top executives. Sometimes it can get a little stressful, but your records indicate you can handle women at this level.

"I guess so," he said trying to hide his apprehension. Taking classes about office work in the Underground was one thing, but actually working in a corporate office would be new. There wouldn't be any instructors to tell him if he did the wrong thing. No do-overs. His real-world work experience was limited to hard-hats, sewer systems, and tarred roads. He trusted his capabilities, but he had never lived outside of East Cambridge, and had reservations about how he would fit into this corporate Midwestern life.

"You're going to do great. We only put people where they fit well. Here's a picture of your 'friend' who supposedly 'interviewed' and hired you," Drew said, handing Nathaniel a headshot of a slightly plump man with a toothy grin and a mustache that attempted to offset his receding hairline. "Garrett Jones" was printed below the picture.

"A former Grounder?" Nathaniel asked, thinking his physique was atypical for the Underground where one had to be in tip-top shape.

"He got out 12 years ago, and now he's married with two kids. He works part-time at Kelly Boys, and is the primary caretaker of the children, of course. A few nights a week, when his family is asleep, he does work for us. Very dedicated man."

Oh, that explained it. Twelve years out maybe Nathaniel would be fat too. The description of Garrett Jones intimidated Nathaniel. What if he couldn't live up to all that – luring a wife and managing a family and this secret work?

"Is there some sort of bigger plan for me after Kelly Boys?"

"Joe," he said smiling and pausing as he addressed Nathaniel with his new name, "Maybe you'll get as lucky as Garrett? You are starting out doing what he did as an Administrative assistant, but we told them you're good at multi-tasking and organizing and that you're an excellent meeting scribe. They were excited about your skills. You may find yourself working on special projects. It's likely you'll eventually snag a permanent position, if you excel, which we hope. Kelly Boys pays pretty well too, which is good because former Grounders tithe. Of course, we encourage you to give more than that, if at all possible. Ten percent is great, but the Underground always needs more money, and after all, how can you put a price on the gifts they have given you," Drew said, and Nathaniel heard the message loud and clear.

"Okay," Nathaniel said. It was just starting to sink in. His life would forever be enmeshed and indebted to the Underground. Payback was just beginning.

Nathaniel drifted off to sleep during the long ride, and when he woke, the shades of the van were up. A warm, natural light bathed his face for the first time since he had entered the Underground.

He looked outside and wished to fly alongside the birds in the distance, free to go anywhere the breeze went.

The emerald suburban lawns slowly gave way to the city sidewalks and dwellings that sat stacked up and crowded. He'd missed the cold winter, which he usually disliked. He preferred to miss it on his own terms, instead of the forced circumstances. He still felt strange about his Underground experience. Kidnapped at first, but now he was part of it, and there was no way to leave. "We'll keep in touch" He heard Chester's voice – a reminder in his head.

Before he knew it, the van pulled in a round driveway of an apartment building, and Simon cut the engine. "We're near The Plaza, the heart of downtown Kansas City culture. It's a great neighborhood, perfect for a single man. The last Grounder who had this apartment just got married so it's open. First month of rent is covered until you get paid. It's a studio that we've had for years," Drew said, handing him a backpack that was heavy. Nathaniel had no idea what was in it, but knew that at least it had a tablet computer of some sort.

"This is it," Simon said, jingling the apartment keys in front of him. "You ready?"

Nathaniel answered with a grin, even though he was feeling less sure than ever before. Was he really prepared for this? Nathaniel didn't know if he could pretend to be a new man who had just turned 21. Would they notice the laugh lines forming around his eyes and know he was lying about his age and about everything else too?

He hid his fears and shook Simon's hand.

"Apartment 8-C. Take good care." Simon said as he clicked the van locks open so Nathaniel could get out.

Nathaniel started to open the door, but Drew put his arm on Nathaniel's, and he stopped.

"One more thing. You may hear rumors about the Underground. Unfavorable things. Unless you speak with someone who you know is a legitimate contact, ignore everything. There are a lot of crazy people out there," Drew said, without any hint of a smile or lightness. His eyes were dark. Nathaniel heard a chill in his voice.

"How will I know who is real and who?"

"You'll know," Drew said, interrupting him before moving out of the way so Nathaniel could get out of the van.

Nathaniel walked across the driveway, feeling shaken by Drew's last words until the warm July breeze enveloped him. He felt like a kid on the first day of school.

The air conditioned lobby felt nice, but he longed to go back outside, to feel the natural air, even if it was hot. He turned back to look out the front door, but the van was gone.

He entered his new home. The lobby looked like an old hotel, badly in need of at least a paint job. Walking to the elevator, he stopped in front of the mailboxes to see one with his new name. It fit in with all the others, printed in the same block style. It was as though he had been living there for a while. That's me, he thought: Joe Merino.

The big, old-fashioned elevator had a wire gate he had to close before pushing the button to his floor. The slow creak made him wonder if he should have taken the stairs, but it slowly made its creaky way up to the eighth floor. Nathaniel tried to look nonchalant while the other person in the elevator – a woman - flipped through her mail. In theory, he knew how to survey women's behaviors and signals. This training taught him to offer the perfect tailored greeting, but he was too scared. The Master Instructors would chastise him if they knew he had wasted this opportunity. Other than the Sexperts in the Underground, he hadn't stood next to a woman since he left. When the elevator stopped at the sixth floor and the woman got off, Nathaniel breathed a little easier. It would take some time to acclimate to the new environment so he could apply all of his new knowledge.

Inside his apartment, there was a galley kitchen with white metal cabinets, tan Formica countertops and a white vinyl tile floor. The bathroom was small, with a shower stall but no tub. The apartment was furnished with a futon bed, and a tiny table with two chairs.

At least it was clean. Compared with his Underground cell, it felt like the Taj Mahal. The hodge-podge decoration was the result of an unnamed trail of Grounders who each left an imprint of some sort in the small efficiency. There was a wooden coffee table that caught his eye first, with inlaid mother-of-pearl elephants. It was beautiful, but it looked funny next to the puffy blue velvet couch that had seen better days, and the plastic cat clock on the wall that had eyes that moved back and forth as each second passed. It was kind of creepy.

He opened his backpack. Sure enough, an electronic tablet was on top. He turned it on and looked at his new files from the Underground. This included Joe Merino's resume, which he would use at the state-sponsored Parties Of Availability. He would attend them until he was engaged. Next, his curiosity got hold of him and he Googled his real name, but there was nothing. It was as if he had never existed at all. He tried not to think about how strange that felt, knowing that he needed to move forward.

He logged onto his new email account and composed a message:

Dearest Shayla,

I missed you more than you'll ever know. I'm sorry I disappeared. I'll explain it to you and make it up to you, if you give me the opportunity. I completely understand if you've moved on or never want to see me again, but I hope that isn't the case.

I love you Shayla Smith with all my heart and soul.

No matter what happens, I want you to know that.

-Nathaniel

He didn't bother typing her email address in the "To" field, but quickly hit the Cancel button. The forced barrier of the Underground was gone. He hoped his willpower would be able to keep him away so he didn't cause trouble for everyone who put their lives on the line so he could have a second chance.

As he prepared to leave his apartment to buy a few things, he reminded himself that there was nobody telling him what to do or where to go. Were cameras embedded in the walls of the apartment? Was every entry of his tablet being recorded too?

Chapter Twenty-Two

"If I go on one date, then you promise to leave me alone?" Shayla said.

"I promise," the Queen said, trying to suppress the joy in her voice. "I'll arrange it."

Shayla said, "No, just send me his information and I'll arrange it."

"Whatever you prefer," the Queen said, thinking that Shayla was finally coming to her senses. Having Shayla back in Washington was wonderful. It was a big step toward getting her to return to the Palace.

"He comes from a good family and is very handsome, and went to finishing school," the Queen said.

"Oh, great. Sounds formal," Shayla said, sounding deflated.

"You're confusing formality with good manners," the Queen defended. She tried to see where Shayla was coming from, but sometimes she just plain did not understand her daughter's attitude. Shayla lived an extremely privileged life. Why did she have to be so negative?

"I'll send you his contact information," the Queen said. If Shayla agreed to go on a date, it meant she was, finally, starting to get over that derelict. The Queen periodically asked Gerald if there was any more news about Nathaniel DeLuca, but apparently the trail had dried up. He was probably living in a tent in the wilderness to avoid being forced to marry that wretched fiancée. In any case, Shayla seldom mentioned him anymore. Thank God.

"And how is Steelco?" her mother asked, taking a sip of tea, from the cup that boasted her crest. Now that she had Shayla's commitment to date a suitable man, it was best to switch subjects before Shayla changed her mind.

"Not so great. I'm a little disappointed, honestly. Lorraine is back-peddling on promises she made when I signed on," Shayla said, annoyed.

"Like what?" the Queen asked. She wasn't really surprised, and figured she'd have to manage this relationship, but didn't think it would be so soon.

"I'm trying to improve working conditions. Do you know there is no overtime pay for steel workers? They often work fourteen hour days, or longer, and get the same pay as if they worked eight. They don't even get breaks. It's not right," Shayla said, shaking her head.

"Those steel workers are amongst the best paid laborers in the country. They have a steady job. Believe me, they are happy. Besides, men like to work hard," the Queen said.

The Queen watched Shayla roll her eyes and wondered if Shayla would ever grow out of her pie in the sky idealism. She was 29. It was time to get real about the world.

"Better working conditions means better productivity. As it stands, there are costly accidents at the plant from exhausted, overworked men," Shayla said with a sigh.

"Steelco's system works," the Queen said, thinking she would need to call Lorraine and insist that she throw Shayla a bone. Otherwise, she could tell Shayla was going to stir up trouble. That was the last thing the Queen needed. She hated to admit that the stress of the recent protests was bothering her, but it was true. She crossed her fingers that the protests were done. She hated keeping all those men locked up and wondered if she was making a mistake. Maybe she should have followed her instincts and killed them as soon as they were captured, but she really didn't want to. She was not a murderer.

A knock on the door interrupted their dinner.

"Come in," the Queen said. Gerald poked his head inside. "Your attention is needed," he said. His even-keeled face gave away nothing, but she knew he wouldn't have interrupted for something trivial.

"What is it?" she asked, feeling her heartbeat quicken. She detested the fear that entered her body lately.

"Maybe we should let Shayla tend to other things," he said.

The Queen thought about it a minute. She could tell he was trying to protect Shayla, but the Queen needed Shayla to begin to help out and partake in the job that would one day be hers.

"Shayla will stay. There is no reason she shouldn't hear whatever you have to tell me," the Queen said. "Unless you have somewhere to be?" she said, turning to Shayla.

"I can stay," she said.

Gerald closed the door behind him before speaking.

"There's another protest; this one is much bigger."

"Become a chosen man: Come to the Parties Of Availability!" Queen Amanda said. The Webavision was larger than life, in the heart of downtown Kansas City. He stopped to watch as the video continued. An upbeat music track blared as the picture panned to a ballroom filled with smiling men and women. "Won't you try it?" the Queen's voiceover continued, with the advertisement ending in a still shot of her face. Nathaniel had to admit the Queen's photo looked like Shayla – from the generous smile to the clear olive complexion, but he knew the similarities ended at their skin.

He stared longer than he should have, as he tried to push away the unrealistic thoughts of Shayla. He had only been out of the Underground for a couple of hours, and his self-control was already being tested. Maybe he could buy a disposable phone and call her using a fake name. Who would know?

POA, The Plaza Ballroom, Every other evening from 5 to 9! was posted next to the picture of the Queen, as though she would be the host or available to date.

He noted the date and time for the party that very evening, but all he could think of was Shayla. He didn't want anyone else, but knew that seeing her was impossible.

He walked to Augustine's clothing store where he was told to shop.

"Something to wear to the POAs?" said the salesman. "Follow me."

All the clothes he tried on felt very un-Nathaniel, but they were perfect for Joe Merino.

"You're going to do great tonight. I can feel it!" the salesman said with a smile after spending an hour helping Nathaniel invest in a small wardrobe.

"You should really check out our Salon-o-Rama," the salesman said after wrapping Nathaniel's purchases. "I think a little eyebrow waxing would do you wonders. Those baby blue eyes need to be properly framed. It's right down the hall. Ask for Sammy," he whispered to Nathaniel as he handed him the packages, along with a 10 percent off coupon.

"Thanks for the tip," Nathaniel said. He timidly entered the Salon-o-Rama. A voice from behind the counter beckoned his response.

"What can we do for you today? Need a new doo? Manicure? Wax-o-rama?"

"I've never done this before. I'm getting ready to go to the POA this evening and really want to look my best. What do you suggest?"

"A facial and an eyebrow waxing. Why don't you come here and Sammy will do you over."

Nathaniel glanced at Sammy who looked a little overdone. He wore not-so-subtle eyeliner, and hair that spiked in all directions with various unnatural shades on different parts of his head. This was not the look that Nathaniel thought would get the Underground stamp of approval. His stomach knotted as Sammy put forth his hand, complete with black polished nails, for Nathaniel to shake.

"Hi, I'm Sammy. And you are?"

"I'm Joe Merino," Nathaniel said.

"Nice to meet you Joe. Facial and an eyebrow waxing?" he said, leading Nathaniel through the salon with his bulky packages in tow.

While other men in the Underground had been required to get eyebrow waxing, back waxing, laser hair removal, and even Botox, Nathaniel had been spared. Maybe I shouldn't do this, he thought, but his feet continued behind Sammy, walking ever deeper into the Salon-o-Rama. It reminded him of the maze-like hallways of the Underground.

He found the facial more pleasant that he would have imagined. With warm, lavender scented towels strewn on his face, he immediately relaxed. Cool cucumbers placed over his eyes followed, along with an incredible face massage that felt perfect with the beautiful classical music permeating the background. All the tension eased out of his temples and lower jaw when the fingers of Sammy-with-the-painted-nails performed their magic.

Once the facial was complete, Nathaniel felt mellow and happy.

"That felt good," Nathaniel said, smiling.

"You sound surprised. What did you think? You're in Sammy's hands and now your skin is glowing. Your pores are opened which means the waxing will go well, too," Sammy said. "It might sting a little," he said, just before ripping the hot wax from Nathaniel's brow. Nathaniel yelped like a kicked dog.

"What the?"

"It hurts to be beautiful!" Sammy sang.

Nathaniel felt new compassion for the poor men in the Underground who were forced to have their backs waxed on a regular basis.

"Oh, sorry. Guess you weren't ready," Sammy said while smoothing some sweet smelling lotion over the shocked area. "Just one more to go."

Nathaniel didn't yell when the other one was done, but it hurt just as much. He couldn't believe that men subjected themselves to this all the time.

"Just a few strays I've gotta fish out," Sammy said, leaning in close with tweezers as he pulled a goose-neck lamp close to Nathaniel's face. Nathaniel closed his eyes and sucked in his breath as he waited for the plucking to end.

"Here you go. You're perfect!" Sammy said, handing Nathaniel a mirror.

"It looks great," Nathaniel said, thinking it looked a little too clean for his taste. Maybe it was something he just needed to get used to, along with everything else. Maybe it would help him meet a decent woman who could potentially be his future spouse. He also hoped it would help steer his mind from the inevitable thoughts of Shayla that he couldn't shake.

Nathaniel stood in the short line outside the POA waiting to check in. Would they know his identification card was fake? Nathaniel held his breath as he waited for the scanned card to go through.

Peering into the party, he saw a Taser whispering to a man whose color drained from his face. Nathaniel wondered what was going on. Was the Taser threatening him for some reason? Nathaniel couldn't understand why they had to be that way, but remembered his mission and looked away.

"Your card?" the hostess said. It had gone through the computer without a problem. That meant that Joe Merino existed, according to the United States.

"Thank you," he said, as he took the coveted identification and put it back in his wallet before entering the ballroom. There had to be at least 500 people. He glanced at the men who were mingling with a carefree air. He studied their stances, their laughs, and wondered if they were graduates of the Underground with more POA experience under their belts. He tried to look relaxed. It appeared that the ratio of men to women was two to one. He tried not to look desperate. The Underground gave him the tools to beat the odds, but he needed to create the opportunities to use his new skills.

"Hi Joe. I'm Mandy," said a voice that reminded him of those ancient Betty Boop cartoons. She sounded much too young for someone at the POA. "I just checked out your resume," she said, pointing to her electronic tablet. It was hard to believe that this petite woman in a fruity printed dress was actually 18, the required age for attendance. "Is there anything else I can tell you about myself?" he asked, knowing she had the advantage of knowing all about him. His knowledge of her was limited to what he saw and she chose to tell. He was also hoping that other women might become interested, now that he was talking with someone. Mandy wasn't exactly what he or the Underground were looking for.

"Well, it says here your mom is dead. I was wondering how she died," she said. This was not the type of interview he expected. Certainly not the type of question he figured would be first.

"Both my parents died in a car crash when I was 18," he said, his eyes sincerely welling up, as he forced himself to think of losing Shayla. "I try not to dwell on it. You've got to be strong and move on," he said, hoping her sympathies would kick in, but all she did was stare at her electronic tablet, which made him feel even more awkward.

"Why do you ask?" he asked, unable to hide his curiosity.

"Do you like cats?" she asked. "I have five cats, and I just love them. Being with someone who appreciates cats is very important to me." Her eyes grew wide, eager for an answer. He wondered whether she chose not to answer his question or whether she had simply not heard. Wisely, he knew better than to ask a second time, even though her next question seemed just as strange.

"I adore cats! I grew up with them, and this is actually the first time I haven't had one. I miss them terribly. What are your cats' names?" he asked. In reality, Nathaniel was indifferent to pets. He didn't really understand people who put so much into the lives of their animals, but he suspected he could learn to tolerate them. He heard the strong voice of his motivational Master Instructor coaching him from behind: "Every opportunity must be followed through. Take an interest in whatever they talk about."

"It was a pleasure to make your acquaintance, Joe. I may be back for you later," she said. With that, she sauntered across the room and immediately began chatting with another man.

"How many times have you been here?" said another woman who approached a few minutes later. Her tone was almost suspicious.

"Actually, this is my first time," he said to the woman who was attractive, but looked to be 15 years his senior. She was well-dressed and amply made-up to temper her wrinkles. At least she offered a more standard ice-breaker than asking how his mother had met her ultimate fate.

"I thought I hadn't seen you before. I'm Claire Jameson," she said, holding out her hand.

"It's lovely to meet you, Claire. I'm Joe Merino," he said, thinking that her slightly husky voice was sultry. She was certainly attractive. Her long auburn locks fell perfectly to the middle of her back. She was a woman of understatement and class, which the Underground had taught him to hone in on.

"Would you like to get out of here? I'd be happy to buy you a drink that has more of a kick than the watered-down, over-priced beverages they serve here," she said staring him squarely in the eyes.

"Yes, I'd love to, Claire," he heard himself say with a politeness that seemed straight out of the Underground classroom.

Nathaniel was quite surprised by her forwardness, but maybe this was how the POAs worked. He wasn't sure she was the best one for him, but turning her down would seem rude, and he could suffer repercussions.

Nathaniel checked out of the party without incident and slid comfortably into the passenger seat of her BMW 7-Series, as though he had sat in one every day of his life.

"I thought we were going to get a drink somewhere?" he said when she pulled into a parking spot of the Plaza Marquis, an apartment complex synonymous with wealth. He read about it in the literature Crosby gave him before he left the Underground. This was certainly a good sign, but he still felt funny that she had been so quick to invite him out and then she was taking him to a residence rather than a bar. He was starting to have a hunch for what she had in mind.

"We are getting a drink here at my apartment. That okay?" she asked casually as she led him to the front of the building.

"Of course," he said. Her unit was beautiful with perfect city views through the large bay windows. He had never been in such an apartment. The clear glass motif offered a modern, minimalist look with glass statues delicately balanced on end tables and bookshelves. He felt like a child in a boutique where it was important not to touch anything for fear of breaking something he couldn't afford to buy.

"Have a seat," she said, motioning for him to sit on the couch, before she disappeared.

She returned with a bottle of wine and two long-stemmed glasses. They sparkled as she filled each one with a deep red wine.

"Cheers," she said, handing Nathaniel a glass and they toasted, their glasses lightly touching which set off a perfect pitch beautifully reverberating from the delicate crystal.

"Thank you," he said taking a sip. She smiled broadly as she inched a little closer to him on the snow-white leather couch. He worried about spilling, but he felt good. It had been a long time since he sat in anyone's living room to relax.

"What do you do?" he asked lightly.

"I am a senior VP over at Crown Center. I work hard, and when I'm not working hard, I like to pamper myself with fine wine and good company. Just as you see." Her compliment embarrassed him. She was clearly interested in him sexually, but beyond that he didn't know. Was she even open to marriage? He tried to put aside his own personal desires, remembering that finding a mate was paramount. Anyone better than Janice was a step up, but obviously he wanted someone with a big income and influence for the benefit of the Underground.

"I certainly like walks on the beach, although there aren't any near here, and I do enjoy an occasional rock concert too. Do you have any more questions?" she asked before draining her glass.

"Well, I do have one more question, actually," Nathaniel said, taking a draw on his wine glass.

"Ask me," she said before topping off his wine glass and filling her own.

"What are you looking for at the POAs?" he asked, looking her straight in the eyes. The question was loaded, and his gaze of intrusion indicated he wanted to know and understand exactly what he was getting into.

"Well, Joe, you're quite a fellow, aren't you?" she said laughing.

He was immediately uncomfortable, afraid that he might scare her off.

"I'm sorry if I seem too forward," he said apologetically. "I hope I didn't offend you. It's just that I'm looking for something long term and I hope we're on the same wavelength."

"I appreciate your honesty."

Nathaniel wondered whether this was true. He became unsure of how reliable his instincts were. This felt like a game, and she had more experience at it.

"This evening, I went to the POA looking for something, and I found you," she said. "I found Joe Merino, a lovely gentlemen who is handsome and witty and kind. She moved closer to him on the couch, until she forced her eyes onto his and she whispered.

"That's enough talking for this evening, don't you think?"

Before he knew what to do, she kissed him. He wasn't surprised, and he wasn't unhappy, but he wasn't thrilled either. For the moment, he decided to let his feelings slide by. His body wanted her.

Her kiss continued as she climbed on top of him. Nathaniel could tell that Claire was used to being in charge, and she certainly was this evening. She pulled up her dress so she could straddle him and lunge her hips into his, a preview of what she would do once they undressed. She wore thigh high stockings that brought Nathaniel's excitement up a level as his thoughts moved back and forth between Shayla and Claire. Claire pawed him aggressively, stopping slowly over his hardness to feel its shape beneath his clothes.

It felt good to be taken. Yes, he needed to find a wife, but right now he wanted nothing more than to plunge into Claire with all his might, and he could tell that's how she would like it.

"That feels so good," he said when she moved her hand on him in a rhythm that made him want to let go. Tonight, he was hers. He closed his eyes and kissed her, pretending she was Shayla, and before long he came with a powerful thrust that made her cry out.

"I came too soon. I'm sorry," he said.

"Enough talking, remember?" she asked rhetorically as she led him to her bedroom revealing a king-sized poster bed.

"Lie down on the bed, on your back," she commanded.

Nathaniel was a little nervous, but did as he was told.

"Have you ever been tied up, Joe?" she asked playfully.

"Once," he said, preferring not to lie. It had been one of the Underground tests, by a large sadistic woman. He didn't love it, but he wasn't going to say that now.

"After tonight, it'll be twice," she said with a devilish grin. "I promise not to hurt you… too much," she said as she pulled some cotton scarves from a drawer.

"I'm game," he said, trying to act casual but when she tied his wrists up with her belt, but he wasn't at ease. She left his ankles free and slowly took off her dress, her underwear, and lastly she slowly removed her bra. Her breasts were pert, and she ran her fingers over the nipples, teasing him. She now wore only her garter and stockings. He had to admit she looked sexy, and he felt the blood rush to his groin.

"Somebody's excited," she said before pulling herself onto him with a force that rivaled the Underground's roughest Sexpert. He closed his eyes and thought of Shayla and his excitement grew. He couldn't help but enjoy Claire as she moved herself up and down quickening her pace. He soon heard her voice of pleasure, but it wasn't the voice he wanted to hear. He opened his eyes and couldn't deny that Claire was attractive, but that's not who he wished to see looking down to him. Still, Claire was kind enough to wait for Nathaniel's pulsation, a well-needed release. After that, she collapsed before rolling over on her back.

"Oooh, you're good Joe! That was just what I needed," she said, laughing.

Nathaniel caught his breath and he hoped she would untie him, but she got up and left the room, returning with a pint of ice cream and a spoon. The devilish look in her eye had been tamed, and her focus was on the ice cream.

"Want some?" she said, playfully licking the chocolate-flecked vanilla ice cream.

"Of course!" he said. She slowly fed him, purposefully dribbling some on his chin. He struggled to lick it. Before he could reach it, she pulled it back and put a big hunk of it on his belly and then proceeded to lick it ever so sensually. Finally, she untied him and wordlessly handed him the ice cream container before she settled alongside him.

After that, she rolled onto her side, moving close to him as she rubbed tufts of his chest hair between her fingers. He thought of getting up, but soon drifted to sleep. Between the wine, the sex, and the ice cream, he was spent.

His sleep brought Shayla to his dream. She was topless, but wore stockings identical to those Claire had.

"Nathaniel, why are you playing these games?" Shayla asked. She ate from a pint-sized container of ice cream. "What are you doing with that woman? Can't you tell she only wants your sex? I want all of you! I love you Nathaniel. I love you. I love you. IloveyouIloveyou..."

Nathaniel woke up next to Claire who was fast asleep. He wondered if Shayla was also sleeping next to a lover who had satisfied her in a way that made Nathaniel nothing more than a distant memory.

"I'll call you," Claire said, the next morning. He didn't know whether she would or not. He hoped she would, if for no other reason than there was no other living soul who knew his alias: Joe Merino.

Chapter Twenty-Three

"I doubt that Grounders were involved in that last protest," Simon said, as though Gerald was some overprotective parent.

"Why are you so sure?" Gerald said, his voice icy.

"The Webavision photos."

"You're kidding, right?" Gerald said, with a biting laugh. "The Webavision photos are your intelligence data? That reflects a fraction of what's out there," he said, unable to filter anger from his voice. He wanted to tell Simon to get his shit together.

"Okay, Mr. Palace, tell me what you know," Simon said.

"There were three hundred protesters. I can't get my hands on the names, but they are supposedly all in custody, spread around dungeons of area jailhouses in D.C., Virginia, and Maryland. From what I can glean, the Queen is trying to figure out what to do with them. Any idea how many Grounders are late checking in?"

"We don't have regular check-ins with everyone anymore. It's too risky," Simon said.

"If they are in custody, they will be forced to talk," Gerald stressed as best he could. Simon didn't immediately respond. Clearly, he didn't know what to say. *Finally*, Gerald thought. *He's listening*.

"Is there anything you can do?" Simon asked, sounding slightly humbled after a pause.

"I doubt it. The Queen is scared," Gerald said calmly, even though he was angry. Gerald couldn't help but wonder when they stopped having regular check-ins and who made that decision.

"That's good. She should be scared because we are going to take over," Simon said with excitement.

Gerald realized just how clueless this guy was. How he had risen in ranks was a mystery. In the olden days… he started to think, but stopped himself. It was a waste to think like that.

"Don't delude yourself. When she's scared, she tightens the noose. You think the laws are tough now? Just wait and see."

"Something smells delicious," Shayla said, as soon as she stepped into the apartment.

"Your mother mentioned that tuna steaks were your favorite, but you are probably smelling the fresh bread."

"I'm impressed," she said, feeling annoyed at her mother for butting in. Did she really have to tell this guy her favorite food? Already?

"Let's just say I'm very comfortable in the kitchen," he said, sounding both modest and confident.

"Glass of wine?" he asked.

"Please," she said, following him into the kitchen as piped classical music paved the way.

"Nice place," she said, looking around. The kitchen wasn't large, but nicely decorated and organized. The living room was homey, tastefully furnished with original paintings that complemented the formal couches and inlaid wood coffee table.

"It came from Singapore," he said, watching her study the table. "As did the dining room table," he said, motioning toward the beautifully set table, cloth napkins and all.

"My phone." she said, pointing to the ringing from her purse. "Work has been crazy."

"By all means, take your time."

Shayla stepped away from the kitchen and opened her phone.

"Hello?" The phone clicked dead. That had been happening with some frequency, and it was annoying. She looked at the number, but like all the other calls, it appeared as some sort of weird scrambled phone number. Somebody was blocking the real number. Could it be Janice? It could be, but that didn't make sense. Would she even know how to block a call? Plus, the few times she called before, she was drunk and rambled, and the last time she called was months earlier.

Maybe these calls had something to do with Nathaniel's disappearance. She swore she wouldn't think about the possibility of him returning anymore. She turned off her phone, thinking it might be time to enlist the help of her mother's head of security to get to the bottom of these crank calls.

"Sorry about that," she said, turning around to see Michael setting down two exquisite plates of food that were as beautiful as any gourmet dinner she had ever seen in the Palace. "Wow!"

"I hope you'll say that after you taste it. Why don't you have a seat?"

Chapter Twenty-Four

"I 've only got a few minutes," Garrett said, after a sweaty handshake. They were at a café down the street from Nathaniel's first assignment.

"I got you an easy job to start. It's at a bank. Think of this as a favor that I might need returned someday," Garrett said, looking at Nathaniel with a distrustful eye. Nathaniel hated the idea of being beholden to anyone, but he knew he'd better get used to it.

"I really appreciate it," Nathaniel said, forcing himself to sound friendly, but he didn't like this guy.

"Any questions?" Garrett asked.

"This kind of work is new for me. Any tips about working at a bank?"

"It's not rocket science. Be extremely attentive, especially to the ladies. That's about it. I've got my own shit to deal with. My two year old has a cold, and I've got to work today and then take him to the doctor and get home and clean the house and put a decent dinner on the table. Otherwise there will be hell to pay. If you really need to contact me, here's my number," he said, jotting it down on a napkin. With that kind of endorsement, Nathaniel thought he would almost rather call the Tasers for help. Garrett nodded, got up and left.

"Thanks again," Nathaniel said, calling after him. This job would be sink or swim.

He watched Garrett's chubby body scurry toward the café's exit and was glad to see him go. He was unkempt; his jacket slightly wrinkled, his pants a little snug. Nathaniel figured they probably fit when he bought them. Despite his looks, Nathaniel knew Garrett was a success as far as the Underground was concerned. He had a job that helped their cause, tithed his salary, and was married.

Nathaniel finished his coffee and walked out the door, nearly bumping into a group of Tasers. Whenever Tasers were in the area, he felt more nervous than he had before he was in the Underground. He breathed deeply and continued down the street. Looking straight ahead, he did his best to shoo away the paranoia that crept into his thoughts.

The bank entrance was a few blocks away. As soon as he stepped inside, he felt immediate relief from the threat of Tasers. The environment felt very professional with a lot of women but many men, too. Just being in the building was pleasant. The high ceilings and pristinely clean bay windows lifted his mood. After months spent with the Underground, he had a job that allowed him to look outside whenever he wanted. He would never again take the sunlight for granted.

"Stand here and when anyone comes in, direct them to the right area of the bank to speak with the appropriate person. Here's the chart, okay?" said Eve, who was assigned to manage him.

"Anything else I need to do?" he asked, wanting badly to do a good job.

"If there is, I'll let you know, alright?" she said, smiling. His eyes drifted to her ring finger and he was sorry to see she already wore a wedding ring.

✣✣✣✣✣✣✣✣✣✣

"We're moving you out of this position," Eve said two days later.

"Did I do something wrong?" Nathaniel asked.

Eve smiled. "Just the opposite. People keep talking about how much they like you as the first face they see. The Bank President's administrative assistant is ill, so they need someone good, pronto. You're movin' up, Joe!"

As Nathaniel rode the elevator to his new job, he thought of all the hard labor he had done at the Cambridge Public Works. He had used jackhammers, fixed broken water mains, and responded to emergencies of all kinds for years. Much of his time was spent underground in the sewers. Now, he was on his way to a skyscraper penthouse office where he would report to a bank president, answer phones, serve lunches, coffee, and run errands. He would be trusted by women in ways that he had never experienced. He had become a white-collar worker, the very kind he and Brigg used to look down on.

And he liked it.

While his work life was progressing, dating was laborious. He religiously attended the Parties of Availability. He often got dates, and even found himself in fancy houses of wealthy women. Still, he couldn't stop wishing for Shayla. He remembered making love in her dingy office. That's all he wanted, even with the annoyances of that tiny room – like the annoying sound of that hissing radiator.

He tried not to think about her, but did look her up on the Internet when he first got out of the Underground. He found a single news report dated just weeks after he went to the Underground. *"Shayla Smith, daughter of the Queen has left the Cambridge Public Works to pursue interests in the private sector."* He read the short article a few times, but it rang false. She was passionate about being a public servant. Why did she leave?

He sighed as he remembered their time together, but living in the past and wondering what the hell she was doing was futile. He needed to lure a wife, preferably someone high-powered and financially successful who would make the Underground happy. He braced himself to enter his umpteenth POA. He had been attending a few a week, for months. He pulled his identification card out of his wallet and went through the registration line before heading to the bartender.

"I know what you want," the bartender said, not waiting for Nathaniel to order.

"That's a bad sign! That means I've been here too often," Nathaniel said, trying to be light.

"Don't worry, it'll happen. Coming here is like throwing darts at a board, you'll get the bulls eye soon enough. Chin up.

This is where I met my wife," the man said, handing him a Manhattan.

"Here comes one now," the bartender said before walking away.

"You work at Kelly Boys?" a woman said, walking up to him, glancing at her electronic tablet. She wore a plain blue dress and sensible black shoes that looked like they came from "The Walking Store." He always thought of those stores for older people, but she looked to be in her early 30s.

"I sure do!" he said, having long since mastered the upbeat cocktail party tone.

"I work at a company that uses Kelly Boys, so I am familiar with the caliber of people working at your company. I'm Lianne, by the way," she said holding out her petite hand. Her light blond hair was cut in a sensible bob that flattered her sweetheart face.

"Well, thank you," he said, before noticing Claire out of the corner of his eye. Claire had never called him as she had said she would. Now she was flirting with another young man, sipping her wine and tossing her hair. Women.

Lianne continued the interview but cut it short a couple of minutes in.

"I'll be right back. I just need to go to the ladies room," she said, but he had heard that line before. He had been to enough POAs to easily tell when someone was going to come back to him or not. Lianne was moving on.

As he took a sip of his drink, he wished to be somewhere else. He really longed to spend an evening at The Black Hole, sitting next to Brigg, clinking a neat glass of Maker's Mark with his friend.

Instead, he nursed his watery Manhattan, retreating to the corner to regroup and reenergize before hoping another woman would approach. All of a sudden, a group of Tasers ran toward the exit as though someone yelled fire. Nathaniel's heart sped. Other people quickly followed suit, swarming the exits, but Nathaniel didn't know why. In the frenzy, many men didn't follow the usual checkout protocol, but Nathaniel couldn't afford to do so. That kind of mistake could invite a visit from the Tasers for breaking the law. It was too dangerous, so he nervously waited in line amidst the chaos. After finally checking out, he tentatively walked toward the exit where a group of men solemnly stood. As he moved toward them, he heard the chants coming from outside. They all watched through the simple glass doors as though it were a movie, but this was very real.

A piece of him longed to run out and join their chorus. He believed in these words more than anything.

Keep Your Laws Off My Body. Equal Rights and Justice for all Men!

Keep Your Laws Off My Body. Equal Rights and Justice for all Men!

Keep Your Laws Off My Body. Equal Rights and Justice for all Men!

It sent a chill through Nathaniel, but he stayed put; getting caught protesting certainly meant immediate castration.

Were these Grounders? They had to be. It was the Underground's mantra, taken from *Reminder of Truth*. He remembered what Drew said just before Nathaniel left the Underground custody. "Don't believe anything you hear, unless it is from someone you know is a legitimate contact. There are a lot of crazy people out there."

He watched the arrests unfold alongside other POA attendees. Torches burned as their cries grew louder until the Tasers began, one by one, pulling the protesters into windowless vans. They padlocked them from the outside and drove off. He had heard of a few protests on the Webavision when he first got out, but that was months ago. They seemed to die down.

"Let's go outside together," said one of the men standing nearby. "We walk out slowly and turn left at the corner," the unofficial leader said.

Nathaniel nodded and a dozen others followed.

As they stepped outside, the pandemonium began to subside, but the Tasers' flashing lights remained strong. They systematically Tased the men brave enough to stand their ground. Nathaniel forced himself to look at the road, rather than the painful scene. As he and the group of men were about to turn off the main drag, he glanced once more, as if to remind himself of why his role in the Underground's mission was vital.

Garrett Jones, his boss, stood tall, looking dazed and angry as blood ran down the side of his face. His rage filled eyes looked shocked as they recognized Nathaniel, but they quickly went dead as a Taser stunned him. He fell on top of two other men, like a pile of dead flies.

Chapter Twenty-Five

"Another one?" the Queen said.

"I'm afraid so. It was in Kansas City, outside one of the city's largest weekly POAs," said her head of security.

"How many people?" the Queen asked. This had to stop! She had to do something.

"A few hundred. As with the others, we rounded them up. They are in local prisons."

"That's good news, at least," she said. "I'll call you back," she said, hearing the knock on the door. She took a moment to compose herself before opening the door. She felt frazzled inside, but smiled as soon as she saw Shayla.

"My dear, how are you? Or should I say how are you and Michael?" the Queen said, wearing her best mask of confidence.

"We're doing fine, I guess," Shayla said. The Queen could see the hesitation and it worried her. Michael was the ideal choice for a son-in-law. He had the perfect balance of obedience and diligence. His lineage was strong and stable. His mother had been active and supportive of the Queen's politics for decades.

"Fine? I thought you said he's terrific?"

"I can't say anything bad about him," Shayla said, but she definitely seemed unsure.

"He's educated, kind, thoughtful, and a great cook and homemaker, right?" the Queen asked.

"I guess so," Shayla said.

"That sounds ideal to me, yes?"

Shayla nodded and the Queen felt her daughter was listening. Finally.

"And how is work going?" she asked Shayla, knowing it wasn't good to focus too much on Michael. Shayla could easily snap into her rebellious self.

"I'm still having problems there," Shayla said, collapsing onto the couch in a defeated manner.

"Really?" the Queen said, truly feeling surprised. She was going to kill Lorraine who had promised she would be more amenable to Shayla's requests. Why was she being so difficult?

"I'm not sure what to do. I don't want to make a big public stink, but these are important worker rights that I'm fighting for and I'm not going to give up."

"Give it a little time," the Queen said, quickly, feeling like her own daughter was playing her. Fine, so long as Shayla was interested in Michael, the Queen would figure out some way to force Lorraine to make concessions around Steelco policies. The Queen needed to keep Shayla happy and calm.

It was only short-term, she would remind Lorraine. Once the Queen lured Shayla to work in the Palace, everything at Steelco could go back to normal.

"If you think things might get better," Shayla said, looking curiously for the subtext of assurance.

"I have a hunch things are going to start going your way very soon," the Queen said, smiling. She never thought she would have to make political deals with her own daughter.

"That would be great. How are things going here?" Shayla asked.

"Another damn protest, in Kansas City this time. I am getting too old for this, but I'm not going to let the bastards get me."

"Maybe it's time to think about making some changes here, too. I could help," Shayla said.

"Don't start with me again. Not tonight, Shayla. Okay? I really don't need it."

"You promised I could run this company my way, and you're stonewalling me," Shayla said to Lorraine, realizing bluntness was required. She looked her dead in the eyes, sitting across from her. The glasses of cold water sat untouched in front of each of them, the condensation slowly beginning to run down the outside of each glass.

"You are doing a fantastic job," Lorraine said, seeming relaxed. She was a little older than her mother, but always looked good. Her eyes were bright and full of energy and her hair was gray, in an elegant bob cut.

"I don't feel that way," Shayla said, seeing through Lorraine's attempt to butter her up.

"I think you're working a bit too hard. You should concern yourself with the big picture instead of all these details," Lorraine said.

"I believe that the big picture is ruled by making sure that the little picture looks good. I've got to have happy workers," Shayla said, feeling like she was talking to a brick wall… or her own mother. She should have known better than to think her mother's friend would keep her promise with regard to even making the tiniest changes to give their employees, mostly men, more benefits. Or anything.

"Our workers are happy," Lorraine said, waving her hand through the air as if this discussion was unimportant.

"I disagree. The steelworkers need shorter work shifts. If they do work overtime, they need to be compensated financially and they absolutely need more breaks. Current working conditions are inhumane."

"Do you want the company to go bankrupt?" Lorraine said sternly, leaning forward, her kid gloves off now as her voice deepened.

"Don't give me that line. This company will not go bankrupt or anything close to that with my proposed changes. The last time I checked, you had more than enough money to keep yourself and your family in diamonds and Rolls Royces forever. You will still be very profitable with these small changes I'm requesting. You and I both know that," Shayla said, holding her ground.

"It's my company, remember that," Lorraine said, her lips pursing together, making her upper lip crinkle.

"That's true, but you hired me to run it. I want to make a public statement about how well we're doing, but I'd hate to have to report anything negative about the company," Shayla said, quietly.

"What's it going to take to shut you up?" Lorraine said, clearly annoyed.

Shayla smirked inside. She had learned her negotiating tactics from watching her mother for many years. Now she felt as if she were using her mother's own weapon against her, or at least against her friend.

"Let me pull together some ideas to present so that we're both comfortable, as far as what we give the employees, okay?" Shayla said, backing off. She had shown Lorraine what she was capable of and now it was time to settle back and implement something small. For now.

"Have it on my desk tomorrow morning," Lorraine said, getting up to leave.

"I just want to say one more thing," Shayla said, as Lorraine turned back to her.

"I did this successfully at the Cambridge Public Works. In the short time I was there, morale improved. Better morale means more productivity."

"Time will tell," Lorraine said, clearly unconvinced.

Shayla saw that she was pushing Lorraine right up to the edge of what she would allow, but what she really wanted was to push the whole company over the edge to a new place; a better place.

"He will make a perfect husband and father," the Queen told Shayla over a pre-dinner glass of wine. Michael was due to arrive at any moment to join them at the Palace.

"Please, mother, I'm not up to that," Shayla snapped.

"Okay, I'm only saying," the Queen said, throwing her hands in the air.

"You're right, though." she said, resigned as she looked out the window. "He would make an excellent father."

"How come you never remarried?" Shayla asked, turning back to her mother.

"I just never found the time," she said with a forced smile.

Shayla was about to ask more, but a knock on the door interrupted them.

"Michael Wilson is here," Gerald said, announcing their guest in a formal manner, even though he had become more like family over the last few months. Gerald stepped out of the way, allowing Michael to walk past. He went straight to Shayla, kissing her on the lips before presenting the Queen with a perfectly wrapped platter of desserts that looked like it came from a bakery.

"Oh my! They are decorated with my crest," the Queen said, delightfully surprised. "Absolutely gorgeous. You are too much!"

"I baked them especially for you," Michael said as he kissed the Queen once on each cheek. Her mother clearly loved the attention, and Shayla felt as if he were courting her mother as much as her.

"You shouldn't have, but thank you. We shall have them for dessert," she said, setting the gift aside. "Let's dine, shall we?" the Queen said as she led them to her private dining suite.

Dinner was pleasant. Shayla noticed that she and her mother got along far better when Michael was present. Shayla couldn't deny his calming influence on her life. He was easy going. He understood when Shayla needed solitude, but was always available when she wanted company. He was attractive, faithful and respectful, thoughtful and sweet. How could she complain? As the evening wound down and they walked to their car hand-in-hand, Shayla made her decision.

"I'm taking you out tomorrow night, so dress up," she said before they went to sleep that night.

"I can't believe I can really see you," Shayla said, looking at Nathaniel who stood in a fog. She tried to touch him, but he was just out of reach.

"Take my hand," she said, stretching it as far as she could. Each step she took toward his direction made him a step farther away. "Don't go!" she said, as an anxious feeling grew.

He didn't answer, but his face was pained. He looked like he wanted to speak, but couldn't. As he reached toward her, she woke up.

When she went to work the next morning, she was even more certain it was time to move on and marry a man who was physically with her and whom her mother accepted. It was easier and practical. And she was starting to feel, in her heart, that Nathaniel was never coming back. While she would never admit this to her mother, it was true.

"Please make a reservation at Restaurant Nora for two for this evening at 7:30," she said to her assistant who nodded agreeably.

As she dressed that evening, her confidence from the prior night faded. She had a new dress purchased that afternoon, black and short, cut above the knee, with a neckline plunging just enough to be sexy and tasteful. She wore shorter heals so she wouldn't tower over Michael. It was as though looking her best would make her feel her best.

"You look stunning!" he said, when he picked her up.

"Thank you," she said, smiling. "You look very handsome, too," she said, and it was true. Even as his hairline slowly crawled toward his crown, he kept it short, which looked tidy and attractive.

After they checked in at the restaurant, she ordered a bottle of wine, and grew nervous. She told herself that nervousness was normal when proposing. She reminded herself that this was what she came here to do and that he was wonderful and would make a great husband and companion. There was no doubt that he satisfied the qualifications to be an excellent husband.

The wine arrived and they each sipped. "Michael, I think we should marry," she said shyly but abruptly, with unceremonious simplicity.

"Yes," he said, smiling broadly, as he tenderly took her hand and kissed it vigorously across the table. "I have been hoping you would ask me since the day we met. I love you so much," he said, passionately. "I would be honored to be your husband." He had no idea of the volatile ambivalence that suddenly flooded her veins.

"I... love you too," she said, feeling the words slip unnaturally across her tongue as she stared at her fiancée.

"Let's wait before announcing anything, okay?" she said. This was not part of her planned proposal, but it had come out and felt right.

"Okay," he said, looking a little unsure. "Is there a reason?"

"Lorraine and I are negotiating some company issues and I want to make sure that everything is ironed out with her before facing the media frenzy that our engagement will undoubtedly bring."

"Sure, my love. Anything you want. We have our whole lives to be together," he said, taking her hand.

As they made love that night, Shayla recoiled inside as Michael tenderly stroked her breasts, before reaching his lips to her nipple, flicking his tongue quickly on the tip before nibbling it softly. She tried, unsuccessfully, to give herself wholly to Michael, not realizing just how much she still longed for Nathaniel. But suddenly, she didn't want Michael, even as she allowed him to move within her, slowly at first, and then with a steadily increasing rhythm, his breath matching every movement until he finally pulsated forcefully inside of her.

"I love you, Shayla," he said again, as his grinding movements finally slowed.

"I love you, too," she parroted, immediately wishing she could take back those words as well as the entire evening. She couldn't have Nathaniel, but that didn't mean that choosing another man, even one with the perfect checklist of credentials for marriage, fixed the longing in her heart.

"You can't tell anyone," Shayla said, sitting on the pink couch of her childhood suite, where she and Gerald met. She had asked him to meet with her privately.

"Of course," Gerald said, reassuringly. "So what's this news?" Shayla knew she could trust him, more than anyone else.

"I proposed to Michael," she said, softly.

"That's wonderful!" he said, but immediately looked at her curiously. "You don't look happy," he said.

"He's a wonderful man," Shayla said, knowing it was true.

"Then why is your engagement a secret?"

She hesitated. She wanted to tell him the real reason, but couldn't quite admit it out loud. "I'm negotiating employment terms for the steel workers and having trouble. I want that ironed out first. Plus, I'm not ready for the paparazzi. News of my engagement will have them all over us," she said.

"Are you sure that's the only reason?" he asked. Shayla remembered how well he knew her.

"I just want to wait a little," she said. She really wanted to tell him, but the words wouldn't come.

"Of course," he said, nodding and she knew he wouldn't question her further. That was one of the things she loved about Gerald. He respected her answers without digging, unlike her mother.

"I especially don't want my mother to know," she said.

"Understood," he said pausing. "You know, Shayla, your father wrote you a letter to be opened upon your engagement," Gerald said. Her heartbeat quickened at the thought of something new from her father. He had been gone for so long. Why was Gerald the keeper of the letter, rather than her mother? It made her think of the last time she saw her father. He had said, "This is just for you. Never, ever show it to your mother or tell her you have it. Promise?" her father asked, as his frail hand held out the black velvet bag. He had been sick for so long, he was skin and bones.

"I'm afraid," she said, as the tears rolled down her cheeks. She looked at his offering, but didn't reach for it.

"There's nothing to be afraid of," he assured her. "It's just private, that's all."

She took the bag and was about to open it when the machine that her father was hooked up to beeped and his sickly body coughed violently. In a whirlwind, she was swooped out of there, but she clutched that velvet bag as she saw her father alive for the last time. She ran to her suite with the bag hid it in the bottom of her toy bin.

Chapter Twenty-Six

Memories of Shayla washed away with each passing day, and Brigg and Chester started fading too. Reality sank in.

Nathaniel would never see anyone from his life in Cambridge again. It was far more challenging now that it was up to him to keep the distance.

He had diligently worked on his new life but was tired of attending the POAs. He had gone on countless dates, and cooked gourmet meals for women who were only after sex. What he really needed was a wife, not another random date from a woman at the POA. Nathaniel needed a break. He picked up a slice of pizza and popped open a beer as he relaxed on his futon bed with a brand new novel by Berrini that made him think of Shayla. Had she already read it?

The phone rang and he sprang from the couch.

"Joe Merino?"

"This is he," Nathaniel said, bracing himself. Fear pulsed through his veins.

"This is Kelly Boys," said an unfamiliar voice. It was Saturday night, and he couldn't imagine why they needed to contact him. Garrett was gone. Nathaniel wondered if they knew. Maybe they just realized he wasn't returning or maybe they were going through Garrett's files and Joe Merino was listed as an Underground affiliate. Nathaniel's heart pumped with fear. Maybe there were Tasers right outside his door, ready to storm in.

"Sorry for the short notice, but your Monday assignment has changed."

"Oh, that's fine," he said, relieved. Couldn't they have just sent him an email? Then again, Garrett usually called with assignment changes. Nathaniel was about to ask about Garrett, but stopped himself. What was he going to say? "What happened after he got Tased and taken away at the protest?" That could be self-incriminating, as they might want to ask how he knew that Garrett was part of the demonstration.

"We're sending you to Washington D.C. for the next week to work as an executive meeting scribe. Your flight is on SuperAir, and it leaves Monday at 6 a.m. Someone will meet you at the airport in D.C and help you out on that end. If you have any questions, feel free to call us."

"Okay," Nathaniel said, feeling out of sorts all over again. He hung up and let it sink in. He would have to cancel two dates, but wasn't sure he minded missing either.

More importantly, his Underground contact at Kelly Boys was gone and nobody else stepped in. What did that mean?

Then there were logistics. Nathaniel had never been on a plane. The Underground had all kinds of courses, but there wasn't anything that covered how to squash the anxiety of your first airplane flight.

✣✣✣✣✣✣✣✣✣✣

After waiting more than a half an hour for takeoff, he was far more nervous than he cared to admit.

"Another Maker's Mark, please?" he asked the steward.

"You sure? Kind of early for so many drinks, don't you think?"

"It's my first flight," he whispered, thinking about the life he used to have. There was never a reason to fly anywhere. Winter vacations in New England were just a drive to a ski area and summers meant hiking in Maine or a beach trip to Cape Cod.

"I'll get you one more, but I don't want to have to carry you out of here," the steward said, half joking.

He thought of Janice. "You know what? Maybe I don't need another," Nathaniel said. He would rather white knuckle it all the way than be a drunk.

"You sure?"

"Yes, thank you," he said, just as the pilot announced to prepare for takeoff.

The flight went smoothly, but he was glad when he landed. Right outside the gate, he saw a man holding a sign with his name.

"I'm Joe," he told the man.

"Do you have luggage?"

"Right here," he said, indicating his carry-on.

"Let's go," the driver said dryly before silently leading Nathaniel to the car. Nathaniel tried to ask a little about the capital, but the grunt-like responses told him this grumpy taxi driver only drove. Just like Simon, he thought to himself.

"Are we going to my hotel?" he finally asked.

"I'm dropping you at Archibald Company," the driver said.

As they drove through the city, Nathaniel drank in the sights, which differed from both Cambridge and Kansas City. It was a clean city. Watching people walk the streets, he noticed a more formal dress, a far cry from Kansas City and even farther from Cambridge.

It was a short drive from the airport to Archibald, which was in a bustling business district of the city. The driver got out of the car, took Nathaniel's luggage from the trunk, and deposited it on the sidewalk. Nathaniel pulled out his wallet.

"It's paid," the driver said without looking at Nathaniel. He returned to the car and drove off.

Nathaniel was about to enter Archibald's building when a jackhammer sound caught his ear, like a familiar tune on the radio. He stopped and turned. A group of Public Works personnel were going in and out of a manhole in the middle of the street. He remembered wearing their uniform: protective eye and ear-wear, and the ever-present hard hat. He didn't miss that kind of work, and yet, a piece of him wanted to walk over to see what they were doing.

He stepped inside, and took the elevator to Archibald's floor. The grandiose reception area had intricately inlaid marble floors and a large floral arrangement on the clean glass counter out front. The three men behind it were all occupied, speaking politely on phones. The first who was free approached Nathaniel.

"I'm Joe Merino from Kelly Boys. I was told you would know where I should be," he said. He was glad to be holding luggage, which hid the shaking of his nervous hands. This was the first time he would work solely as a scribe.

"Follow me," one of the men said.

As he followed the man down the hall, Nathaniel imagined himself bragging to the women at the next POA. Being a scribe had caché.

"Here you go," said the man who had led him through the maze of hallways filled with glass offices and conference rooms where the "skirts" appeared to be hard at work.

"I'm Dan, by the way. Can I get you something? Coffee? Water? Something to eat?" It was strange to be on the receiving end of the work he was accustomed to doing.

"I'd love a cup of coffee, if it's not too much trouble," Nathaniel said. "Actually, I can get it myself if you'll just point me to the coffee station." Surely, Dan had plenty to do. Nathaniel knew this from firsthand experience.

"Don't be silly."

"Are you sure? I really don't mind getting it," Nathaniel said, feeling awkward no matter what he did.

"Cream and sugar?"

"Yes to both," Nathaniel said.

He put his suitcase in the corner and admired the large room. He counted 18 chairs around the conference room table before sitting down. It all seemed too pretty to disturb. The black lacquered table shined beautifully without a single fingerprint on its glossy veneer. He carefully unpacked his laptop and pad of paper before sitting down.

"Here you go," Dan said, handing Nathaniel a mug wafting with fresh-brewed coffee.

"Thank you very much," Nathaniel said. "Do you know what I'm supposed to do now?" Nathaniel asked.

"I'm sorry. I don't. But I know the management group has signed this room out all week, and I'm sure they'll be in within the next 15 minutes or so," he said, looking at his watch. "I'd just sit tight. Give a holler if you need anything though," Dan reiterated, smiling as he left.

Nathaniel drank his coffee and felt guilty for this plum assignment as he looked at the original art on the walls. Sometimes he just didn't understand art, and now he grappled to find the beauty in the odd and probably expensive collage of ripped and broken canvases dipped in oil paints.

All at once, a group of women came through the door chattering and laughing casually as they planted themselves around the table and continued their conversation as if Nathaniel were invisible.

"Hi, I'm Gladys," one of them finally said as she held out her hand. "You must be the Kelly Boy." Nathaniel stood up and put out his hand. She was petite, and she looked him squarely in the eyes as her strong handshake surprised him. She wore a flattering, business appropriate red suit.

"It's nice to meet you Gladys. Yes, I'm Joe Merino from Kelly Boys," he continued. "Do you know when I'm supposed to start taking notes?" he asked.

"We're still waiting for a few others, but they should be here soon, and then we can get started," she said, sitting beside him. Her perfume reminded him of Shayla's with that same hint of honey vanilla. It was distracting.

"Don't be nervous, I'll take care of you," she joked sensing his concern.

Was she flirting?

A few minutes later, all seats were filled.

"Okay, ladies," Gladys said. "Let's get down to business. We've got a lot to cover this week. Here's the agenda." She handed out sheets of paper. "We are fortunate to have our boy Joe from Kelly Boys here to take notes, so best behavior, please," she said. "No off color jokes in front of him, even though he's adorable," Gladys said, triggering light laughter around the table.

He tapped their names as attendees into his laptop on a chart so he could easily document their ideas. A number of them were very beautiful. In fact, this was about the best stock of women in one room that he could imagine: bright, successful and attractive.

Maybe he would get a date. First things first, he had to do a great job.

At the end of the day, his fingers were as tired as his brain. He was grateful for the Underground training.

"Joe, would you like to join me for a bite to eat?" Gladys asked. "I could show you some of D.C.'s finest hotspots."

He wanted to. Very badly. But he had to come across as professional first and foremost, to build her respect. He didn't need another woman wanting him only for sex. "I would love to," he said, balancing on a tightrope beneath which his professional and personal life spread out beneath him, "but I should really reorganize the writing I did today so it's in good shape for you tomorrow."

"All work and no play makes Joe a dull boy!" she joked, waving her finger.

"I just want to make sure I get it right," he said, feeling the ache in his neck from hours of bending toward the ergonomically incorrect screen.

"Get your coat," she said. "I'll meet you in the lobby. I'm taking you out tonight, and it's not up for discussion."

They went to Snake Oil, a hopping club right near the National Zoo where all the dishes had names that referred to clichéd business opportunities. There was a chicken sandwich called, "Wanna Buy a Piece of a Bridge in Brooklyn?" And a burger with sweet potato fries called, "I'll gladly pay you Tuesday," among others.

Gladys was a class act with an easygoing air that Nathaniel liked. And the restaurant fit her perfectly.

"How do you like Archibald?" he asked.

"I've been there for seven years and let's just say they've been good to me. Just look at today. I met you and here we are having dinner," she said.

"I am glad you invited me," he said, genuinely happy.

At the end of the evening, she leaned over to kiss him. Nathaniel enjoyed Gladys's soft lips on his. She smiled as she pulled away and turned to leave. Nathaniel stood outside his hotel, watching her walk away.

He took in one last breath of the hot summer night as he enjoyed looking at the city street before him; yet another new place he had never imagined himself.

"Hey, Joe," she said, turning and yelling in his direction from down the street.

"Yes?" Joe said. She was far more relaxed than your average white collar woman. She reminded him of a football player telling him to send her the ball. And he liked it.

"You like opera?"

"I've never been. There isn't a lot of opera in Kansas City."

"Good, you'll come with me tomorrow. I've got tickets for a star-studded benefit of La Traviata, and I won't take no for an answer," she said, flashing a big grin.

"How can I say no to that?" he answered back before he waved goodbye and walked away. He knew this was an important invitation, but it wouldn't be until the next evening that he would see just how important.

Chapter Twenty-Seven

"It's supposed to be a fabulous production," Gladys said, as they made their way down the street. She wore a strappy magenta gown that had a tasteful slit half-way up her toned calf. She was transformed from her business persona. "I'm so glad you were available to join me," she said.

"Me too," he said. "I must confess, my theater experience was limited to one trip as a kid to see the Nutcracker." Brigg's mother had taken them to the Wang Center, in Boston, as kids. He would never forget the 20-foot-tall Christmas tree that magically grew out of the floor like a dream. He nearly mentioned the details, and then realized how easily the truth might slip out about his true origins. He needed to be guarded. Always.

"That was your only time?" Gladys said, giving him a come-hither look that made him blush. They moved slowly through the crowd. Gladys knew many of the patrons who waved to her, as they made their way toward the lush velvet seats that signified the comfort of wealth and privilege.

"This place is unbelievable. I could just stare at these murals on the ceiling all evening," he said, wondering if he should tone down his working class excitement.

"I like the idea of showing you new things that make you happy," Gladys said, moving her body close to his and smiling as she looked into his eyes.

Nathaniel was grateful that the lights dimmed at that moment. The voices hushed, and the operatic experience kidnapped his senses. This was no Nutcracker. The men and women stood gallantly on the stage, entrancing the audience with pristine voices that filled the Washington Opera House.

After the first song, Nathaniel tore his eyes from the stage and looked out over the audience sitting perfectly still in their finest eveningwear, and jewels that dazzled under the dimmed lights.

His eyes moved from person to person on the opposite side of the balcony and came to a dead halt at a woman who wore a necklace that held a shocking resemblance to Shayla's necklace that he remembered from their evening at the hotel. She told him it was one-of-a-kind, a gift from her mother's favorite jewelry designer. Could it be?

He looked at the woman, sitting beside a tuxedo-clad man. As he leaned into her, placing his hand on her lap, she turned momentarily away from him and Nathaniel saw that tiny beauty mark peeking out from the base of her neck and realized it was Shayla. It could only be Shayla. Here was the love of his life, directly across the balcony from him, sitting with another man.

The moment froze and the music seemed to stop. He begged her to look at him. This way, Shelia. Here, my love! But she continued to stare at the stage. He wanted to leap across the balcony and kiss her full red lips, and hold her forever.

Maybe he could go and wait by the door where her seat was… how could he get away from Gladys without drawing attention? Escape plans flooded his mind. One way or another, he was going to get to her before they left here. He had to.

At the end of a song, the audience applauded and Shayla did too, her eyes leaving the stage and scanning the crowd. When they caught his gaze, she froze, her eyes wide and her lips parting slightly as her rapid clapping slowed. They stared at each other throughout the singing of Dite Alla Giovine, the voices singing a version of their own heart wrenching truth.

"I'll be right back," he whispered to Gladys who nodded to acknowledge him but kept her eyes on the performers. "Men's room."

There was a bar just outside the exit from his section and he quickly borrowed a pen and napkin on which he scribbled: *Joe Merino, Omni Hotel, Room 304, 8 p.m. tomorrow. I'll explain everything.* His heart raced as he folded the napkin into a palm-sized nugget. He scurried to the door he knew she should emerge from. There were a few others milling about in the theater hallways, all focused on cell phone calls.

He stared, unfaltering, at the door. He couldn't worry about what Gladys would think if he was gone too long. He would feign illness if need be. He had found Shayla, and hoped it wasn't too late. It was as though he could feel her excusing herself before she daintily walked, ever so slowly, to minimize disturbance as she made her way to the exit. Was he imagining this? He looked at his cell phone and saw he had been outside for five minutes, but it felt like an hour. He would give her another five minutes and then go back inside, knowing she didn't want to see him.

A moment later, the door opened and out she came. As soon as the theater door closed behind her, she stopped. They stood apart, staring at one another. He wasn't sure how to begin. This was certainly not the place to describe the jungle he had been through most of the last year. He cautiously walked toward her. Once he was close enough, he spoke gently.

"I believe this is yours," he said as held out the napkin to her. His hand jittered slightly with a nervousness that he did his best to harness. He wanted to kiss her, to hold her, to inhale her inviting perfume, but he wasn't sure she would want him anymore. He held his hand out for what seemed too long, waiting for her to take the napkin.

She made sure her hand brushed his. "I guess it is," she said taking the wadded napkin. Touching his fingers reassured her that this was really him, that those were absolutely the calloused hands of Nathaniel DeLuca, made rough by years at the Cambridge Public Works. They were also the hands that held her so intimately and touched her with such passion. She had prayed for his safe return, dreamed about it, but she had stopped believing, and now he was right in front of her.

"You enjoying the performance?" he asked her.

"Very much so, but I should get back to it," she said before reluctantly turning away. The reality of his touch gave her a chill as she turned toward the ladies room, clutching the napkin tightly.

Only when she reached the privacy of a bathroom stall did she dare to open her palm and reveal the message he had bestowed.

She wondered why it said Joe Merino. Tomorrow night would provide her with the answer. Room 304 at the Omni Hotel. The thought of being alone with Nathaniel stole her breath, momentarily, as she fought back the tears. She closed her eyes and focused on the evening at hand, as best she could before returning to sit next to the man she had promised eternity to only weeks earlier.

"You okay, my love?" Michael whispered to her when she sat back down.

"Oh yes," she said, trying to stay present. Michael took her hand and she wanted to pull it away and tell him her heart belonged to another man. As he lovingly caressed her fingers, she squeezed his hand for just a moment, knowing that it was necessary. She could only think about Nathaniel. Why was he there? She looked at him for the remainder of the performance, as the swell of beautiful voices carried them across the balcony to each other. She glanced at Michael, from time to time, to see if he noticed her eyes weren't focused on the stage, but he was enraptured with the opera. As Shayla looked at Nathaniel, she remembered his touch and that perfect evening in the hotel as they made love again and again, before he disappeared. She couldn't stop herself from wanting more, and knew she had to pull herself back to reality, and to Michael. The deafening applause at the end of the performance grounded her, and she began to clap, too, returning her eyes to the stage at last.

"That was unbelievable," Michael said. "I've never seen such a perfect operatic performance and I've seen La Traviata many times." His voice slid into a perfect Italian trill when he mentioned the title. She knew that Nathaniel wouldn't have said it the same way, and suddenly Michael sounded pretentious.

"I'm so pleased we came," she said. If he only knew how pleased! "Do you mind if we skip the reception?"

"Whatever you'd like, my love. Are you not feeling well?"

"Just tired," she said, as they made their way to the exit. She didn't know if Nathaniel would be at the benefactor reception, but if he were, she didn't think she keep herself away from him. And if paparazzi were in the vicinity, that could spell trouble. After all, he had been missing for so long.

In the limousine back to her apartment, she wished she could drop off Michael at his place and go home alone but that was impossible. She held Michael's hand, but looked out the window, imagining Nathaniel's pleas for forgiveness as he begged her to understand why he left, as he begged her to understand why he needed her back. She saw herself protesting, but only briefly, before she gave herself to Nathaniel, in every way.

"You were the most beautiful woman there," Michael said, reaching to gently move her chin toward his.

He kissed her with a passion that felt genuine, and she let herself go and kissed him back, knowing what he wanted. She wanted it too, just not from him.

"I want to make love to you," he said, as they pulled up to her apartment, and she smiled somehow knowing she had to put on a show.

She unlocked her apartment and as soon as they were inside, and kissed her again.

"Take me," she said, pulling him into the bedroom as she quickly slipped her dress over her head, in desperation to feel Nathaniel, not Michael, against her body.

"I love you," he said.

"Don't talk," she whispered. She didn't want to hear his voice. She wanted Nathaniel. She turned off the light and pulled him into her, telling herself that he was Nathaniel, until she believed it and moaned with the success of a deceitful pleasure. Her private reminiscence of Nathaniel was always the true beacon behind her orgasms. She pushed the scents and sounds of Michael from her mind and kept her eyes shut. Michael's movements quickened with a passionate force that her body enjoyed.

Her mind was focused elsewhere, on someone else. She knew

that no matter where Nathaniel had been and why he was gone, it didn't matter. Shayla wanted him back.

Just hours earlier, Nathaniel thought Gladys might be a potential spouse, but as she kissed him goodnight with intent, he felt nothing. He thought she was attractive, but felt no desire of any kind.

"I'd love to come up and see your room," she said quietly after finally pulling away, "but I've got to be up early in the morning. Besides, I don't like to mix business with pleasure, and you've still got three more days on my watch. After that, it's another story."

"I understand," he said, relieved, and zipped out of her car and into his hotel.

He slept fitfully, dreaming of Shayla all night, waking up hard. He wanted her so badly. The next day it took everything he had to stay focused on the job. The women argued more than the previous days as they tried to come up with different strategies to take Archibald to the next level.

"You look tired, Joe," Gladys said during a meeting break, when the two were alone in the conference room.

"I didn't sleep well," he said. "It was such a great performance. My mind wouldn't quiet down, I guess," he said.

"I'm sorry," she said, as though it was her fault.

"No, I had an amazing time," he said quickly. "I'm so grateful you invited me. I just need a little sleep."

"Well, you shall have the evening to yourself. Tonight is girls' night out," she said,

Nathaniel's heart sprouted wings. He wouldn't have to make awkward excuses about being unavailable. "Have a wonderful time!" he said. But he was pulsating with thoughts of the evening ahead with Shayla.

Nathaniel left work at 6 p.m. and walked toward his hotel, feeling uneasy. He was on guard for the Tasers, as there always seem to be a rash of them around this time of day. Today there were none. Maybe it was a lucky sign. He passed the Blue Café, a bar that reminded him of the Black Hole. He ducked inside and felt comforted by the divey interior and decided to grab a bite. It would be better than going straight to his hotel and pacing for two hours.

He sat on a worn, red vinyl stool near the bar and it gave a loud squeak, causing several guys to turn toward him.

"Sorry," he said, as they stared with a hint of disdain. He was dressed for the office, and everyone else wore blue collar garb, some with the Washington Public Works insignia. "I'm one of you!" he wanted to say, as they turned away. He felt so alone as he turned his attention to the Webavision. The Queen's face smiled broadly as she answered an interviewer's questions. She talked about how successful the POAs were and declared that marriage rates were rising. He couldn't stand to watch and turned away. He started to worry about Shayla. What if she didn't show up? He reminded himself that if she hadn't wanted to see him, she never would have walked out of the opera's first act. Curiosity might only keep her there long enough to get an explanation, but at least she would show up.

Nathaniel didn't know what to tell her, but he wouldn't lie, even if he didn't reveal everything. He needed her love, her forgiveness, and the warmth and peace he hoped she would offer. Even if they had to be secretive again, that would be okay. It wasn't ideal, but they had lived through it before.

Chapter Twenty-Eight

Shayla told Michael that evening that she needed some time alone.

"But we made these plans so long ago," Michael said. "And my Uncle is making us dinner. Can you have your alone time tomorrow?" he said. It was the first hint of impatience he had ever expressed, and she couldn't blame him.

"I'm just not up to it," she said. "A rain check. Dinner at the Palace." This would be a rare opportunity, and Shayla hoped it would make up for the last minute cancellation. Yes, she felt badly, but no, nothing was going to keep her from Nathaniel at the Omni Hotel at 8.

"I'm disappointed," he said, and she could tell he was beyond disappointment as she hung up the phone. But she pushed thoughts of Michael from her mind as she rushed to the Omni hotel. She was early, but knew he would be there. Disguised in a hat and sunglasses, she walked through the lobby with her head down. It was five minutes to 8 p.m. when she knocked on the door.

"Shayla," he said, and she felt a flutter in her stomach at his voice speaking her name. A well of emotion surged in her as she stepped inside, pulled the door closed and fell into his arms. Her fantasy of making him explain or apologize before she took him back wasn't even a whisper in her mind. She needed him.

He hugged her, holding her close so she could feel his heart beating as if it were in her own chest. Her love for him burst into its second bloom as he kissed her and they stumbled toward the bed, quickly removing one another's clothes with a primal passion. Desire boiled inside her belly.

"I missed you," she said.

"I'm so sorry," he said, as he wordlessly unbuttoned his shirt. She took him in with her eyes before they kissed again. She felt the roughness of the skin on his hands, like a residue of his years at the

Cambridge Public Works, and it made her want him more.

She led his hand to the front of her blue jeans and he began to unbutton them.

"Lie down," he said as he helped her remove them, along with her underwear that revealed a triangle of softness that she pulled his hand toward. Shayla groaned with pleasure, as his fingers explored her with the perfect touch.

She reached to touch his hardness with her hand, and gripped it as she moved up and down the shaft with an undeniable urgency. After all the aching nights of dreams and fantasies about reuniting, she couldn't believe they were together.

"I need you now," he said suddenly, pulling her hand away from him. She wanted him more than she had ever wanted any man.

She lay back and opened herself to him. He entered her slowly at first and his love for her made him move with a rhythm that satisfied them both. She bellowed as a ripple of ecstasy tore through her over and over and he shuddered with it too as she felt his hot, wet pulsation flood her body.

They collapsed in a beautiful exhaustion, entwined in one another's arms. They were peaceful. They were complete. They lay silently for a long while, caressing each other. Shayla was afraid to speak. The moment was so perfect and she wanted it to last forever. She was afraid of what he might say. She was afraid that something might keep them apart.

Still, she wanted to know. Why had he disappeared? Why did he give her a note the night before, like she was a stranger? And why did it have another man's name?

"I've missed you so much," she said, finally breaking the silence, meeting his eyes, as she basked in the warmth of his arms. "Why did you leave?"

His forehead reached down to softly meet hers. Their eyes locked together, as though averting this gaze might pull them apart all over again. Shayla finally broke away, carefully and slowly, not wanting to separate herself from the pull of love that was as strong as the moment she first felt it.

"It wasn't my choice," he said solemnly.

"What happened?" she said, her heart beating quickly as she feared it might not be easy to hear.

"You can't tell anyone what I'm going to tell you or that you even saw me. Our lives are at stake."

"I promise," she said quickly.

"Especially not your mother," he added.

"Definitely not my mother," she said, even as she worried about the ramifications of keeping that promise.

"I was kidnapped. I couldn't contact you and didn't even know where I was."

Shayla's eyes filled with tears. She listened as he recounted select pieces of his journey to the Underground, their mission, and how he came to D.C. as Joe Merino. He spoke slowly, stopping at the evening of the opera.

"I couldn't take it when you left," she said. "I had to leave the Public Works. I had to leave Cambridge."

She didn't want to tell him about Michael. Not yet.

"I'm never going to let you go again," Nathaniel declared.

"I love you, Nathaniel," she whispered, surprised at how easily those words came, and how much she meant them. "But I have to tell you something."

"You can tell me anything."

"You were gone for a long time. I thought you might be dead. I was horribly depressed and my mother pushed me. I'm dating someone."

"Is that who you were with at the opera?" Nathaniel said, as his caressing hand moved away.

She nodded, afraid that they wouldn't be able to move past the next thing she had to say, but she knew there was no way around disclosure. "He's my fiancée, actually. His name is Michael. He's a wonderful man. But he's not you."

The idea of Michael sat in the silence between them.

"The moment I saw you at the opera… " Shayla said.

"I'm sorry about all of this. I really am," he said, taking her hand.

"I knew right then, looking out across the opera house beside my fiancée, that I only wanted to be with you. Even before I knew what you had been through," she said.

He smiled and stroked her face.

She continued, "It sounds like it was awful."

He nodded solemnly. "I haven't spoken to Brigg either since the day I left. I think about him all the time," he said looking straight ahead, remembering their carefree days as kids.

"We'll need to think about this," she said.

"We've been silent before, and we'll do it again if we need to," he said, caressing her bare shoulder. "At least now we can make love in a bed," he joked as he drew her near.

She nodded. "But we must be careful. More so now than ever before," she said. And he nodded back.

They held each other closely through the night, until Shayla awoke at 5 so she could get home before work.

"I don't want to leave. I'm afraid you won't be here later," she added.

"I promise I'll be here. At least until tomorrow. Then, I need to go back to Kansas City."

"Unless a certain Steelco executive calls up Kelly Boys and requests your services," she said.

"Really?" he asked. "Unless you need a meeting scribe specifically, I can't see how that would work."

"I'm the CEO, remember? We always use temps, and I will put together a profile of what I need that caters specifically to you," she said.

"That would be incredible," he said.

"I'll see you tonight," she said. "8 p.m. here?"

"Yes, we'll have room service and a full evening together," he added. They kissed once more, and Shayla tore herself away.

"Hello, my lovely wife-to-be. How are you today?" he asked with his usual adoration. It was his routine midday call.

Shayla wasn't ready to deal with Michael, but avoiding him would make matters worse.

"Hi, darling," she managed, the words sticking in her throat. "Sorry, I was just looking at a finance report and the numbers startled me," she said, as she realized some explanation of her silence was required. Hiding her new reality was more difficult than she had anticipated.

"Nothing bad I hope?"

"Not too bad, though things are a bit crazier than usual today," she said hoping to fend him off quickly. She twirled her hair nervously, thankful he couldn't see. He knew this trait and would have wondered what troubled the woman he worshipped.

"What would you like me to cook tonight? Duck confit? Salmon with hollandaise? Anything you want," he said. Michael's stint in chef school meant he frequently created mouthwatering gourmet meals with the full romance of tall candles and fine wine.

"I hate to do this, but tonight isn't going to work," she said, trying to quickly think of a good excuse. "There's something that just came across my desk, and it must be done by morning," she said, feeling guilty at the lie.

"You still need to eat, my love."

"That's true. But, if I have dinner with you, I'll just be tempted to take the whole evening off and play with you," she said, hoping the flattery would deflect any suspicion. She hesitated, then added, "Tomorrow we can have the whole evening to ourselves."

The desire to spend a romantic evening with Michael was far away, but she knew it was vital. She was, after all, supposed to marry him. She needed to be careful and remain outwardly attentive while she figured things out. In a certain way, she knew there really wasn't much to figure out. She had to marry Michael. That's the way the world worked and just admitting that to herself made her die a little inside. She knew she wouldn't give up Nathaniel, but she hated the dishonesty.

"Okay. If you really can't make it tonight, tomorrow will have to do. I'll miss you." Disappointment saturated his voice.

“Can I come over late? You know, just to stay over?” he added.

“I’ll call you if I get done early.”

“Okay,” he said, sadly.

“I have to run,” she said.

“I love you.”

“You too,” she managed before clicking the call away.

Sometimes Michael could be so clingy, she thought to herself. She couldn’t catch her breath for a moment at the thought that maybe there was a way to undo this mess. Maybe there was a way in which she could get out of marrying him, without hurting him. As she wondered, her assistant came in with an envelope.

It had proofs of their engagement photos. Michael insisted they have them taken, so they’d be ready for their announcement to the world about pending nuptials. It had taken an entire Sunday afternoon of clothing and location changes.

Shayla looked at the top photograph in the healthy stack of glossy 5x7s. Their broad smiles glowed, although hers felt forced. It reminded her of when she was a little girl. She smiled for the press photos, but hated the paparazzi. For some reason, her mother adored it.

The photo captured what appeared to be the perfect couple sitting in the park with the glorious backdrop of a summer day. He wore a smart summer suit, and Shayla wore a sundress that Michael had picked out. She felt the dress was too conservative, but Michael was insistent and she didn’t want to hurt his feelings.

She couldn’t bear to look at the rest of the photos, and tucked the envelope into her desk drawer, knowing she would not mention the proofs’ arrival to Michael.

She only wanted to focus on her evening ahead with Nathaniel. Attaching her mind to that thought was much more enticing. Besides, she had a call to make.

“Kelly Boys, Kansas City. May I help you?”

“I’m calling from Steelco in Washington D.C. and I need a temp, most likely for a few weeks. I've heard you have some special meeting scribe candidates. Can you send me the best resumes you have? In fact, if you have someone who specializes specifically as a meeting scribe and can do weeklong meetings, that is precisely what I'm looking for," Shayla said, before requesting specific credentials that perfectly mapped to Nathaniel's skill set. "I need someone starting Monday, by the way," she added, knowing his schedule freed up that day.

"Not a problem. I'm looking and see there are a number of top candidates we have and I'll email those right over," the man said before hanging up.

Not an hour later, a wave of relief washed over her when Joe's resume was in the small batch sent. She handed the resume to her assistant to finish the rest of the details.

That night, she left work at 6 p.m., and ran home to put on a tawdry black bra with holes around the nipples and crotch less panties. Just the thought of revealing herself to Nathaniel with that element of surprise made her excited.

She arrived at the hotel with one of her best bottles of Cabernet in her bag. She walked nonchalantly across the lobby and into the elevator, doing her best not to draw attention to herself. She wore blue jeans and no makeup and a Red Sox baseball cap. She never wore a sports team hat. Hopefully, people wouldn't even think it might be the Queen's daughter.

"Shayla?"

Shayla heard the voice just as she was about to reach the elevator. For a split second she thought about not turning around, but that would be worse. She knew that voice...and when she turned around, she saw the Palace's old head chef.

"Josephine? How are you?"

"I'm fine! It's nice to see you. What brings you to the Omni?" Josephine said, giving Shayla a confused look as Shayla adjusted the hat that she hoped would act as a disguise. It wasn't exactly Shayla's style.

"Oh... I just am here because a friend is visiting, so I was coming to say hello," she said, trying to hide her nerves, worrying that Josephine sensed something.

"Well, please come down to the restaurant with your friend. I'm the head chef here, you know. I promise to make something special, like seared tuna. I remember it's your favorite!" she said, making Shayla nervous. She didn't want Josephine to remember anything, especially running into her at the hotel. She could see the gossip news of her eating at the hotel with Nathaniel when Michael read the story.

"I probably can't tonight, but promise to come another time!" she said.

"I'll look forward to it," Josephine said, looking at Shayla in a funny way as Shayla ran to catch the elevator.

"Take care," Shayla yelled just before the elevator doors closed. She sighed in relief as she pressed the third floor button.

When she knocked on the door of room 304, it opened quickly.

"Do come in," he said with a big smile, as he gestured a welcome with his hand. As soon as the door closed, their immediate embrace made it clear making love would precede dinner. She could feel him, like steel, rubbing against her thigh. She could barely take off her clothes in time.

"Is that what you wore to the office?" he asked, amused, when he saw her bra.

"Yes. This is what I always wear for work. Why?"

He laughed before kissing each nipple that peeked out the holes of her bra.

She insisted on wearing her crotch less panties, and Nathaniel didn't protest as he slid his fingers between the folds that lay just inside the black lace. She watched him enjoying entering her with his fingers, with a quickness that made her come.

He drew her to the bed and took her quickly, with a rough passion that thrilled her, although she hadn't remembered Nathaniel being aggressive in this way. She enjoyed the rawness of his desire and his command of her body.

"I'm going to want to do that again, you know," she said to him as soon as they finished.

"I'm sorry I came too soon," he said.

"No, you came just right. I'm just going to want it again. And again. And again.

"Good," he said, smiling. "Me too. We have all night."

"Are you expecting someone?" she said, hearing a knock at the door.

"Don't worry. It's just room service," he said, grabbing a robe.

"I'm going to hide in the bathroom, just in case," she said.

"Good idea," he said, as he waited for her to shut the bathroom door so he could open the door to the hallway.

"You can come out now," he said, as soon as the room service delivery person left.

"Ooh, you've even got candles," she said.

"I bought them today. I wanted tonight to be special," he said, drawing her close and reaching his hands inside her robe to feel the smoothness of her skin. "I wish I could make up for the lost time," he said.

"Let's not think about the past," she said.

"Thank you for giving me another chance," he said before slowly backing away and pulling out her chair around the beautiful table that had two covered trays. He dramatically revealed their contents.

"Beautiful presentation," she said, smiling as she looked at the pasta primavera and the steak and salad plate.

"I didn't know what you wanted," he said, taking a seat across from her after lighting the tall candles and dimming the lights.

"It's all perfect," she said. He smiled at her, wondering if she would still feel that way by the end of the evening.

"I just wanted to talk to you more about what I told you yesterday," he said, skirting around what he really needed to say.

"Which thing was that? That you loved me? Or that you thought I was too sexy to go outside," she said, laughing.

"This is serious, Shayla," he said.

"Of course, what is it?" she said, leaning forward, her silken hair falling around her shoulders, with a just-got-out-of-bed look that he found incredibly sexy. He reached across the table and took her hand, caressing it slowly with his fingers, as he looked into her eyes. Her smile vanished.

"I want to make sure you haven't told your mother about me or the Underground. And that you won't. Not ever," he said.

"Of course I haven't. I know how dangerous that would be. You made that quite clear," she said sounding irritated.

"I'm sorry. It's just that I feel bad asking you to keep my secrets from your mother," he said.

"Nathaniel, it's fine. Right now, my mother has her own troubles. There are protests against mandatory castration. She doesn't talk to me about it, but I can tell it's reaching a stressful point for her," Shayla said, pausing.

Nathaniel saw the sadness in her eyes.

"I thought there were only a few protests?" he said putting his hand on hers across the table. His heart beat quickly. How much should he tell her? He certainly knew a lot more about those protests, including at least one of the participants.

"I don't know how many there were, but I feel like she's waiting for another one, even if she won't say so. She's such a control freak, and she's had the entire country under her thumb for so long, but it's changing," Shayla said, sounding worried.

Nathaniel sat silently. He had planned on telling her more about the Underground, but changed his mind, wanting to spare her the stress. Even if Shayla might agree with the Underground politics, in theory, it didn't mean she wanted to hear their ultimate goals were to not only banish castration, but overthrow her mother's regime.

"What?" she said to him. "You look as if you've seen a ghost."

"No, no. I'm just stunned and grateful to be here with you right now," he said, caressing her hand.

"I want to show you something," she said getting up from the table and bringing her pocketbook to the bed. She motioned for

Nathaniel to sit next to her and handed him her velvet bag with a copy of *Reminder of Truth.*

He took it and turned it over in his hands. "I haven't seen this book in a long time," he said, carefully turning the pages. "I've memorized certain passages." He didn't mention that the walls of the Underground were lined with quotes from *Reminder of Truth.*

"Now I have something to tell you that must not be shared with anyone," she said.

"You have my word," he said. "What?" His heart started to pound.

"My father gave me *Reminder of Truth* on his deathbed," she said, looking at Nathaniel. His eyes grew wide in disbelief. "No, of course, my mother doesn't know…I've had it since I was 10. I didn't know why he gave it to me, exactly, until a few weeks ago. I told Gerald about my engagement to Michael, in confidence. He swore he wouldn't tell my mother and I trust him more than I trust her. He gave me this letter from my father," she said, showing the hand-written letter to Nathaniel.

Chapter Twenty-Nine

"It's good to see you too, mother," Shayla said. The Queen noticed how relaxed Shayla looked.

"Dare I say, you look quite happy," the Queen said. It had to be because of Michael! Good. She was finally moving on from that Nathaniel person.

"You know, I really am," Shayla said, nodding.

"So, any news?" she said to her daughter.

"About what?" Shayla said, a sour mood blossoming on her face.

"Why do you have to use that tone with me? I don't want to fight with you, Shayla," the Queen said, and she meant it. Shayla plopped herself down on the couch across from her mother before taking a few crackers and cheese off the platter that sat on the coffee table between them.

"I don't want to fight either, mother," Shayla said, before eating a cracker and looking away.

"Good, well, then, tell me how are things going at work?" the Queen asked with interest. She had spoken with Lorraine, quite bluntly, the previous week.

"Actually, it's getting a little better. Lorraine isn't happy with how I run things. I can see that, but I'm making changes. I honestly don't know why she hired me. I feel like she hates me sometimes," Shayla said, looking pensive as she ate a carrot.

"Nonsense," the Queen said. "Lorraine likes you very much!"

"Then she hates my ideas. She gave me a fraction of what I asked for. But I suppose it's a start," Shayla said, looking defeated.

"Lorraine is nothing, if not fair," the Queen said. She saw Shayla roll her eyes, but let it go. She didn't have the energy to argue with her. Still, she wanted to appease Shayla, if at all possible.

"What about you, mother. How is it going for you?" Shayla asked.

"I'm fine. Everything's fine!" she said.

"C'mon, Mother. I watch the Webavision. I've seen the news," she said quietly.

"You can't believe everything you see on the Webavision. Didn't you learn anything from me?" the Queen said snidely.

"What about the protests?" Shayla said.

"It's nothing. They've died down," the Queen said, noticing Shayla size her up.

"What about that petition that's circulating?" Shayla asked, and the Queen heard a nearly accusatory tone.

"What are you talking about?" the Queen said.

"The one to end castration. C'mon mother, it's just me here," Shayla said.

"Yes, yes, I know about that. It's a petition that nobody wants to sign with their real names," the Queen said. "My dear, someday you will learn about the many people with no backbones. You think this is the first time this idea has surfaced? You wouldn't remember the last time because you were just a little girl. They petered out then and they will peter out now, too. Mark my words," the Queen said. If this movement of people didn't fizzle on its own, she'd have to stomp it out herself.

"Hello, my love," Michael said to Shayla as she walked in the door of his apartment. She used all of her effort not to turn away and allowed him to kiss her on the lips.

"What's the matter?" he asked.

"Michael, we need to talk," she said.

"Okay. We can talk over dinner. I've made a reservation at…"

"I want to talk to you here," she said, sitting down across from him, the kitchen island between them.

"Okay, take off your jacket at least and have a glass of wine," he said. Shayla set her summer sweater on the island, beside her purse. She had hoped to ease into it, but she knew he loved her in a way she could never reciprocate, and it gave her a feeling of urgency.

"Michael," she said, but couldn't say more. She knew she was going to break his heart which was never her intention. She looked down at her own hands against the backdrop of the seashore colored granite countertop that was his canvas for many beautiful meals he'd served her. She remembered watching him knead bread and pour wine and try his absolute best to make everything perfect. He'd done nothing wrong. He didn't deserve this, but she needed to be true to herself.

"What is it?" he asked studying her carefully and trying to read what she was about to say.

"I can't marry you."

"What are you talking about?" he asked skeptically, his eyes stuck open wide in wonder, his mouth contorted in disbelief.

"I can't marry you," she said, shaking her head back and forth as the tears began to fall. She sniffled and willed the tears to stay at bay, at least for now.

"I can't marry you," she said again. No matter how many times she rehearsed, it didn't matter. It couldn't be sugar-coated in any context that would make sense to him.

"You proposed. We're getting married!" he said, taking her hands roughly in his and squeezing them all together, as though that made it certain to happen. She pulled her hands away as gently as possible.

"No. We aren't," she said, gathering her composure. "I care for you and never meant to hurt you, but I know what I want to feel when I get married, and I don't feel that with you. I wish I did. I thought I did. I tried. I'm so sorry."

"Please Shayla. Give it more time. I love you." A tear escaped his eye.

"It's not meant to be," she said.

"That's it. The end?" he said, a tint of anger in his voice.

She stood and turned to leave, wishing she could be fairer to him. He was an innocent in all this. He let go of her, and she grabbed her things and hurried out the door.

✣✣✣✣✣✣✣✣✣✣

"What on earth is the matter with you?!" It was the unmistakable crow of her mother on the other end of the phone, tearing into her without even hello. Shayla looked at the clock, and saw it was 1:30 in the morning.

"I'm sleeping," Shayla said, feeling groggy.

"Well, wake up! I just got a long distraught email from Michael saying that you proposed and that you two were engaged, which was news to me, and now you broke off that engagement for no apparent reason. What the hell is going on with you? How could you do that? He was perfect for you!" the Queen yelled.

It seemed as if her mother cared more for Michael than Shayla.

"Can we please talk about this tomorrow?" The attitude didn't surprise her, but she didn't think it was necessary to talk about this in the middle of the night.

"I'd like to talk about it now," her mother said. Shayla sighed. As much as she wanted to click the phone closed and pretend this was a small part of a bad dream that would bc gone by morning, she might as well let her mother go on. To finish with this inevitable lashing meant she was one step closer to a normal life with Nathaniel.

"I broke up with him, but it's not because I don't care about him. I absolutely do, certainly a lot more than you do."

"What's that supposed to mean?" the Queen said.

"It means that I broke off the engagement to be fair. I just don't love Michael. I thought I did, but I really don't. Sure, he's sweet," she said as her voice trailed quietly.

Her mother said, "And good looking and loving and trustworthy and from a good family and smart and kind and a great cook and a perfect gentleman! What more do you want?! What more could any woman want?!"

"It's not your business. This was between me and Michael and I'm not going to discuss this with you," Shayla said.

"It became my business when he sent me this long email,"

the Queen growled.

"I'm sorry about that," Shayla said, her voice growing calm. "I really am, but I don't want to live my life with someone I don't love. Something is missing. Can't you understand that?"

"You're just scared. It's perfectly natural," she said dismissively. "The two of you glow together. I don't want you to make a decision you'll regret."

"Mother, that's precisely why I broke up with him."

"You know, I really don't see that. I just don't understand you, Shayla."

Chapter Thirty

Office of the Queen's Royal Spouse,
Sir Edward Smith, II

My Dear Shayla,

Congratulations on your engagement. I'm sorry I can't meet your future husband. I have no doubt that you've chosen well.

Before you marry, I thought you should know more about your lineage, from my side of the family. As I write this, you are too young to understand, but I gave you Reminder of Truth and trust you have read it and kept it from your mother, as I instructed.

It is a special book in its own right, but even more important for you to know about. Your grandfather, Edward the first, is the author. He could not stand by and watch the injustices that your mother, and prior generations endorsed. He did more than just write that seminal book. He started an organization that you may, or may not, know about. By the time you read this, it may be disbanded or it may be ruling the country. It is called the Underground. You should be proud that your bloodline founded it.

I am weak and my time is short on this planet, but wherever I am, my love will always be with you and I hope your life is beautiful, full of peace and joy. Even at the age of 10, I can already see your gifts, and know you will go onto do great things.
Much love,
Father

As Shayla refolded the letter, the creases well-worn, and replaced it inside the velvet bag along with Reminder of Truth, she was grateful to have it. She felt sad that her father would never meet Nathaniel, but she knew he would have approved of her choice.

She was unsure how she could make Nathaniel her husband, but she was going to figure it out no matter what. They'd be photographed when things went public, and at the very least Janice would surely call the Webavision in a drunken rage to claim that the Queen's daughter had stolen her fiancée.

Then again, who would the Webavision believe? The Queen's daughter, or a wretched drunk.

"I'm so happy that we're going to be together, We'll actually be able to live together. No more hiding," he continued, as he hugged her.

"Do we have to talk about that right now?" she said, sounding a little grumpy. "I'm trying to enjoy today," she said, looking into his eyes, pulling him close, forcing his arms to wrap around her. He held her tightly, inhaling her vanilla scent that he had missed when they were apart.

"I am enjoying today, but I'm thinking about our future, too," he said, caressing her arm. "I can see us married with children," he said, feeling happy at the thought until her body tensed.

"I'm just not sure," she said.

"Not sure about what?" he asked, feeling uneasy. Was she not sure she wanted to marry him? Not sure about their love? One way or another, he needed to marry, and while it would kill him not to be with Shayla, he had to protect himself, ultimately. He turned to face her so he could look into her eyes. It reaffirmed his knowledge that she loved him deeply. He saw it, even with her wariness in talking about the future.

"I'm sure about you, Nathaniel, but…"

"But, what?!," he said. His heart pulsed quickly, from fear, not passion. Isn't that why she broke up with Michael; so they could be together? He had spent his entire adult life worrying about castration, never-mind finding true love and fulfillment. Everything he wanted was in his arms. He refused to let it slip away again.

"Calm down!" she said, sitting up to face him. "You're an outlaw, Nathaniel. If they find you, they'll kill you. I'm the enemy. Can't you see that I am fully committed to you? I am. But that doesn't mean we can have a public relationship. As soon as there is talk of me marrying, there will be a lot of attention and photographs. People study those photographs. You've never been in the spotlight that way. I have been there most of my life. The press will dig into your background… your fictional background, and think about what they'd find, what would happen."

"I look different now. I'll grow my beard back. Dye my hair…"

"Nathaniel, you disappeared. Do you honestly think a little hair dye would make you unrecognizable to all the friends and family back in Cambridge? You can't afford that. And what about the Underground? You think they'll just look the other way? They'll want something," she said, exasperated.

"Shayla, I have to marry. You know that! What the hell am I supposed to do? Put yourself in my shoes, here. I'm still in great danger of being castrated! If I don't marry you, then…" Nathaniel couldn't finish.

"For now, I'll keep you on as a temp. We'll go along the way we have been," she said. "But long term, I don't know."

"What are you saying?" he asked.

"What I'm saying is I don't know how to fix this," she said.

✣✣✣✣✣✣✣✣✣✣

"I'm dating a wonderful man and I'd like you to meet him," Shayla asked, hoping her mother would realize that Michael was really out of the picture. She twirled the phone cord, nervously, and felt glad that her mother wasn't there to see.

"Who is he?" she said with a formality that Shayla recognized. It was the tone she fed to visiting diplomats and businessmen she didn't particularly like.

"His name is Joe Merino," Shayla said hesitantly. She still hadn't grown accustomed to thinking of him as Joe. He would always be Nathaniel to her. "I met him at Steelco. He's wonderfully sweet, completely charming and highly intelligent," Shayla said feeling proud.

"What does he do?" the Queen asked.

"Actually, he's working as a temporary worker, mostly as a meeting scribe at Steelco," Shayla said, hoping her mother would find that palatable, but knowing she probably wouldn't.

"A temporary worker? Where is he from?" the Queen asked. Shayla could picture her mother's face, matching her skeptical voice.

"Kansas City. Is that okay with you?" Shayla asked in an accusatory tone, feeling like she wanted to slam down the phone.

"Why do you always have to get snippy with me?" the Queen asked with a fake innocence.

"Because you are giving me the third degree," Shayla declared forcefully.

"Dear, I was just asking a few questions. Is that so awful? Look, I'd love to meet this man. I have dinner with the ambassador of Cuba, who is visiting this evening, but I am free for lunch tomorrow."

"That sounds great," Shayla said before getting off the phone and turning to Nathaniel.

"Tomorrow, lunch, you will meet my mother," she said smiling.

"I can't wait," he said, rolling his eyes, before hugging her.

"Let's just take this one step at a time. It might not be so bad," Shayla said, taking comfort in Nathaniel's strong arms wrapped around her, his fingers still rough from years of hard labor. Would they ever be smooth? She hoped not. He had to change his identity, but underneath it all, he was still the same man she fell in love with.

"I need you to do me a favor," she said to Gerald who she summoned as soon as she got off the phone.

"Yes, your majesty," he said, standing before her.

"I need you to look into a Mr. Joseph Merino. That's M-E-R-I-N-O. All I know is that he's from Kansas City, temping at Steelco and Shayla is smitten with him. Find out what you can, ASAP," she said, writing "Joe Merino" in block letters on a piece of paper that she ripped off and handed to him.

"Of course," he said.

"He's coming to lunch tomorrow. Shayla is dating him," she said, wearily. "Did you know?" she added, observing him keenly. While she trusted Gerald implicitly, so did Shayla. Perhaps she confided in him.

"I had no idea she was dating anyone, your majesty," he said, unhesitating, his eyes locked with hers.

"I'm not optimistic. I suppose this is a step up from that chap from the Cambridge Public Works, but she always seems to pick men beneath her," the Queen said, shaking her head. She was still bothered by Shayla dumping Michael, seemingly out of left field

"Let's hope he's a good fit," Gerald said.

"She hardly knows him. I find her dating habits odd. She's all over the place. First with that laborer, then Michael, and now back down the ladder to a temporary worker?" she said to Gerald, shaking her head.

"Maybe she's finally getting ready to settle down. After all, she's 29," Gerald said.

"I think she's naive. No matter how many times I've tried to explain that people are out to take advantage of her, she doesn't pay attention," the Queen said, growing weary of Shayla's childish attitudes.

"I promise to get right on this and get back to you later today," Gerald said before turning to leave.

"Gerald?" she asked, and he turned back toward her.

"Yes, your majesty?"

"What do you think?" she said.

"About what, exactly," he said, his face unreadable – as always.

"Shayla and her dating choices."

"I have faith in her abilities to discriminate between someone who is genuine and one who is manipulative," he said, not missing a beat.

"Thank you for your opinion," she said. Maybe she was too hard on her daughter and maybe she should reserve judgment, at least a little bit until she met him. "As soon as you have that report," she said, smiling.

Gerald nodded without emotion and was gone.

Gerald was certainly used to keeping secrets and lying to the Queen, but usually the lies were dictated by the Underground. This time, he was making up the fake history of Joe Merino.

"He is from a middle-class family in Kansas City, was able to finish high-school and has been working for Kelly Boys for many years. Just as Shayla indicated, he specializes as a meeting scribe, especially for large groups. He is noted for his accuracy in those environments," Gerald said, as he surveyed the Queen's reactions.

"Hmmm… No Taser record?" she asked, squinting, which was her tell-tale sign of great pondering.

"No, your majesty," he said, trying to decide whether to fabricate additional details about him. "He is nearly 22 years old and has attended many POAs in Kansas City."

"Dating history?" she asked.

"He has dated a number of women via the POAs and the women who choose him are often business women," Gerald said.

"Yes, but they don't keep dating him, now do they? Nobody has proposed to him, to the best of our knowledge, isn't that true? There must be something wrong with him," the Queen said, clearly searching for any crumb leading toward disapproval.

"Permission to speak frankly, your majesty?" he asked. His heart beat wildly, as he rarely offered his opinion without her asking, but knew he needed to put her mind at ease about Joe Merino.

"Of course, Gerald. Please," she said invitingly.

"I think he is a fine young man, and Shayla seems happy," he said, trying to choose his words carefully while maintaining the neutral facial expression he honed over the years, to mask his truth.

"Thank you, Gerald," she said, in a way that he knew meant the Queen didn't want to hear anymore.

He nodded, feeling relieved, and slightly concerned, as he opened the door to leave.

"One more thing. May I have the written report of all you've found out about Joe Merino? I'd like to look it over a bit," the Queen asked casually. Gerald's heartbeat quickened as he answered.

"I don't have it with me, but..."

"Actually, never mind. You told me all I need to know," she said interrupting him, sounding defeated, as she waved him away.

He stepped outside her office, feeling the small beads of perspiration at his temples, and hoped she hadn't noticed. He was pretty sure she bought his story. In any case, he had done all he could, but he still had to report back to the Underground.

He left the Palace later that day to take a walk. The brisk autumn Washington D.C. air was refreshing.

"I think I convinced her that Joe Merino is a good guy, or at least he's not a bad guy," Gerald told Simon on the phone.

"Let's hope so because he's going to be there tomorrow and it's a miniscule window to win her approval."

"What happens after tomorrow?" Gerald asked.

"I'm not at liberty to say," Simon said, curtly.

Gerald thought this was getting ridiculous. He had dedicated his entire adult life to the Underground, and felt severely insulted that all-of-a-sudden, this young guy comes along and starts acting like Gerald isn't trustworthy. Simon seemed to be on some sort of power trip that made Gerald want to pummel him sometimes. Of course, there would never be that opportunity. They'd never met face-to-face and probably never would.

"Understood," Gerald said with the air of professionalism that revealed nothing. "One more question, sir," he said.

"What is it?"

"May I reveal myself to Joe Merino when he arrives?"

"Absolutely not!"

"I was simply asking," Gerald said, holding back his anger. When he dealt with Chester directly, there was a great deal more respect, but that contact ended nearly two years earlier.

"It's too dangerous," Chester had said.

Not only did he miss the respectful exchanges, but he missed his friend. Their bond went back to the castration recovery room where they met, laying side by side. Gerald trusted Chester, but he couldn't say the same of Simon.

Despite orders, Gerald had half a mind to call Chester at the bakery. He took a deep breath, and reminded himself of the goals.

Simon was just one cog in the wheel. The years of sacrifice involved many, and Gerald needed to take one more for the team.

Chapter Thirty-One

"I can't wait for you to meet Gerald," Shayla said, her eyes bright. Nathaniel didn't feel the luxury of any excitement with regard to his pending visit to the Palace, no matter how wonderful Gerald might be. All he could think about was the Queen and the dangerous waters he would enter the moment he stepped into the Palace.

"What if she finds out who I am and turns me directly over to the C Center?" he asked Shayla.

"You're with me. My mother would never hurt anyone I care for, no matter the circumstances. Don't be so nervous," Shayla said, as though he was being silly. What person wouldn't be nervous meeting the Queen? And he wasn't just anyone. He had secrets.

Nathaniel admired Shayla's confidence, but wasn't certain that Shayla's upbringing could give her clarity about the Queen.

"Come here," she said, hugging Nathaniel. He knew she was trying to reassure him, but he would need more than a hug to feel at ease in front of the Queen. Despite Shayla's insistence that her mother didn't care about a missing manual laborer from Cambridge, Shayla didn't know the truth and couldn't possibly think of her mother objectively.

"What should I call her? Your highness? Your majesty? Ma'am?"

"Call her 'Your Majesty.' For now, that is. In time, things will be different," she said before kissing him passionately. He didn't share her casual attitude toward his visit to the Palace. He couldn't help but think about the Underground, and he was downright terrified. They explicitly forbade him from contacting anyone he had ever known prior to entering the Underground.

He didn't seek out Shayla, but even though their reunion was serendipitous, this was only true to a degree. The Underground certainly wouldn't condone what he had divulged to Shayla.

Had the Underground caught wind of the fact that he was dating the Queen's daughter? He hadn't heard from them since Garrett disappeared.

Sometimes he felt a set of eyes on him as he walked down the street and felt like he was being followed. Was it his imagination? If it was real, would they punish him for divulging Underground secrets to Shayla?

"You're going to be wonderful. Use your gentlemanly skills. I love you, Nathaniel DeLuca," she whispered softly. He looked into her eyes and his worries fell away as he grew hard.

"I love you, too, Shayla Smith," he said before kissing her as he guided her hand toward his fly. She unzipped it and wrapped her hand around him, moving quickly as he looked into her eyes.

"I want you, now," he said. She led him to the bedroom and they each threw their clothes onto the floor. "I can't wait," he said, moving to take her.

"Lie down," she said, teasingly, as she pushed him away. He quickly climbed on the bed, and she slowly kissed him on the mouth, as she lightly touched his balls, causing him to moan quietly.

"I can't take your teasing," he said.

"I'm going to make you wait," she said, laughing, as she kissed him one more time before moving down to take him in her mouth, fully, deeply, over and over.

"I'm gonna come," he said to her, and she withdrew her mouth and smiled at him.

Before she knew it, he grabbed her hips and positioned her on top of him. She cried out in pleasure as she moved up and down, feeling him inside of her in a way that felt just right. He couldn't hold back and she felt the warmth as he finished. She collapsed on top of him.

"Sleep tight, my love," she said, as he fell asleep wrapped round her.

"*...Remember, I might need the favor returned,*" *Garrett said, his face bloodied, as he looked into Nathaniel's eyes.*

Nathaniel bolted upright, his heart pounding as he looked around the room. He was in Shayla's bedroom, and there she was sleeping peacefully beside him, the sheets having fallen off, exposing one of her perfect breasts. He lightly touched her, just to be sure she was really there. He looked at the clock. The red digital numbers read 3:15 in a blood-red color that reminded him of Garrett's bloody face. He looked away and flinched, accidentally hitting Shayla.

"What is it?" Shayla said.

"Just a bad dream," Nathaniel whispered, trying to downgrade it to Shayla and to himself. He wondered what was going to happen when the Underground found out he was sleeping with the enemy's daughter.

He heard Shayla's breaths return to a slow peaceful rhythm, but his eyes remained wide open.

Until he went into that Palace, and returned home in one piece with Shayla on his arm, he would not be able to shake these thoughts.

With Shayla's hand entwined in his, Nathaniel walked down the Palace corridor. The intricate plaster medallions that sat in the middle of the ceiling complemented the crown moldings that were unlike anything Nathaniel had ever seen. The grandeur was beautiful – and intimidating. As they made their way closer to the security desk, he felt Shayla pick up the pace. His instinct was to run the other way, as he felt like he was entering a prison where he'd be interrogated.

"Good afternoon," Shayla, the guard said smiling, not acknowledging Nathaniel in any way.

"How are you today?" she said, with as happy a tone as he had ever heard her utter.

"I am well. The Queen is expecting you, of course."

"Thank you," she said just as Gerald walked toward her.

"This is Joe. Joe Merino," she said, feeling his new name become more natural as she said it.

"Nice to meet you, Joe. I'm pleased you've decided to join us.

The Queen apologizes she can't be here to greet you, but she is finishing up an overseas call."

"Oh, I certainly understand," Nathaniel said. Nathaniel couldn't help but notice that he was a Spot. The purple tattoo appeared to be old, blurring at the edges, but clearly visible nonetheless.

"Come and I will make you comfortable," Gerald said, turning to lead them.

"Actually, I was going to give Joe a little tour of the Palace. I want to show him my quarters," Shayla said.

"Of course," Gerald said, formally as he motioned for Shayla to lead the way. "Would you like me to escort you?"

"I'll just walk him through and then meet up in mother's main living room in a little while," she said to Gerald who nodded and walked in a different direction.

Nathaniel watched him walk away. From Shayla's description, Nathaniel thought Gerald would be more relaxed and casual, but he was very formal. Maybe he was different when he was alone with Shayla, and not officially working. His intimidating height also struck Nathaniel. He had to be 6 foot 3.

"How'd I do?" Nathaniel whispered to Shayla when Gerald seemed out of earshot.

"You were perfect," she whispered back, before kissing him on the cheek.

"He's not what I expected, kind of off-putting," Nathaniel said.

"He's serious, but kind and gentle," Shayla said with affection.

Although Nathaniel knew it would be lavish, he was not prepared for the Palace to be so intimidating. The walls were decorated with breathtaking portraits of previous queens, large and luminous.

There was even a childhood portrait of Shayla, looking unhappy.

When they reached the portrait of her father, Nathaniel stopped.

"What is it?" Shayla started to ask, but then she noticed what he was looking at. "You would have liked him and he certainly would have liked you," Shayla said quietly as her father's towering likeness looked down on them. Nathaniel noticed a glimpse of Shayla in the shape of his face and the dark hair color, perfectly coifed. He looked more serious than the portrait of the Queen. Nathaniel understood why. Living a double-life left little room for laughter.

Shayla squeezed Nathaniel's hand and led him forward.

I hope he will watch over me from wherever he is, Nathaniel thought as they walked away.

"Well hello, darling," the Queen said as she walked toward them. Her smile was perfect, just like he'd seen in every photo of her. It was strange to see her in person. She was shorter than he imagined, but her presence was pronounced, accentuated by the shimmery silk sari that made her sparkle in a way unlike anyone he'd ever seen.

"Hi mother," Shayla said, before quickly embracing her mother. A brief brushed ceremonial kiss on each cheek completed the greeting.

"Mother, this is Joe Merino," Shayla said, standing back, smiling proudly.

"It's a pleasure," the Queen said, holding out her perfectly manicured hand that was cold to the touch.

"It's really an honor, your Majesty. Thank you for the invitation," he said, stopping himself before he laid it on any thicker than he already had. Relax, he told himself. He bowed his head, showing proper respect to her, the way Shayla rehearsed him.

"Shall we dine?" the Queen asked.

"Thank you," he said, as the Queen led them to the dinner table, just as two white-gloved servants quietly entered. One had a bottle of wine and a pitcher of water and the other had a basket full of bread that smelled like it was just out of the oven. They sat silently as the servers poured water and wine and the bread server placed a steaming roll on each bread plate. Nathaniel couldn't help but notice the Queen's crest embossed on the perfectly sized roll. It was the same crest that was on Shayla's father's jacket from the portrait they passed in the hallway.

"So Joe, how did you decide to work for Kelly Boys?" she asked with the interest of asking someone the meaning of life.

"Mother… please. This is not an interview!" Shayla said.

"Shayla, it's okay," Nathaniel said putting down his fork. He heard his Underground instructor whisper in his ear. "*Look them in the eye with confidence, and the other person will sense it.*"

"I have been working for Kelly Boys for a while and I enjoy the variety of the work and the travel that allows me to see different places," he said holding her gaze dead-steady.

Nathaniel carefully selected the correct fork and took a bite from the bed of greens that was laid in front of him.

"This is delicious!" he proclaimed when the silence in the air felt like it had been there too long. He was conscious of his words, trying hard to be polite, without fawning over her every word. He knew a woman like the Queen would sense any bit of dishonesty.

"I'm glad you're enjoying it," the Queen said. "Now tell me about Kansas City. Of course I've been all over the country, but I don't know what it's like to really live there," she said, looking keenly interested.

"Kansas City is a wonderful place. It really is. The people are nice, the city is beautiful, and there is plenty of parking," he said in a joking tone. "Unlike the many other areas of the country."

"I guess so," the Queen said, smiling, but it looked forced to Nathaniel. He felt like a dork for mentioning parking. Of course she didn't have to worry about that. It was his nerves making him too talkative, and he knew that he should be mindful of that.

When the four course lunch was complete, it was nearly 3 p.m.

"We should really be going," Shayla said.

"Well, it was lovely to meet you. I do hope we'll see you again, yes?"

"I certainly hope so," he said.

"Mother, how about the Queen's ball this coming Saturday?"

The Queen's smile lessened a bit and Nathaniel felt the air get sucked out of the room.

"Well, the invitations have already gone out and, well…"

"It's perfectly fine. Some other time then," Nathaniel said, not wanting to anger the Queen after lunch had gone reasonably well.

"Oh, come on, mother. I'm sure there is enough food for me to bring a special guest," Shayla said, and Nathaniel felt the challenge in the air. Shayla told him that their relationship was tough sometimes, but seeing it first hand was more uncomfortable than he imagined.

"Of course, Shayla. We can certainly arrange that," the Queen said, with flawless dignity. "I'll get Gerald to escort you out," the Queen said, as she was about to push a button on a panel in the room that boasted many.

"We don't need an escort. We'll see you on Saturday," Shayla said with excitement. Nathaniel was nervous as hell.

Chapter Thirty-Two

"What did you think?" the Queen asked Gerald.

"He seemed like a fine young man," Gerald said.

"Well, something jumped out at me," the Queen said. "That's no Kansas City accent, that's for sure," she said.

"He did mention that he's worked all over the country, for Kelly boys," Gerald said, hoping she would let it go.

"Perhaps you are right, but when you get a chance, can you go ahead and send me the information from that background search you did? I want to know exactly who my daughter is involved with, and who I am exposing my guests to at my annual ball."

"Of course, your majesty," he said, feeling glad that he had taken the time to at least jot down notes about what he had said in his oral report to her.

"Thank you, Gerald," she said. "And one more thing, would you make sure and keep an extra eye on him that evening?"

"Of course, your majesty," Gerald said, before the Queen turned and walked away, retreating to her private quarters.

It was raining, but Gerald put on his rain gear and took a walk through the park outside the Palace to make the phone call.

"It's better than we could have asked for," Gerald said to Simon. "Shayla forced her mother to allow her to bring him to the Queen's ball. It's her largest event for local supporters each year. She'll be far too busy to keep an eye on everyone," he said.

"Finally, some luck on our side," Simon said, sighing. "Speaking of which, is there any word about the protesters she had captured? We've got hundreds of men missing."

"I don't know anything. I imagine they are either still locked up or dead. I can't ask her. It would raise too much suspicion," Gerald said.

Nathaniel rose early the next morning and went back to his hotel to get fresh clothes before work. The unexpected sight of Simon in his room, sitting on a chair, caught him by surprise.

"Good morning, buddy!" Simon said, his feet propped up as he sat leaning back on the easy chair by the window, his arms behind his head. Despite Simon's relaxed look, there was nothing relaxing about this visit.

"Come on in and close the door, son. I'm not going to bite you."

Nathaniel did as he was told. He knew it was no coincidence that Simon showed up the morning after he met the Queen. Clearly, he wasn't being paranoid. The Underground was keeping tabs on him, after all.

"Come. Sit down," Simon said, gesturing to the edge of the bed. I've been here all night waiting for you," he said with a smile. "I'm guessing you got lucky, and I even think I know who the lucky lady is. It looks like you're doing pretty well for yourself here." Simon gestured to the niceties of hotel life, the perfectly pressed shirts peeking from the closet, and the lined up row of shoes for every occasion that sat on the edge of the room.

"I'm okay. Settling in."

"Well, good. Through the grapevine, we hear you are doing quite well."

"Yes, sir," Nathaniel said with resignation. "*I may not see you again, but I will track your whereabouts. I know you'll do well. I have great faith that you will help our cause, will help your brothers all around you.*"

Nathaniel heard Chester's words echo in his mind, before they parted in the Underground. Now he understood the purpose of their meeting Chester wanted to make sure Nathaniel understood that he would be called on. The balloon payment of Nathaniel's Underground education was coming due.

"We need a little favor from you, son. You don't mind, do you?"

Nathaniel sat down. He dreaded this day, but wasn't surprised. "Good." Simon shifted in his seat, and the mood changed with him, as the smile dissolved from his face.

Simon took his feet off the chair and sat up, leaning a little closer to Nathaniel. He removed the dark glasses, focusing his serious eyes on Nathaniel. He continued speaking in a voice so quiet Nathaniel strained to hear.

"You've done a great job of getting in with Shayla. Chester is very pleased with that. Very pleased. Nobody could have done it but you. Our favor is very simple. We need you to put a little something in the Palace for us when you go to the party on Saturday."

"What is it?" Nathaniel asked flatly. He felt like he was on autopilot.

Simon moved closer to Nathaniel.

"It's a bomb," he whispered before moving back, sitting up straight. He cracked his fingers one by one, slowly, giving Nathaniel a moment to absorb his words. Nathaniel hid behind a closely guarded stone face that masked his true terror. He anticipated the favors they would ask would not be as simple as helping a community fundraising carwash, but he never expected this.

"When will it go off?" he asked quietly, once again on autopilot.

"Well, it'll go off after you set it. You'll have 30 minutes to get out of there. Then… ka-boom," Simon said, mimicking an explosion with his hands. He spoke about it lightly, as though he were talking about making popcorn.

"How do I set it?" Nathaniel asked.

"I was just getting to that part. I'll show you right now." Simon said removing a brown paper bag from his coat pocket. He pulled out two credit card sized items and a thin wire with plugs on both ends.

"Take this plug and put it into each of these items here, you see, and then… voila! It's all set and the timer starts ticking. Then, stick it to the back of a toilet. It's that easy," he said with sarcasm clearly in his voice. "It's as easy as eating a big juicy apple pie. Even easier really. Not as messy, until cleanup time," he said making a scowl that frightened Nathaniel.

"Can I leave once it's set?"

"Of course! Jeez, son, do you think we'd kill you? What kind of folks do you think we are? You're one of our own. Our kin! You leave as soon as you set it," Simon patted him heartily on the back.

"By yourself," he added quietly, and Nathaniel knew there was no way he would leave Shayla there. He knew that escaping with the Queen was out of the question as she was the obvious target. How would that work, anyway? With all her security, there was no way he could swoop her away from her own party, the biggest of the year. Besides, what would he do with her? Ask her to eat dried fruit while they camped out on the side of a river in the country, hiding out like fugitives trying to avoid castration?

"Any other questions," Simon asked casually, as though it were the end of a high-school physics lecture and he wanted to ensure the audience fully understood his lesson.

Nathaniel thought about asking exactly how much damage the bomb would do and how many people it was likely to kill, but decided against it. What difference would it make? The more he knew the harder it would be and he realized there was no choice.

"No, sir," Nathaniel said solemnly.

"Good. Well, here you go," Simon said quickly tossing the small bag to Nathaniel with a chuckle. Nathaniel barely caught it, and was dumbfounded that this was the same Simon who escorted him to his home in Kansas City, setting him free like a butterfly only months earlier. Nathaniel felt doomed. The price of life through the Underground was higher than he imagined.

"Good to see you again," Simon said as he walked past Nathaniel, leaving him alone with the bag, and the task of murder at the top of his to-do list for Saturday evening. Nathaniel could hear Simon whistling the National Anthem as he sauntered down the hall.

Nathaniel collapsed onto the bed, as his frenzied thoughts ran through the process, putting all emotion aside. Go to the Palace, plug the wire and cards together, tape it to the back of a toilet in the men's room, and get out of there with Shayla.

Just a single day earlier he had pinched himself to see if the happiness he felt was real, and it had been. Now, he felt his insides being torn up over the crime against humanity, against his lover and her mother that he was to commit in less than 72 hours.

After work that day, he met Shayla in her office at 5 p.m. As usual, the office door was closed and locked before she issed him.

"What would you like for dinner? I can get take out from wherever you want," she said, growing used to the idea that they might never go out in public together. She didn't care. Being wined and dined at some of the spectacular and romantic restaurants that the D.C. area paled in comparison to having Nathaniel by her side.

"I don't really feel well. I think I'm coming down with something. Maybe I ate something bad," he said, feeling guilty about hiding the truth.

"Hmmm, you do look a little pale."

"I think I just need to sleep," he said, hoping she would suggest he go back to his hotel alone.

"Then you'll just have to come back to my place so I can take care of you. I'll force-feed you something to make you all better," she said jovially, her arms clasped together behind his neck as she looked up at him with loving innocence he couldn't return.

"Are you sure? What if it's a virus or something. No reason for both of us to be sick. Maybe we shouldn't chance it," he said turning his head away. He couldn't look her in the eye.

"Nonsense. I'm sure it's nothing like that. I know just the thing to help you get better," she said, reaching behind him and squeezing his behind hard and quick.

Chapter Thirty-Three

Nathaniel left most of the meal on his plate.

"Is my cooking that bad?" Shayla asked in jest.

"No, it's delicious. Really," he said unconvincingly. "It's just that I don't feel well. I think I need to go to sleep."

"I know what will make you feel better," she said as she began to unbutton his pants, placing her hands snuggly inside. He gently took her hands away.

"Geez, you really must be sick," she said, surprised.

"That's what I tried to tell you," he said with annoyance. It was a tone he had never used with her, and he felt bad about it.

"Alright. I was just trying to make you feel better, but if you need to sleep, then sleep. I'll just go and read for a while before I join you."

"Sleep well. Feel better," she said a short while later. She kissed Nathaniel softly on the forehead before turning out the lights.

His sleep wasn't restful as his nightmare came alive. He saw himself place the bomb before barely escaping with Shayla.

The explosion sent body parts everywhere. Hands still wore diamond rings. Arms still wore bright designer fabrics. Heads without bodies cried out to him, but it was too late. He looked over at Shayla who cradled the bloody stump of her mother's head. As she held it out to Nathaniel and asked him why, through her thick veil of tears, he awoke abruptly with a scream that brought Shayla upright.

"What is it?" she asked frantically.

Unable to reconcile his task with the thought of murdering his lover and her mother, he told her what had happened. It spilled out of him in fragments, until he could speak cohesively. She turned on the bedside light and listened with wide eyes as he recounted the previous morning's events in detail.

"I'm so sorry, Shayla. To bring you into this. To be part of it at all. I don't know what to do, but if I don't do it, they'll kill me! They will!"

"We'll figure something out," she said, sounding shocked.

"Besides, if I don't do it, someone else will! That's one of the few things I know about how the Underground works. Goals are met, regardless of obstacles. Whatever the cost. It might not happen this Saturday, but make no mistake that it will happen."

Just then, his phone rang. Given the events of the day and the unidentified caller, he felt he needed to pick up, even though it was 3 a.m.

As he answered, he heard the crackle of a bad phone connection, but there was a clarity to the voice that yelled his name.

"Joe! It's Garrett. You must help us! We're in the dungeon in Kansas City. There are hundreds of us. We're dying! Send help!" he heard before the phone call clicked to a dead silence.

"You look like you saw a ghost," Shayla said.

"I think I just spoke with one," he said before recounting the snippet of a phone conversation he had just had.

"I know just the person to help us," she said, seeming almost smug, which puzzled Nathaniel.

"What on earth are you talking about?" he said, feeling ill at the stack against him. There was nobody on earth who could prevent this eventual act.

"There is one thing I haven't told you either," she said. Nathaniel was fearful, but sat up straight as he couldn't speak.

"Gerald is in the Underground. I've known him my whole life but only found out recently. He can help us," she said.

Nathaniel needed a minute to take it all in, as his disbelief in what he heard was beyond his imagination.

"What can he do?"

"Think about where he works. We can have our own plan," she said.

"May I please speak with Chester?" Nathaniel said. He felt his heartbeat quickly. He knew it was extremely risky to call Chester, that he was explicitly instructed not to, but he had no choice. With Garrett in a dungeon and no way to contact Simon, he was in a corner.

"This is Chester," said the friendly voice that he longed for.

"Joe Merino here. Sorry to bother you, but I must talk to Simon, immediately and I didn't know who else to call," he said.

As quickly as the chipper voice had warmed him, there was a chill as the call abruptly ended with a click. Nathaniel felt deflated as he threw the disposable cellular phone he purchased into a dumpster on his way to work.

It wasn't the response he hoped for, but he still hoped that he would get a visit from Simon, and soon, even as he dreaded it.

"You're not going to do this," Shayla said. She called him as he walked back to his hotel. He could hear she was in problem-solving CEO mode.

"Of course I'm not going through with this. I'm no murderer. Maybe I should just run. I'll leave tonight and just go away," Nathaniel said.

"You are the one who made it clear that the Underground carries out their plans, no matter what," she said, accusing.

"That doesn't mean that I can do it!" he said.

"Look. I'm trying to figure this out. Don't yell at me!" she said.

"I'm sorry. I just don't know what to do. Think of Garrett and all those men. They may be starving or tortured. I have no idea, but we can't stand by and do nothing," he said.

"We don't know where Garrett is exactly. Why don't we proceed with the plan that I came up with last night?"

"It won't work," he said, as he approached his hotel.

"Get in," he heard as a black van approached and the door opened.

"I gotta go," he said, and clicked his phone closed before climbing inside.

"This had damn well better be good," Simon said.

Chapter Thirty-Four

As he walked into the Palace for the second time in two weeks, Nathaniel couldn't enjoy the beauty of the silk wallpaper and oil paintings that lined the hallways. He could barely take pleasure in having Shayla on his arm, dressed in a form-fitting vintage gown that made her look like a movie star.

Each step was an effort as he tried to make it through the evening without drawing attention to himself.

"You're going to be fine," she said to him, as if she could feel his fear through her skin. All he could think was that he should be consoling her.

Nathaniel entered the ballroom to a backdrop of live jazz, sprinkles of laughter and clinking glasses. He wanted to take Shayla by the hand and run the other way, but instead he allowed a smile to form on his face. He walked toward the Queen pretending that the gala was a pure joy to attend.

"You look beautiful, mother," Shayla said, admiring her mother's new pear-colored sari with gold threads. It glowed when the light hit it.

"Thank you, my dear," the Queen said, turning to Nathaniel. "My daughter certainly looks stunning, doesn't she?" the Queen said. There was something that terrified him further, in that moment, as the Queen faced him. He knew she couldn't possibly know what was coming, but her eyes on him weakened his confidence.

"It is wonderful to see you again, your majesty," he said. Just as he was about to bow, another couple approached the Queen. As quickly as she turned toward him, she was gone, gliding through the crowd with everyone patiently waiting to have a moment with her.

"That's probably the only time we'll talk to her tonight. She's busy at these functions," Shayla said quietly to Nathaniel after the Queen stepped away. Nathaniel took little comfort in

Shayla's declaration.

"Are we ready for the party?" Gerald said, approaching Shayla and Nathaniel, moments later. Nathaniel was still dumbfounded that Gerald was in the Underground.

"We're ready," Nathaniel said, reaching to shake his hand, which allowed Gerald to give him a beeper that would alert them when they needed to get moving. This was a world away from his Underground training of romancing women and cooking vegan delicacies. He was out of his league and felt uneasy about it, but there was nothing to do but put aside his fears.

Throughout the evening, Nathaniel was glued to Shayla's side, greeting her mother's old friends and supporters until he felt that buzzer go off in his pocket. He jumped. He gave Shayla a nod, and the smile on her face fell, for just a moment before she pasted it back up. Nathaniel walked slowly toward the ballroom exit where Gerald was waiting.

"Mr. Merino, may I escort you to the exit?" Gerald said, dead-pan.

"Thank you, sir," Nathaniel said, glancing gain at the Spot on Gerald's neck, yet another reminder of why he was taking such a great risk.

✣✣✣✣✣✣✣✣✣✣

"Mother, it's Gerald, please come quick!" Shayla frantically said once all the party was over and all the guests were gone.

"What's the matter?" her mother said, with a concern Shayla hadn't seen on her mother's face since Shayla's father was near-death.

"He's in my suite. He isn't well!"

"Let's get the doctor!"

"No, you must come now," Shayla said, grabbing her mother's hand, forcing her to walk quickly through the hallways.

"What happened?" the Queen asked.

"I don't know, but he has been asking for you for the last hour and I promised I'd bring you just as soon as you were free,"

Shayla said. Shayla slowed her pace a little as they passed a few servants, not wanting to cause alarm with them.

"Good evening," Shayla said to the servant, forcing a smile as they passed and curtsied to the Queen.

"Do you think it's something he ate? Where is Joe anyway?" the Queen asked.

"He's with Gerald. I didn't want to leave him alone," Shayla said, her heart pounding as she lied to her mother. It's for a good cause, she reminded herself.

"Hurry" the Queen said as Shayla's trembling fingers punched in the code to get into her suite. When the door opened, the Queen ran inside and Shayla was behind her, closing the door as quickly as it opened, her body blocking the door.

"Where is he?" the Queen said, as she frantically surveyed the room. There was no sign of Gerald on the perfectly made bed or the empty couches. "What's going on?"

"He's in the bathroom," Shayla said, just as planned. She had told the men that she didn't want to watch.

"Gerald!? Are you okay?" the Queen said, near-tears as she ran across the room and pushed open the door that was slightly ajar and disappeared inside.

Shayla's body trembled as she double-checked to be sure that the suite door was closed and locked. Gerald was the only other one with a code to enter, as they had just reprogrammed it to avoid any chance for a cleaning crew to come through unannounced.

Shayla heard her mother's quick, muffled scream, before a rustling that she knew was a struggle. She heard the tear of fabric, undoubtedly the beautiful new silk sari. She almost ran across the room and into the bathroom, but couldn't. She didn't want to see.

Shayla slid to the floor, unable to hold her body upright any longer. Her body shuddered as she sobbed, hoping she wasn't making a mistake.

Chapter Thirty-Five

"Now you know what it's like to have a silver duct-tape for a mouth," Simon said. "You've ordered this very thing for countless decent men over the years, so I'm assuming you don't mind it. At least you are having this experience privately. The men are usually paraded in public and every goddamn person who sees them knows they're on their way to get their balls chopped off!" Simon's voice rose as he moved closer to the Queen until he was inches from her terrified face.

Simon smiled before backing away.

"Maybe we'll take you out on the balcony and duct tape your mouth closed. That's what you do to others. That seems fair, don't you think?" he asked, knowing she couldn't answer. "Maybe I should take your photo and we'll start that way. Smile for the camera," he said, pulling the cell phone out of his pocket as he prepared to take a photo. "Just kidding!" he said, when he heard a knock at the door.

"Just a second!" he yelled as he put the phone back in his pocket. "Maybe it's your savior?" he said to the Queen as he got up to answer it.

"Come on in," Simon said, greeting Shayla, immediately getting serious. When he was alone with the Queen, that was one thing, but he wasn't stupid enough to taunt her in front of her own daughter. Simon still couldn't believe that Shayla had agreed to be part of this. He was impressed. This apple had certainly fallen far from the tree and he respected that a great deal. Even though the Queen was the devil, from where he sat, he still knew that to Shayla, she was mom.

"How is she?" Shayla said, alongside Nathaniel, both dressed in street clothes.

"She's fine," Simon said, as Shayla looked at her mother.

"Looks like her eyes are going to bug out of her head.

Please take the tape off her mouth," Shayla whispered to Simon, so her mother couldn't hear. Simon had to admit that Shayla was right. The Queen's eyes were bulging, but to him they looked like their wrath was aimed at her daughter.

"No screaming. I'll take this off and keep it off, but if you misbehave. Can you be a good Queen?" Simon whispered in the Queen's ear, so Shayla couldn't hear.

The Queen's head didn't move. Her eyes narrowed for a moment, but Simon could see that she knew who had the upper hand. Despite his hatred for her and all she represented, he couldn't help but notice her beauty. And even though he detested what she represented, he found himself feeling something for her. Was it a respect for her determination? He wasn't sure. He saw her face relax before a barely perceptible nod.

He ripped the tape off her mouth, hoping that would rip away any feelings of sympathy, or any feelings at all that he felt for her.

"Who the fuck do you think you are, you piece of shit," she yelled at Simon. There was a venom in her voice that even surprised him, as his heartbeat quickened. She was tougher than he thought. "Shayla, get over here and untie me. Now!" she screamed.

Simon's instinct was to put that tape right back over her mouth. That's what he would have done with a back-talking Grounder, but this was the Queen. He looked to Shayla for direction, but first noticed Nathaniel had taken residence on the couch in the corner. Simon considered doing the same, but thought better of it. He had to keep the upper hand, and that meant remaining in a close physical proximity to the uppity subject.

"I need you to do something for me, first, mother," Shayla said, slowly approaching her mother from across the room. Simon watched her take each step, tentatively at first, but then there was a purpose in her stride until she stopped in the middle of the room, dead straight in front of her mother and crossed her arms. Good. Shayla was displaying strength, confidence, and control.

"I will do nothing for you until you untie me!" the Queen yelled.

"Keep your voice down or the tape goes back on," Simon said

evenly. He didn't want to step on Shayla's toes, but keeping order was vital.

"What the hell is going on here?" the Queen asked. "Untie me, this instant," she said, her voice quieter, but her message no weaker.

✣✣✣✣✣✣✣✣✣✣

"We're not going to simply untie you until you agree to our conditions," Shayla said flatly.

"You'll be sorry, my darling daughter," the Queen said, with contempt.

Shayla hated seeing her mother this way. The long front wrap of her beautiful new sari was torn, her hair slumped to one side, and her face looked like a new crop of wrinkles had erupted since the previous evening when the party ended.

"Are you going to keep yelling or are you ready to hear what we need you to do?"

"Who is the we?" the Queen asked. Even when her mother was tied up, she didn't give in.

"Do you know what the Underground is?"

"Of course I know! It's a lame group of men who think they can take over the world. Don't tell me my own daughter is a member," the Queen said with contemptuous laugh.

"You will do want we ask," Shayla commanded. Nobody else dared speak to her mother that way, but it felt necessary.

"Tell me what you need," the Queen said sarcastically, looking away.

"You must release all the prisoners from the protests," Shayla said. "We need you to record a speech saying that they are free to go. That's for starters."

"I'll tell you what I need. You better let me out of here before people come looking for me. You think the Queen just disappears and nobody notices? There are people who will come looking for me very soon. Gerald doesn't let me out of his sight for five minutes," she said, looking unconcerned.

"Who do you think Gerald works for," Simon chimed in, folding his arms in a satisfied stance.

"What have you done with Gerald?! Did you torture that wonderful man?" the Queen asked, exasperated.

"It's not what we have done with Gerald, but it is what Gerald has done for us, for years, decades, your majesty," Simon said, annunciating her title with his own sarcasm. Shayla shot him a look that shut him up.

"What are you talking about? He'll be here any minute," the Queen said, but Shayla saw her mother's nerves begin to unravel. She was about to start to cave, at least that's what Shayla hoped.

"Mother, he's part of the Underground."

"You are bluffing. Gerald is the most loyal man on the earth"

"Loyal to the Underground, just like your husband," Simon said.

"How dare you talk about my husband in the same breath as that disgusting organization," she growled.

"Grandfather was a founder of the Underground and my father – your husband – played a very big role in that," Shayla said, and her mother's face turned the color of rage itself.

"I don't believe you. If Gerald is a member, why isn't he here telling me himself, and as far as your father is concerned, I'm disgusted with you for making up lies about him. He's not here to defend himself. You may be my daughter, but you are pathetic!" the Queen said.

Shayla ran to the corner and grabbed her purse off the couch and pulled out the velvet bag. Reminder of Truth tumbled out and Nathaniel picked it up as though it was the most precious artifact, but that is not what Shayla was trying to find. She pulled out her father's letter and carefully opened it and marched over to her mother and held it squarely in front of her face, turning the letter as her mother tried to avert her gaze from the words as though it was acid in her eyes, but she finally looked. Shayla knew her mother recognized the unmistakable handwriting so she couldn't deny Shayla's declaration when she finally read the letter.

"It's the truth. Face it! Now, I need you to agree to make a video statement to release all of the prisoners and denounce the Tasers' behavior during the protests. Those men are rotting and starving because they dared to express themselves," Shayla spat, realizing she needed to be more composed, as she felt Nathaniel's hand on her shoulder. She reached back to give his hand a quick squeeze as she glared at her mother. "That's for starters. If you agree to that, we'll untie you, let you get yourself together and put on makeup. We'll film your speech right here."

"You have allowed these people to brainwash you! Your boyfriend is in on this, too?"

"That's Nathaniel DeLuca, mother. My boyfriend from the Cambridge Public Works. He's part of the Underground too," Shayla said, feeling proud.

"I knew it. I knew that there was something off. He doesn't have any Kansas City accent."

"You will do as we say," Shayla said with a deep anger lacing her words.

"What if I don't?" her mother said, the look of pain transforming to a kind of resigned glaze that wouldn't allow anything to penetrate.

"We'll kill you," Simon said evenly.

"I am the Queen and when I get out of here I'm going to kill you," she said, with a fiery vengeance.

"Mother, I am demanding you make this statement," Shayla said.

"Or you're going to kill me?" the Queen said in a mocking tone, as if it was the most ridiculous thing she had ever heard.

"I won't stand in anyone's way."

"You little... you don't have the strength... you're weak... too much of your father's blood made you a crybaby when you were young and too soft-hearted now. You won't let it happen, even if you don't like the laws I uphold," the Queen said to Shayla.

Shayla took all her energy to keep the pain from her face. She felt like her mother was inside her belly with a knife slicing everything that held her body together from the inside out.

"This isn't a joke, mother. It's time for things to change. Daddy used to try and tell you this and I've been trying to tell you too, for a long time," Shayla said calmly.

"Is this from your little boyfriend over there in the corner who has brainwashed you into allowing your mother to be murdered?" the Queen asked, trying to crane her neck to see him.

Shayla looked at Nathaniel who gave her a loving look, but said nothing.

"This is from me and all the men in this country. They are entitled to be heard and to make decisions about their own bodies. Mandatory castration is wrong. You can either make a statement to release the prisoners who speak up about it and begin the proceedings of getting rid of mandatory castration, and stay as the Queen or you will be killed. If you do stay as Queen, all your meetings and decisions will be controlled by us. You have 12 hours to decide. It's your choice. In that one way, you are still in control, but this is your final chance. That's a promise," Shayla said, feeling weak, even as her words pierced the air.

"You don't know what you're talking about," the Queen yelled as her speech turned into a curdling scream.

Simon ran over with a new piece of duct tape and placed it tightly over the Queen's mouth as she squirmed. Shayla couldn't bear to look at her mother anymore.

"You tried your best. Now you should leave," Simon said in a gentle voice to Shayla. Without looking up at him, she nodded and headed toward the door, along with Nathaniel.

As they stepped out of her suite into the hallway, one of the servants walked by.

"Hello, Miss Shayla!" she said, smiling, like it was any other day.

"Good to see you," Shayla said, before turning the other way. As she felt Nathaniel's arm around her, helping her stand, she felt more grateful than ever to have him close.

Chapter Thirty-Six

"I don't know if I can do this," she said to Gerald before breaking down on the couch in her mother's living room. Shayla had spent countless hours on this couch witnessing her mother upholding mandatory castration laws. Now, the tables were turned. Shayla was in control and the Queen was locked up as a hostage in Shayla's childhood suite.

"Shayla, you don't have to do this," Gerald said, which he knew was only partially true. With or without Shayla, the Underground would do what it wanted from now on. With Shayla willingly on board, it was going to be a heck of a lot easier.

"I don't want my mother to die, but I don't think she's going to give in. You should've seen her. You know how she is," Shayla said through a blur of tears. Gerald saw the little girl he had helped and comforted countless times, but he also thought about his mission with the Underground.

"I want you to remember why we gave her this ultimatum. Remember what I went through," he said, his voice cracking with emotion that he tried to banish long ago. He rarely thought about those days of physical and mental anguish. Shayla looked at him and he took a deep breath, composing himself. "I can tell you what it was like, if you want," he said, unable to hold back. No matter his mission, he did care deeply for Shayla and he knew she cared for him. He didn't want to have to choose between Shayla and the Underground.

She shook her head no. "I don't need to hear the details. I know it is wrong. Between my two parents, one taught me what is right and the other what is wrong," she said, nearly in a whisper as the tears slowed. "I know the difference and that I'm doing the right thing," she said.

"You're a good person, a courageous person," he said.

"Thank you, Gerald," she said before leaning to hug him.

He didn't know who was comforting whom. A knock at the door pulled them apart.

"It's probably Nathaniel. What are we going to do? I can't go home. I need to be here."

"You two can stay in here," Gerald said as he opened the door to let Nathaniel in. He rushed over to Shayla.

"Are you alright?" he asked, but she just shrugged.

"I can't sleep in my mother's bed," Shayla said to Gerald.

"Of course not. There is the small guest suite off the dining room. Why don't you two stay there? I'm going to my quarters," Gerald said, "but I'll have my phone. Call if you need to talk later tonight. Otherwise I'll see you in the morning."

"We'll be alright," she said, squeezing Nathaniel's hand and smiling at him a little.

Gerald looked at the two of them for a moment and felt a pang of envy. He wanted to love someone and have children, but the government had stolen those choices from him.

As he stepped outside and closed the door, he felt sadness. He recovered from the castration surgery 25 years earlier, but emotional recovery for Spots was close to impossible.

"I'll take that tape off, but no screaming and no funny stuff," Simon said as she rolled her eyes at him. He knew it had to hurt when he took the tape off, but she didn't complain about it, stoic that she was.

"I have to go to the bathroom badly," she said.

"Just a minute," he said before heading toward the bathroom and removing anything she might think of using against him: nail scissors or products she might try to spray into his eyes. "What are you doing?" the Queen asked impatiently.

"Making it safe for you. I left you some toilet paper, but other than that, the place is clean. Don't dilly dally. I've got a knife and guns," he said, quickly picking up his shirt so she could see the holster and know that he wasn't messing around.

“So do your business fast,” Simon said.

“Are you going to untie me so I can have a little privacy?” she asked.

“I’ll untie your hands in the bathroom,” he said, as he put his hands around her wrists – which felt delicate, but strong beneath his grip. She winced quietly but didn’t complain.

Simon respected strong women, and had to admit that the Queen was the toughest he had seen, maybe ever. It surprised him. As he walked her into the bathroom, hands behind her back, her perfume got into his nose and he was glad she couldn’t see him close his eyes as he felt himself weaken. Despite everything, he admitted to himself she was a beautiful woman, on the outside.

Chapter Thirty-Seven

"I won't do it. I'd rather die. That would make me a martyr and you nothing more than a murderer," she said the next morning once Nathaniel, Shayla and Simon were all present.

"What about all those men who are dying in the dungeons all over the country? Who is murdering them?" Shayla said, tears in her voice.

"What about them?" The Queen said matter-of-factly, and Shayla knew there was no hope. Her mother would rather give her life than break a principal she believed in.

Shayla's lip quivered as she turned away. Nathaniel tried to offer comfort, but there was nothing to ease the fact that her mother was choosing to die. Shayla looked at Simon, but he gave no visible reaction.

The Queen's hands were tied in front of her, rather than behind as they were the previous evening. She almost looked content with her hands in her lap. Her disheveled hair hung straight and unstyled. She never went in public without her hair swept up, just as she was never seen in anything other than a sari, and it certainly would not be a torn one.

"That's that," Simon said, and the Queen looked entirely startled as he pulled a syringe from the leather pouch he had on the coffee table near the couches.

"I can't look!" Shayla said.

"Don't you want to say goodbye to your mom, Shayla," the Queen said with a load of contempt.

"Mother, please! Just make the speech!" she said, begging.

"I can't make a speech I don't believe in," she said, looking at her daughter. Shayla swore she saw a hint of a tear in her eye, but it couldn't undo all the wrongs her mother had done by not repealing mandatory castration. Beyond that, there were the imprisoned men, suffering at her mother's hands, simply because they spoke out against the Queen's laws. Shayla knew the men deserved equal rights, but she also believed that everyone had a right to speak their minds. Too many atrocities against men had been allowed.

"If you won't make the speech, then I will," Shayla said. "Goodbye Mother. You had your chance to live, but you are a selfish, evil woman who is willing to let innocent people die." She spun on her heels and marched out.

"I can't believe you're doing this to me after…" the Queen yelled just as Simon plunged the syringe into the Queen who went limp.

My fellow citizens, I inform with great sadness that my mother, our Queen for more than a quarter century, has died. It is a shock to everyone, but she has had a heart attack. Ironically, she died on the eve of an important announcement she wished to make. I am here to deliver her message. My mother, our Queen, found out just yesterday that there were many men who were captured unnecessarily, unintentionally, without the support of the government after attending a number of rallies many months ago. You may have heard of these rallies to foster male rights. In Washington D.C., Kansas City, Missouri, Atlanta, Georgia, in San Francisco, in California. Men were unfairly imprisoned. Today they will all be free. Their families will receive restitution as they regain their strength and footing in communities across America. We shall unite and move forward under my leadership as I assume the throne. Change is coming, but please give me time to grieve for the loss of my mother and your Queen.

Equal Rights and Justice for all People.

Thank you. Good night and God Bless.

"And, cut!" the director said just hours after Shayla left her mother, slumped over in the bubble-gum pink chair of her childhood suite that had always been a haven. Shayla knew she would never set foot in there again.

"It's going to air in ten minutes. Let's go watch it," she said to Nathaniel and Gerald.

"I had the green suite setup for the two of you, figuring that you wouldn't want to stay in your mother's suite or, obviously, yours," Gerald said.

"Thanks, Gerald. I appreciate it. You want to come with us?" Shayla asked him, looking exhausted.

"No, that's alright. You two need some time," Gerald said, looking at both of them. "I have some things that need tending, but let's connect at dinner? I'll bring it to the green suite myself," Gerald said.

"What about... are there arrangements...? Must there be a viewing for the public? She always said she wanted to be cremated and I want to respect that," Shayla said, nearly breaking down.

"We'll talk about that at dinner. Right now, get some rest. It's been a long couple of days. I've already called Lorraine, and she knows you're not coming back. If there is anything else you need before dinner, don't hesitate to call," Gerald said before hugging Shayla.

Nathaniel felt uneasy about how fast everything happened. One minute he's in the Underground with a new identity, and now he's stowed away in the Palace with Shayla at the country's helm. He felt like such an outsider as he stood by, but when Shayla began to walk out of the room, he followed. After all, he certainly had no idea where the "green suite" was. The Palace was huge.

He tried to keep up with Shayla who walked very fast on this day. It was as if she were trying to get away from him. For the first time, he hesitated before taking her hand and decided against it. They walked quietly as they twisted through the Palace hallways. Days earlier, he and Shayla strolled through these very hallways for the first time. Their hands were intertwined and Shayla stopped often telling stories of her childhood, and pointing out her favorite paintings.

"Here," she said finally, stopping in front of a door. She punched in a code that triggered the clicking of a door unlocking. Nathaniel followed her inside. It was beautifully decorated in various shades of green, from emerald to sea foam, with doors off the main room presumably to a bedroom and bath.

"Are you okay?" Nathaniel asked feeling nervous in her presence in a way he had not experienced since that first day they met.

"No, I'm not okay," she said, breaking down. "I just ordered my own mother killed."

"It's not your fault," he said, reaching to comfort her, but she flinched.

"It has to be somebody's fault. She didn't die of old age or even disease or a car accident or anything other than a decision I made, along with you and everyone else in that room."

"I can't imagine what you feel like, but I'm sorry, truly sorry. I love you," he said, but she didn't turn to him like she usually did. She didn't move closer. She sat on the couch with her head between her knees and cried.

"I'm not hungry," Shayla said to Gerald a few hours later as he wheeled a cart into the suite.

"Eat something. At least some bread. You need your strength. We all need our strength, together," Gerald said looking at Shayla and Nathaniel, both seated across from him. He held the basket out to her and she pulled apart the flower of white linen that was closed around the bread to keep it fresh. She pulled out a roll and took a rabbit-sized nibble.

"Thank you," she said to Gerald. "I thank you both."

"You're very welcome, but we, along with all the other men in the country, are the ones who will always thank you for your courage," Gerald said.

"I thought I was doing the right thing, but now I wonder," she said, setting the roll down on her plate.

"Eight hundred and seventy two men were released from the dungeons of prisons all across the country today. You saved eight hundred and seventy two lives today alone! You will save many more as you go on."

"I never wanted this responsibility. What if I can't do it? My mother might be right. I'm not tough like she was. I couldn't make the decisions she made. What if there are riots?" Shayla said.

"Those men should never have been imprisoned and you know that. They were released after watching your speech. There haven't been riots, but there are Webavision photos of people making posters and writing on sheets that they are hanging from bridges all over the country saying: "Long Live Queen Shayla."

"Really?" Shayla said. She looked at Nathaniel and he could see a glimpse of the love that they had shining through.

"I'm sorry," she said to Nathaniel as soon as Gerald left with the dinner tray.

"For what?" he asked.

"I wasn't very nice earlier. This isn't your fault."

"You have nothing to apologize for. You've been under tremendous pressure. You are strong, at least as strong as your mother, but with your father's conscience. I love you and always will love you," he said.

She walked over and kissed him with a passion that felt freer than ever.

"Just give me some time. I'll get through this. We'll get through this," she said.

She led him to the bedroom and he kissed her while unbuttoning her shirt and then unhooking her bra, but he stopped when he saw the tears slowly escape her eyes.

"Are you alright… we don't have to…" he said, wiping her tear away with his finger.

"I want to. I'm happy and sad all at the same time," she said.

"Why are you happy? Because you helped all those men?"

"Partly, but I'm also happy because I can really be with you, without hiding. I can be with you as Nathaniel DeLuca, as my husband."

"But I didn't even propose yet."
"Men don't propose."
"They do now," he said, getting down on one knee.

Chapter Thirty-Eight

Simon was still amazed about the events of the last few days. If someone told him that the Queen's daughter was the polar political opposite of her mother and she was going to be the new Queen in less than a week, he would have laughed at the absurdity.

Now he was on his way back to the Underground to find out what was next. Chester told him that this was only the beginning. The castration laws weren't officially changed, even though the C Centers weren't currently performing castrations. Until there was true equality, the Underground would remain intact, with some major regrouping.

They'd be working directly with Shayla, and he looked forward to the next chapter. Perhaps there would be less driving. He wondered if he and Eudora would settle down into a little house with a yard and a garden and a white picket fence. That thought made him chuckle.

He still had one more delivery, his most important, and he almost felt sentimental. That wasn't like him.

As he turned off the highway onto the bumpy road for the millionth time, he noted the Midwestern skyline that began to set over the Kansas plains. His passenger should be awake by now, but he didn't even hear a peep from the back.

When he pulled into the Underground garage, he got out of the driver's seat and opened the van doors. Her eyes were open, but she looked sleepy. That's what the shot did, so he wondered how she would be in a few hours or a few days. It was certainly going to be interesting.

"I'm going to take that tape off, okay, but no screaming or biting, alright?" he said, feeling a kindness toward her that he had never thought the Queen would elicit from him. Her nod was gentle and he slowly took the tape off her mouth.

"Where are we?" she asked, looking at him in a way that made him pause.

"You'll find out in just a minute," he said quietly, feeling something that he wasn't sure how to describe. This bothered him a little, but this wasn't the time for thinking. "You alright?" he asked.

"I'm okay, thanks," she said, with a small smile that he couldn't help but return.

"It's a big step down," he said, helping her from the van. She looked around the garage but didn't say anything as he gently took her arm and led her toward the waiting elevator. When he pushed the button, the elevator's usual cricks and cracks sounded as they descended, their ears popping as their eyes held onto one another until the ding of the bell alerted them the doors were opening.

He led her down the hallway and saw her head turn to read the mantra of the Underground, crudely painted in large letters next to the podium where the guards usually sat.

Keep your Laws off my Body. Equal Rights and Justice for all Men.

Just then, they stepped out from behind the podium.

"Your majesty, I'm Crosby and this is our leader, Chester. Welcome to the Underground."

Acknowledgements

I'd like to thank the many people who have contributed to making this book release possible.

First and foremost, I'd like to thank my dear friend, Shira Block McCormick. I feel deeply blessed to have you in my life. For thirty years you have guided me and shared your wisdom, which helped me to become a better person and writer. Thank you for reading countless drafts, for your patience, tireless assistance, infinite encouragement and editing prowess.

I am so grateful to Amy Batchelor, Brad Feld, Cathy Hunter Gould, Deahn Berrini, Jennifer Pitts, and Jenny Lawton for your constant support from the very beginning.

I thank Renee Bacher, Christina Tiemann, Kim Fay, Halley Suitt Tucker, and Wendell Wellman for invaluable feedback and for giving me the confidence and courage to put this story out into the world.

Gratitude to Heloisa Duarte Fitzgerald, for not only encouraging all my creative endeavors, but for your inspired photography that I feel honored to use on the book jacket as well as on my website.

Thanks to Jenny Hudson, of merrimackmedia.com, for your dedication to creating a great book and beautiful website and for making the book production process seamless. Thanks to Donna Berger for your lovely print book design. Thanks to Paul Beeley of create-imaginations.com for your gorgeous and inspired book cover art.

My family always supported my writing. My father, Rabbi Paul Levenson, and my mother, Marlyn Katz Levenson made sure that every room of our childhood home dripped with books. My mother also endured weekly trips to the library with all four, less than well behaved, kids to foster a love of reading. Special thanks to my sister Yonah Levenson Hirschman for proofreading and editing various versions of this book, and to my brother Dode Levenson, whose writing accomplishments far outweigh my own. You helped me learn about plot, dialog, and writing a synopsis. You also encouraged me to keep going just when I needed it. Thanks to my brother Bobby Levenson for reading an early draft and cheering me along from the sidelines.

I thank my unbelievably wonderful aunts, Judy Clapp and Irene Rimer. You have both been invaluable in my life in so many ways including offering encouragement with my writing endeavors.

I'm also very blessed to have families that extend beyond my homestead. My yearly pilgrimage to Ashokan Fiddle and Dance Camp has been a vital part of recharging my batteries, particularly when I was discouraged. I especially want to thank Betsy Kubick, Debra Clifford, Dotty Moore, Eric Brock, Kathleen Moore, Rebecca Kalin, and last, but not least, my dear friend Rebecca Unger a.k.a. Dr. Reba.

The New England Chapter of the Romance Writer's of America has been instrumental in my education about the business of writing and finding like-minded friends who are extremely funny and supportive. Both traits are important when surveying the publishing arena. I could not have done this without the help, encouragement, and wisdom of some key people who are part of this amazing organization, including Annette Blair, Janet Campbell, Jenny Brown, Jessica Smith, Marie Force, Mike Myers, Pam Claughton, Traci Fleischman and Valerie Harris.

A number of people believed in me when I didn't think I could continue to work on this project. I have never forgotten their encouragement. Thank you all for your love and support: Alexa Albert, Amy Goldminz, Avi Weiss, Bonnie Watson, Carol Miller, Claire and David Weis, Darryl Settles, Dave Jilk, Deb Elliott, Dell Lunceford, Eve Goldminz, Fernando Albertorio, Hank Kniskern, Hank Phillippi Ryan, Helena Collins, Jennifer Cohen Katz, Jennifer Coon-Wallman, Joanna Meiseles, Jodi Solomon, Jodi Turek, JulieNussbaum, Kathy Van Patten, Larry Coury, Lisa Owens, Lori Rutter, Lynne Levenson, Marci Sapers, Michele Janis, Michael Tucker, Michael Walsh, Michelle Katz, Mike O'Connor, Nina Ghareeb, Pam Janis, Paul Nowinski, Paul Sandberg, Peggy Conant, Paris Stulbach,

Valerie Sandberg, Sandra Herman, Simone Hnilicka, Susan Ruf, Tori Stuart, and Will Herman.

I also want to thank two significant people who fueled my writing aspirations: I was very fortunate to take courses in college with Pulitzer Prize winner Madeleine Blais more than twenty years ago. Her ability to tell moving, true stories about people with a beauty and sensitivity is unmatched.

I must also thank my previous agent, Marly Rusoff, for believing in my storytelling. I will always be thankful for my experience working with you.

I want to thank my husband, Warren Jay Katz, who I love with all my heart and soul, for inspiring me to pick myself up and keep learning and working hard.

Finally, I want to thank all readers who continue to support writers in all ways. I sincerely hope you enjoy my stories. Many more are on the way.

Sincerely,

Ilana Katz Katz
Boston, MA
www.ilanakatz.com
ilana@ikatz.com
twitter: @katzkatz

Made in the USA
Lexington, KY
08 February 2019